THE CARE PLAN *for* GOD'S PEOPLE!

How We Think and Lives Matters!

THE CARE PLAN *for* GOD'S PEOPLE!

FROM A TO Z

"For I came that they may have life and give it abundantly"

Miss Asondra StarN'air

Helper of Humankind

Library of Congress Control Number: 2022910777

HARDBACK:	978-1-959143-07-9
PAPERBACK:	978-1-957575-65-0
EBOOK:	978-1-957575-66-7

Scripture taken from The Holy Bible, The ESV® Bible (The Holy Bible, English Standard Version®). ESV® Permanent Text Edition® (2016). Copyright © 2001 by Crossway, a publishing ministry of Good News Publishers. The ESV® text has been reproduced in cooperation with and by permission of Good News Publishers. Unauthorized reproduction of this publication is prohibited. All rights reserved.

Ordering Information:

For orders and inquiries, please contact:
1-888-404-1388
www.goldtouchpress.com
book.orders@goldtouchpress.com

Printed in the United States of America

CONTENTS

THE INVITATION

JESUS SAID TO Them, "I am the bread of life. Whoever comes to me will never go hungry and whoever believes in me will never be thirsty" (John 6:35).

Repeat after me: Lord, I am a sinner. I believe in the Gospel of Jesus Christ and that you died for my sins. I repent for the ways I have lived my life down here on earth, Please forgive me, and I want to change. Today I want to make you Lord over my entire life now.

Teach me your ways, I want to obey and serve you for the rest of my days.

In Jesus name, Amen.

If you just prayed that prayer, you just got born again,

Welcome! Come inside...

Here's to Everybody, Everywhere,

Looking for a fresh start and are seeking the Lord—those of us who have finally realized we just can't make it on our own. We need God, we need a care plan.

And to all those parents, single moms, especially—like me—who need regular reminders to stay focus and strong, we must carry on. I'm so excited because **The Care Plan**'s got us all covered from **A** to **Z**. Question is, are you with me? If you are then, let's go and..

Get **The Care Plan,**
Open **The Care Plan,**
Do **The Care Plan,**

Is with You.

And may God be with us all!

Amen.

INTRODUCTION

WHO AM I, and where did I come from? Well let me introduce myself to you, my name is Miss Asondra StarN'air and I come from God, I am a helper of human kind. But I'm also an everyday person just like all of you, I have challenges too.

I am a woman of the faith, a born again Christian, and now a minister of words, I write books for the Lord, my purpose is twofold, one to encourage you to be the best you can be always and two, help win as many souls for Christ as I can.

So "The Holy Spirit" and I came up with **The Care Plan**. And now we're introducing it to all of you. **'The Care Plan'** is a life assessment of some basic human fundamentals practices all people from every part of the globe could use to bring forth positive change in how we think and handle every day matters or struggles. And we all have them, don't we? Well then this book is just what the doctor ordered, I call it, "my doctor Jesus book", because it was inspired by God to be a ministry book for all those in need of a savior, his son Jesus Christ. I'm just the messenger and the one God chose to write **'The Care Plan'** and it was an honor too! However, it must be stated clearly that this book is not to replace the bible, if you want to grow fully in Christ, you must read his word, and therefore you must read the Holy Bible. **The Care Plan** is just another way to help encourage and strengthen your walk with Christ, and give you some practical advice for your everyday life. So please, use and enjoy it for that purpose only. But read your bibles daily!

Back to **'The Care Plan'** Okay, so now, let's talk about what you will find inside **'The Care Plan'** for all of you, I have put together a care plan using all the alphabets—an idea that works quite well, I must say so myself. Each letter is to help you get better at living for Christ. Some of the letters have more than one word chosen because I felt the need to cover different subjects—for example, the letter ***M.*** There are so many important things God wanted me to address: men, money, marriage, just to name a few. Again, some of the letters will have more pages.

Along with each letter and topic, I have provided scriptures and, after that, a reflection journal page so that you can track your growth and development.

The Care Plan is also an interaction book between you and God, I did it that way so that you two would bond and start to become very close to each other, my hope is for you and Jesus to become as one. Finally, at the end of the book, I felt the need to include a daily care plan for the morning, afternoon, evening, and bedtime too. All designed to get you in the habit of checking in and out with Christ all through the day and before you fall asleep, how neat!!!

What is so exciting too is that, this book is not just for you and me, it's for **Everybody, Everywhere!** All one has to do is, take action, "Go":

Get The Care Plan
Open The Care Plan
Do The Care Plan

Is with You!

Let's get started because how we think and live matters! Let's Go..........

Introducing THE CARE PLAN

for

God's People!

Miss Asondra StarN'air

THE CARE PLAN for God's People!

How We Think and Live Matters!

"Knowing these teachings will mean true and good health for you."
Proverbs 4:22

Read Your Bibles **Everyday!**

ATTITUDE

I ONCE HEARD it said, "Attitude is "Everything"! And it's true. But the ultimate attitude is the one Jesus had, which can be found in Matthew 26:39. Jesus cried out, "My Father, if it is possible, let this cup of suffering be taken away from me. Yet I want **Your Will** to be done, not mine."

In life, we will have trials and tribulations, the Bible tells us so. Things will happen, and many times by no fault of our own, especially to those living for Christ. But, remain calm, cool and collected. God knows and sees everything! I know your heartaches; "ME TOO" I deal with some of the same stuff, life can be tough. Those who belong to this world can be low down, dirty and cruel but, we *must* still take on Jesus-like attitudes. We must begin to study the ways of Christ and apply his attitude toward whatever comes our way.

Taking on his attitude is not an option for those who claim they are Christians. We are taught to tackle things and situations differently from the world. Therefore, the ultimate attitude toward life, the one Jesus laid out for us in his Word, should not only be the blueprint for us to follow but the goal as well. Becoming more and more like Jesus in all that we do is sure to set us apart from the world and counterfeits.

So next time you find yourself dealing with ungodly behaviors, along with slanderers, persecution, betrayal, jealousy, hatred, unfair losses, schemers, bullyers or whatever else, **'Attitude is Everything'!** Everyday remember **Jesus Christ** "Our King." Before Jesus took his last breath on the cross he spoke these words to those who crucified him "Forgive them for they know not what they do" "NOW" sister and brothers, let that be **'YOU'!** Let it be us, **"In God We Trust!**

Next, if the issue is not a person, but a thing? No problem, it ain't a thing! Because there's nothing God can't undo, The Care Plan has that covered too. Let's talk about it, are you single and lonely, wishing you had your one and only? Are you having financial difficulties, health issues, struggling to pay rent or the mortgage, car troubles, are you suffering from a loss of a job. a relationship gone bad, broken heartedness, weight issues, shattered dreams, and extremes; don't give up or be mean, remember **Attitude is Everything!** But here's the solution to it all, *Seek the kingdom of God above all else and live righteously, and he will give you everything you need.* Including a great attitude! Matthew 6:33. Remember we belong to Christ now which means, we have the Attitude of Christ. We are choosing to follow him and live right! We are to be in the world but not of it anymore. We can not do the things we use to do, and you all know what I am talking about don't let me spell it out!

Don't practice sin, Godly attitudes always wins!

Put on the new self, which is being renewed in knowledge after the image of its creator. Colossians 3:15

Attitude Care Plan

- Stay in the Word. It's your sword, a way to keep the devil from running havoc in your life.
- Our attitude should be "No weapons formed against me shall prosper."
- Keep praising God. In spite of your situations and problems, they will come and they will go. "Weeping may endure for a night, but joy will come in the morning," my friend (Ps. 30:5).
- Keep an attitude of gratitude. Maybe God is using this as Jesus training for you.

For example, I was persecuted and mistreated so bad in the caregiving field, especially by my own people, and I suffered in every way, financially too. Read my first book, *A Caregiver's Bible to Excellence.* God took all that pain and suffering and created a first-time author out of me, but if I had not gone through those dark valleys, those trials and tribulations trusting and relying on Jesus to pull me through, I would not be writing today. I kept my focus on him, I had his attitude, father forgive them for they know not what they do was all I could think of too as I suffered. I was in pain but through it all I had forgiving attitude, and so must you. And another thing I did was hold on tightly to his word. I kept repeating over and over again to myself these promises of God: He will give me beauty for my ashes, He will help me, He will provide for me, and He will never forsake those who love him. And I said to myself, also, this, "God I trust you, you must be allowing this for a reason" hurts like hell, but let your will be done. My attitude like Jesus, became focused on God, not the problems or the people. So when it comes to the Ultimate Attitude, the one that Christ used to defeat this world, my advice is this, suffer like 'HE' did and live. Rise again, and again, over power your flesh with agape love. "Um hum", love those who mistreat or hurt you. Be Christ- like, And remember Jesus heart felt words "Forgive them for they know not what they do" that attitude will do wonders for YOU!

ME TOO!

Make These Your realities day and night

- A trusting attitude
- A dedicated-to-Christ attitude
- An all-knowing attitude
- A forgiving attitude
- A positive attitude
- A grateful attitude
- A loving attitude
- A peaceful attitude
- A Bible study attitude

Get The Care Plan
Open The Care Plan
Do The Care Plan

Is with You!

My Care Plan

From now on, I commit to ________________________________

____

____

____

____

____

____

I will make necessary changes because ____________________

____

____

____

____

____

I will allow God to ______________________________________

____

____

____

____

I want to be more and more like Jesus in this area because _________

____

____

____

____

____

My prayer is ____

____

____

____

____

Reflection Diary Journal

Date ___________

Father God,

In Jesus name, Amen!

THE CARE PLAN for God's People

How We Think and Live Matters!

"Knowing these teachings will mean true and good health for you."
Proverbs 4:22

Read Your Bibles Everyday!

BOLD AND BRAVE

HAS THERE EVER been a time in your life when you didn't think you could do something or had what it takes to succeed, yet something inside you kept pushing you toward that very thing/desire? Or perhaps maybe it was something you wanted for your future, like a home or college degree and you looked at your circumstances and said, "Not Me." My life is a mess and besides, it's only me. I have no help, no significant other, these are a few examples. You may have different ones. Wait, how about this one? Has there been a time in your life when you thought your dreams can no longer come true because you have too many children, you're up in age, single, often depressed about something, this or that or the other, perhaps some of you feel "what's" the use", I'm big, too overweight, unattractive, boring, not good or smart enough. Let me tell you this, all lies, yes those are all lies don't believe that crap. Those are not the thoughts of our creator, those are the thoughts of the evil one, Satan, trying to steal rob and kill all that God has planned for you. "Wake Up Everybody!"

We have The Holy bible and **The Care Plan**, both working together, hand on hand. I am now one of his messengers, God sent me to tell you this, **"Get Up and Fight"!** Be bold and brave in the Lord, God has the last say in your life, not you or your circumstances. Romans 8:37, "No in all these things, overwhelming victory is ours through Christ, who loves us."

In the book of Joshua, God had to kind of push Joshua a bit too, like he's asking me to push all of you. In biblical times, Moses was the man, but now Moses is dead and now God wants Joshua to lead. But like some of you, Joshua lacked confidence and I suspect too, that Satan knew this and also start messing with his mind. Like he's trying to mess with yours. Rebuke him! Anyway, Satan the devil. probably said to Joshua "you'll never be as good as Moses, you're too weak, you're this, you're that, and what about this, Joshua, you're ah no name, 'ha ha' Moses was much loved and popular, you're not. And besides, who could live up to Moses and all he has done for God's people? I tell ya, that is a tall order to fill, but, God told Joshua "MOSES IS DEAD"! In other words, "I need YOU *now*. You will be the new leader." God also said a few more encouraging things to Joshua. He said this also: "There shall not any man be able to stand before thee all the days of thy life. As I was with Moses, so I shall be with thee. I will not fail thee nor forsake thee. Be strong and of good courage" (Joshua 1:5-6)

What I am trying to get you to see is, if you are a true follower of God, you already have the victory and all your heart's desire. Remember, God said, "Seek ye first the kingdom of God and his *righteousness*. And all these things will be added unto you."

Be Bold and Brave, if God calls you, "Go For It! Like Diana Ross, say **"It's My Turn now!"** Hold God accountable to his promises, but you'd better be living right too, you can't be living like the world does and expect blessing to come your way. Therefore, be done with un-holy living, fornication and fleshly desires. Make sure **'YOU'** yes, **'YOU',** you're on **The Care Plan** now, make sure you are constantly in his Word, and praying too. Furthermore, be sure to check in and out with God throughout your day. listen and learn, hear what the Lord has to say. And with your whole heart, love Our God in every way! At night, later for the clubs and the streets, spend quality time with him. Stay holy don't give in or cheat. Put into practice boldness and bravery, cross over to the other side! If you are doing all that and reading your bibles and constantly working **The Care Plan** then you're playing with a winning hand! *Go for it!* God is with you all the way, "you true and faithful servant." Now for those who are still lost and living like the world does all I can say to you is Repent! Allow the Care Plan to help you start to move in the right direction for a more peaceful and healthy life in Jesus Christ.

Don't be afraid anymore, be Bold and Brave give Jesus a try now,

"Repent", and stay on **'The Care Plan'** God's son will be with you. Remember Jesus has the whole world in his hands.

Bold and Brave Care Plan

- Be strong and of good courage.
- Sit and talk with God about what you want and need.
- Just believe, all it takes is the faith of a mustard seed, that's all!
- Start moving boldly toward the thing you want.
- Keep God fearing people around you; people who love to see you succeed.
- Create vision boards.
- Go take pictures of the things you want and post them on a vision board or by your nightstand.
- Develop the "believe it before you see it" mentality.
- Remember, in order to become bold and brave for the Lord, we must fully trust him and we must read his word on a regular bases. That is how we build our faith and become courageous and ready to take on whatever life brings our way.
- Righteousness has great rewards. Work toward a Jesus lifestyle.
- Pray about everything; take it all to the King.
- Ask yourself, "Is this what God really wants for me, or is it what I want?"
- Know that whatever the task you're facing—whether it's school, A job, a journey or a dream—you can do all things in Christ who strengthens you; not some things but, *all* things.

Make These Your realities day and night

- I have the mind of Christ.
- I am more than a conqueror.
- I am blessed.
- If God is for me, who can be against me?
- Fear doesn't live here anymore.
- My old life is over.
- I am a new creature in Christ.
- I'm the new 'Leader', God has chosen!
- I shall take back everything the devil tried to steal.
- I'm going for it now, circumstancs and all!

Get The Care Plan
Open The Care Plan
Do The Care Plan

Is with You!

My Care Plan

From now on, I commit to ____

____

____

____

____

____

I will make necessary changes because ______________________________

____

____

____

____

____

I will allow God to ____

____

____

____

____

I want to be more and more like Jesus in this area because __________

____

____

____

____

____

My prayer is ____

____

____

____

____

____

Reflection Diary Journal

Date ___________

Father God,

____

____

____

____

____

____

____

____

____

____

____

____

____

____

Amen.

THE CARE PLAN for God's People!

How We Think and Live Matters!

"Knowing these teachings will mean true and good health for you."
Proverbs 4:22

Read Your Bibles Everyday!

COMMITMENT TO CHRIST

"The world's sin is that it refuses to believe in me"
says the Lord! (John 16:9),

AFTER ALL THAT'S been said and done, people still want to live for themselves, do things their own way. They don't want the church, not even God telling them how to live their lives; it's true, this world doesn't believe in our messiah "Jesus Christ". Many say they do, because it sounds good and it is the thing to say, but when you're not looking, they've gone astray, Jesus cries out and put it's this way: The world sins is that it refuses to believe in me" John 16:9

Look, anybody can play church and many do. But the truth is in the lifestyle. The daily walk, forget about the talk, let's see your faithful and true walk!

How "Committed to Christ" are you?
What are you willing to do?
Are you building, to be among the who's who?
Really, Is it all about Christ or about **"YOU"?**

This is what I have learn over the years ,if we want to be blessed and receive all the promises of God including eternal life, we must be committed to him and his word on a daily basis; end of story, besides, he's heard it all! I am not here to police you or make you commit to Christ or read his word, "but that would be nice". But I am here to say this, Jesus is The Messiah, The Savior of The World. The men of this world can't save us. Education, degrees, money, big homes, clothes and fancy cars "all junk", can't save us. People can't save you, I can't, your momma can't, your spouse can't, your pastor can't, we are not the way. We are not the "Star", we are not the "Light" without humbleness and "Commitment to Christ" nobody will see God. Nobody! Think about that tonight!

Commitment to Christ Care Plan

Christ Care Plan is simple, Pick up your cross and follow me, says the Lord. I don't look at porn, cuss, lust or watch sex filled T.V.. Nor do I hang out with unbelievers that party and get high . My vision is upward in the sky. Have nothing to do with such evil and wicked living anymore, if you say it's "Me" you adore.

Humble. thy self, knees on the floor, time for repentance and I shall remember your sins no more.

Lastly, commitment to Christ means leaving many things behind including family if need be, "You" cannot be my disciple says the Lord unless you love me more than yourself ; your family, (your mom and dad) and your children and your spouse, (everybody). your fake friends, your job and co-workers, party-life, sex, desires, everything and everybody! **Luke 14:26** read it , you're going to need it!

Make These Your Realities Day and Night

- Set time aside for God each day.
- Develop a prayer life.
- Read and study the Bible.
- Go public with your faith.
- Be obedient to what the Word says
- Do not lean on your own understanding.
- Allow the Holy Spirit to guide you.
- Remember, action speaks louder than words.
- Keep dying to self, die daily.
- Live for Christ, get born again, stop playing game with your life.

Get The Care Plan
Open The Care Plan
Do The Care Plan

Is with You!

My Care Plan

From now on, I commit to ____________________

I will make necessary changes because ____________________

I will allow God to ____________________

I want to be more and more like Jesus in this area because ____________________

My prayer is ____________________

Reflection Diary Journal

Date ____________

Father God,

____

____

____

____

____

____

____

____

____

____

____

____

____

____

Amen!

THE CARE PLAN for God's People!

How We Think and Live Matters!

"Knowing these teachings will mean true and good health for you."
Proverbs 4:22

Read Your Bibles Everyday!

DISCIPLINE, DISCIPLESHIP, AND DEDICATION

DISCIPLINE, DISCIPLESHIP, AND DEDICATION, these are the 3D vitamins **The Care Plan** prescribes for you, and to be taken every day for life, so that you can run in such a way and win.

> *Do you not know that in a race all the runners run, but only one gets the prize? Run in such a way as to get the prize. Everyone who competes in the games goes into strict training. They do it to get a crown that will not last, but we do it to get a crown that will last forever. Therefore I do not run like someone running aimlessly; I do not fight like a boxer beating the air. No, I strike a blow to my body and make it my slave so that after I have preached to others, I myself will not be disqualified for the prize.* 1 Corinthians 9:24-27

So there you have it, in order to win over sin, and dominate the flesh **"Discipline"** and strict training is required. Children of God, listen carefully, **"WE"** must focus all our attention on pleasing God, not man. Next, comes **"Discipleship"** Jesus said to him, (to **Everybody, Everywhere**, he's talking to you, he's talking to me) "No one who puts his hand to the plow and looks back is fit for the kingdom of God" Luke 9:62. If we are going to serve him, we must serve him all the way, we cannot let others get in the way. Sometimes we may have to tell loved ones goodbye. Whatever we have to do, we belong to God first. Lastly, We must be committed in our walk, **"Dedication"** is a "MUST"! In everything we do, we "MUST" do it as if we are working for the Lord. It is written, The Lord is our Shepard and we shall not want Psalms 23. You shall love the **LORD** your God with all your heart and with all you might. "These are the words, which I am commanding you today. Deuteronomy 6:4-6

3D Vitamins

A spoonful to be taken **“Everyday!”**

Ingredients: Discipline, Discipleship, Dedication.
Side Effects: May not be able to function without Christ.
Benefits: Eternal Life!

Discipline, Discipleship, and Dedication Care Plan

Make These Your Realities Day and Night

- Get fit in Christ and stay fit in Christ! Be a disciple for life!
- Read his word constantly, don't swerve to the left or right.
- Ask God to place in your heart his desire for you.
- Go all the way with God; so God can go all the way with you!
- Get rid of all your idols and ungodliness too.
- Ask the Holy Spirit to remove all unrighteousness out of your life.
- Put into practice, Discipline, Discipleship and Dedication to the Lord.
- Take Your 3D Vitamins "Everyday" and Pray!

Core message is this, we can't hold onto the life we once had and serve God too—not happening! 'We MUST Change!"

Get The Care Plan
Open The Care Plan
Do The Care Plan

Is with You!

My Care Plan

From now on, I commit to ____

____

____

____

____

____

I will make necessary changes because ______________________________

____

____

____

____

____

I will allow God to ____

____

____

____

____

I want to be more and more like Jesus in this area because __________

____

____

____

____

____

My prayer is ____

____

____

____

____

____

Reflection Diary Journal

Date ___________

Father God,

Amen.

THE CARE PLAN for God's People!

How We Think and Live Matters!

"Knowing these teachings will mean true and good health for you."
Proverbs 4:22

Read Your Bibles Everyday!

EDUCATION

Work hard so you can present yourself to God and receive his approval. Be a good worker, one who does not need to be ashamed and who correctly explains the word of truth.

—2 Timothy 2:15

THERE ARE TWO worlds of Education, God's and the world, and we need them both. But my wisdom says God's Kingdom first! And here's why, GOD is the one who created all of us and the world and everything in it. Therefore, he knows what's best for all of humanity.

> Romans 8:27-31, *He knows us far better than we know ourselves, knows our pregnant condition, and keeps us present before God. That is why we can be so sure that every detail in our lives of love for God is worked into something good. God knew what he was doing from the very beginning. He decided from the outset to shape the lives of those who love him along the same lines as the life of his Son. The Son stands first in the line of humanity he restored. We see the original and intended shape of our lives there in him. (Keep reading) After God made that decision of what his children should be like, he followed it up by calling people by name, after he called them by name, he set them on a solid basis with himself. And then after getting them established, he stayed with them to the end, gloriously completing what he had begun.*

How Beautiful Is This! So, What Do You Think? With God On Our Side Like This, How Can We Lose?

We Can't Lose! Listen, It Is True, That We Still Have To Live In This World, But Remember That We Are Not To Be Of It, God Has The Final Say In What We Are To Become. Go To School, Yes, Get A Good Job—Certainly, Of Course, That's What God Wants Too, But Still, Include God In Those Plans, Make Certain That Your Plans Lines Up With His. Don't Be One Of Millions Out There, Who Hate Their

Jobs Later On, — Their Lives Too! Do **The Care Plan** Don't Let Me Have To Say, **"I TOLD YOU"!**

Listen, **The Care Plan** Cannot Stress Enough How Very, Very Important, It Is That We All Look To God For Everything, He Already Knows What We Will Do, What We Will Be, Yes God Already Knows Our Destiny. Keep God First Place In Your Life, He'll Take You Places You Never Dreamed Of. Receive This Message, It's With Love!

"Education" is more valuable than material things. Having wisdom and understanding is better than having silver or gold.. So go for it!
Proverbs 16:16

Education Care Plan

Make These Your Realities Day and Night

- I'll say it again and again. Read your Bibles daily; study to make yourself approved.
- Stay in school, further your education.
- Go to college or trade school, get a good job!
- Strive for excellence; do it in Jesus's name.
- Don't quit. Unless God sends you on another mission, don't quit.
- Ask God what he wants you to major in, not your parents or others. Ask God.
- If school is not for you, don't be discouraged. God will still use you! God can use a butcher, baker, candlestick maker, and he does, I use to be a baker!
- Remember God already knows the plans he has for you, you just have to start spending more time with him to find out.
- Lastly, if you want all to go well in your life, you must not practice sin, you must live according to what is written. I'm just sayin! Come out of the world, focus on being a Child of God.

Whatever your path in life, keep God with you, keep him first!

> "Be strong and very courageous. Be careful to obey all the law my servant Moses gave you; do not turn from it to the right or to the left, that you may be successful wherever you go. Keep this Book of the Law (bible) always on your lips; meditate on it day and night, so that you may be careful to do everything written in it. Then you will be prosperous and successful. (God's people) Have I not commanded you? Be strong and courageous. Do not be afraid; do not be discouraged, for the Lord your God will be with you wherever you go." **Joshua 1:7-9**

Make These Your Realities Day and Night too!

- I love reading God's Word.
- I found out there really is power in his Word.
- God's Word is a lamp unto my feet.
- In God, I move and have my being.
- God knows the plans he has for me.
- I trust God completely.
- I am saved by the blood of Jesus his word matters
- The Bible is my:

"**B**asic
Instructions
Before
Leaving
Earth" book.

Remember, read his word, it works and stay focus:

Get The Care Plan
Open The Care Plan
Do The Care Plan

Is with You!

My Care Plan

From now on, I commit to ______________________________

I will make necessary changes because ______________________________

I will allow God to ______________________________

I want to be more and more like Jesus in this area because __________

My prayer is ______________________________

Reflection Diary Journal

Date ___________

Father God,

____

____

____

____

____

____

____

____

____

____

____

____

____

____

____

Amen.

THE CARE PLAN for God's People!

How We Think and Live Matters!

"Knowing these teachings will mean true and good health for you."
Proverbs 4:22

Read Your Bibles Everyday!

FAITH

I have been crucified with Christ and I no longer live,
but Christ lives in me. The life I now live in the body,
I live by faith in the Son of God,
who loved me and gave himself for me.
—Galatians 2:20

DID YOU KNOW, you got to have Faith? Faith is the fundamental foundations of our existence, in other words we cannot underestimate what God can do in our live whether you are a believer or not, Faith saves the day. And more than that, Faith is the only way!

The bible says Faith is the substance of things hoped for, the evidence of things not seen. Hebrews 11:1. Now what does all that mean? I'll explain it like this, Faith causes us to act on things we have not experienced yet, to believe promises in the bible that haven't been fulfilled yet, and to trust in God and his Son Jesus Christ, when our situations hasn't changed yet! Put simply, so that even a child could understand, I think faith is 4 words, those 4 words are: 'In GOD We Trust!'

We trust him completely, no matter what the blues, bad news, or how we've been persecuted and used. Through all of life's joys and pains, we don't give up, our faith remains the same, 'In GOD We Trust'! And where there's that kind of trust, faith shows up and do its thing, you'll be able to move mountains and understand why the bird in the cage sings!

So today if there is anybody out there, suffering from say a job loss, a relationship gone bad, health issues, financial hardship, divorce, loss of a love one or spouse, death of a pet, loneliness, depression, family problems, substance abuse or just worn out by everyday life, and that can happen, especially if you don't have faith.

Quickly, here's what you do, pray for more faith, ask the Holy Spirit to strengthen your faith so that you can have peace in your life once again. Can I say this, living in this world is not easy, I don't care how successful some of you may be, everybody, everywhere will have troubles, the bible says so, look at the president, look at the rich and famous too, nobody is exempt, nobody, not even **YOU!**

But let me tell you what "The Savoir of the world' can do and will do; well, I won't tell you, here, I'll let him speak for himself: *Come to me all you who are weary and burdened and I will give you rest. Take my yoke upon you and learn from me, for I am gentle and humble in heart, and you will find rest for your souls. For my yoke is easy and my burden light."* Matthew 11:28-30

How wonderful and amazing is that! Those words are like sweet music to the ears! Nothing else to say, You Got to have Faith! So get those gloves on, be with Jesus today, let him and his word remover all the years of pain and suffering that this world and others has inflicted on you. In Jesus name, forget about everything unkind that was ever done or said to you, all lies, it isn't true, Jesus loves you. Let him into your heart, trusting that He will do what his word says He will do. Faith is an attribute 'the holy spirit' wants to instill in all of us, so, **The Care Plan** wants to help. First don't forget to keep taking your

3 D vitamins, along with that I want you to for one full year and beyond, say this seven times daily and before you fall asleep at night: ***Life Will Never Be To Much, Because "IN God I Will Always Love and Trust!"***

"All Together"

In God we Trust, In God We Trust,
In God We Trust, In God We Trust
In God We Trust, In God We Trust
In God We Trust!

Faith Care Plan

Remember You Got To Have Faith! And remember this also, **Faith Without Works Is Dead!** Today, start reading your bibles if you want to start living the faithful and blessed life! Learn too, all you can, about the promises of God and what you need to do to receive them.

I have put together **The Care Plan**, to help us and with Christ on our side there's absolutely nothing we can't do. From this day forward, lets keep our focus on working together in the body of Christ and help be there for one another, remember, we are sisters and brothers. Together **"WE"** can win! Faith comes by hearing and hearing by the word of God . And I can hear *Him* say, *"Tell the people I love them, tell the people I'm here!"*

> *He said to her "Daughter, your faith have healed you, Go in peace...*Mark 5:34
>
> *Then He said to him, "Rise and go; your faith has made you well"* Luke 17:19

Everybody, Everywhere, are you ready to do the work, if so then we must put our trust and faith in God and accept His son Jesus Christ and make him Lord over our lives. Right now, not tomorrow **"NOW"!**

- For God so loved the world so much that he gave his only begotten Son, that whosoever believe thin him should not perish, but have eternal life. John 3:16

- For everyone who has been born of God (gave this world up) overcomes the world. And this is the victory that has overcome the world — our faith. 1 John 5:4

- What good is it, my brother, if someone says he has faith but does not have works? Can that faith save him? if a brother or sister is poorly clothed and lacking in daily food, and one of you say to them, "Go in peace, be warmed and filled," without giving them the things needed for the body, what good is that? So also faith by itself if it does not have works, is dead. But someone will say, "you have faith and I have works. Show me your faith apart from your works, and I will show you my faith by my works. James 2:14-26

- And whatever you ask for in prayer, you will receive, if you have faith. Matthew 21:22

- For the righteousness of God is revealed from faith to faith, as it is written "The righteous shall live by faith. Romans 1:17

Make These Your Realities Day and Night

- Abraham believed God, now so do I.
- I can turn any problem or situation around in Jesus's name.
- God is faithful to me, I am faithful to God! In God I Trust!

- I exercise my faith by facing everything that comes my way without fear.
- From now on, I'm trusting God, so therefore, I'm going for it. I'm stepping out on faith, buying that house, I'm going back to school, I'm moving on..., I'm taking that new opportunity, I'm beating this cancer, I can make it without that toxic relationship, I will get back on my feet—whatever life throws at me, I can beat! My faith is fierce "I haven't felt this kind of power in years!" "Fear, get Outta here!"

I got the faith, I'm keeping the faith, my situations not taking its place, I'm a winner, I'm running my race! While I'm running, I'll tell Everybody, Everywhere, my friends and family too, to:

Get The Care Plan
Open The Care Plan
Do The Care Plan

Is with You!

My Care Plan

From now on, I commit to ______________________________

I will make necessary changes because ______________________

I will allow God to ______________________________

I want to be more and more like Jesus in this area because ________

My prayer is ______________________________

Reflection Diary Journal

Date ___________

Father God,

____

____

____

____

____

____

____

____

____

____

____

____

____

____

____

Amen.

FEAR

FEAR OF: **F**ALSE- **E**vidence- **A**ppearing -**R**eal and that's exactly what the world and Satan have used to deceive all of us fear. In fact, fear has become a god within itself, it's a fake god, but unfortunately, these fake gods are ruling and destroying people's lives every day. In order to defeat these imposter's, you must learn to do battle in the mind. There is a book out there called ***Battlefield of the Mind,*** written by Joyce Myer, a cool, calm and collected charismatic Christian author and speaker, also the president of Joyce Myer Ministries. In it, she gives applications on how to defeat fear and win back your mind and she also shows you how to take back all the power God wants you to have. I will not step on her toes here, heaven knows, she's been through enough and so have I, probably all of you too. God chose HER for that book, not me, that book is Excellent! I love Joyce Myers, she means more to me than she knows. God, you said ask anything in my name and believe and it shall happen, well I'm asking to meet her one day. I have learned a lot from her, and that book 'Battlefield of the Mind'. Joyce Myer ministry has helped me in so many ways, I would like to encourage all of you to tune in on her television series 'Enjoying Everyday Life, check your local listing you will be glad you did.

Back to fear, fear is not from GOD. Fear is something from the devil, because it is written, (right Jesus) Right! that God did not give us a spirit of fear, and timidity, but of power, (right Mrs. Myer) Right! power of love and a sound mind. 2 Timothy 1:7. If this is so, then fear has to go! Just like I said in the beginning, fear is an illusion. It is **False Evidence Appearing Real**, no matter what your circumstances, the real **GOD** is always going help you out and take good care of you no matter what. Realize this, and start to agree with me too, that, if you are full of worry and fear you are hanging out with the wrong god, because the real **GOD** we served, don't know what fear is. It doesn't exist! And how profound is this, no matter what life brings, good or bad, happy or sad, good mood or pissed off and mad, And for some, **"Money"** or wishing you had, but with Christ by our side we can still move on and be glad; it's only temporary anyway. Like the seasons, your situation will change 'whatever it is'. The bible tells us that in this world we will have trials and tribulations (problems) and his people are to trust in him to help get us through such difficult times, He will help make things right. But we have a job to do as well , we must fight the good fight of Faith! **"Fight"** do battle in your mind, destroy fear, don't let fear hide. Keep those gloves on and whip that fake god's behind, **"Knock Him out"** make him go blind. Don't let fear stop you from crossing the finish line. With God on our side, who can be against us? **"Nobody!" "Trust GOD"**, give it time. Again, **Knock Fear Out, Make It Go Blind.** After you knock fear out here's what you need to do:

Get The Care Plan
Open The Care Plan
Do The Care Plan

Is with You!

Fear Care Plan

Make These Your Realities Day and Night

- First of all, tell the devil, "Get behind me, Satan. What you said is *not* written."
- Say, No weapons formed against you shall prosper.
- When thoughts come in your head, ask yourself, "Whose thoughts are these, mine or God's?" If it's not God's, it's of the flesh or Satan's. It's just this simple: rebuke it.
- If God's not in it, don't begin it, don't agree with those thoughts, rebuke fear, do let fear win.
- Learn to think about what you're thinking about, and pounder this too: If God did not give me the spirit of fear, why am I lying here? Why am I keeping people in my life that are destroying me and keeping me in bondage and upset all the time? Why can't I control my mind? I'll tell you why, fear comes in all forms, it's sneaky and cleaver. Fear can become a person and convince you to becomes it's lover, many times we let fear walk straight through our doors. Fear is not a friend, trust me, it will burn you in the end.
- Realize this as well, fear is also an indicator you still don't fully trust God. So go back and read all the scriptures on fear and turn that fear into faith. You can do it, you must do it. Your mountains depend on it. Your bills depends on it, your health depends on it, your everyday life, happiness and future depends on this, fear or faith, you choose!
- Take to heart, what I told you, **"FEAR"** is **F**alse **E**vidence **A**ppearing **R**eal, so get busy, rebuke it, say, to that fear, get out of here!
- Fear not, For I am with you says the Lord. Isaiah 41:10 .We must remember that God will alway protect , provide and look out for those who live for him.
- Fear's job is to make sure you don't succeed at nothing. Therefore, don't hang out with fear, hang out with **FAITH!**

- Get Joyce Myer's book, **Battlefield *of the Mind***, today, don't wait!
- Replace fear with faith don't wait!
- Anything you are afraid of, conquer it!
- On the positive side, "The Fear of the Lord is the beginning of knowledge, but fools despise wisdom and instruction." Proverbs 1:7
- Lastly, in life we all will have trials and tribulations of various kinds, Jesus said so, and he wants to remind us that some of the things that happen to us may also be a testing of out faith. So if we allow fear to overtake us during this time, we still have work to do and hard lessons to learn. Remember this, Faith produces steadfastness and Fear produces pain and defeat. "Pray" don't be weak, don't go out like that, ***"Get Up On Your Feet!***
-

Make These Your Realities Day and Night

- I have all I need; I won't worry about tomorrow.
- I am in excellent health. Even if I am not, I will say it and witness my own healing!
- I can be single and happy too. I'm trusting God for my soul mate, not me.
- God is my provider, not man.
- I have no fear because I trust God.
- Thank you, God, for giving me the mind of Christ.
- I love reading my bible now!!! I'm so excited, I'm hooked!
- Now I do everything to protect what I have with God, I have faith, fear don't live here anymore!
- From now on, when I feel fear trying to get in, I will grab my bible and read God's word. There is no fear in love, and God is love. I will run to God and his Word because I know that perfect love for him cast out all fear.
- **F.E.A.R, NO MORE!** I refuse to live in **F**alse **E**vidence **A**ppearing **R**eal, I'm not leaving **GOD** for that. No, **"No Deal!"**
- My faithful and obedient walk with Christ is worth telling Everybody, Everywhere to:

Get The Care Plan
Open The Care Plan
Do The Care Plan

Is with You!

You Got To Have Faith!

- Faith that the situations will change.
- Faith that God will help turn things around in your favor.
- Faith that God is in control and he will not let you fall
- Faith that our problems are never too big or small, God can fix them all.
- Faith that broken hearts do mend.
- Faith that when we stumble/back slide he'll forgive us and help put us back on a righteous path.
- Faith in sorrow, healing tomorrow!
- Faith in your finances, you will be the head and not the tail!
- Faith in your goals, and dreams, grades too, on the test, you'll do well!
- Faith in Faith!

God Will Never Leave or Forsake Us.
In God We Trust!

My Care Plan

From now on, I commit to ______________________________

I will make necessary changes because ______________________________

I will allow God to ______________________________

I want to be more and more like Jesus in this area because __________

My prayer is ______________________________

Reflection Diary Journal

Date ___________

Father God,

Amen.

THE CARE PLAN for God's People!

How We Think and Live Matters!

"Knowing these teachings will mean true and good health for you."
Proverbs 4:22

Read Your Bibles Everyday!

GRACE

WHAT EXACTLY IS grace? It's the free and unmerited favor of God as manifested through the salvation of sinners and the bestowal of blessings. Here's another way to understand it: God never gives up on us, his grace overlooks our shortcomings, he will always forgive us, —he knows our hearts and how to help us find our way back home. He's a merciful God, his grace and mercy is new every morning, "EVERYDAY"

Having understood what grace affords us, we should be thankful and full of gratitude. Because God did not have to give his grace to us, we are sinners—all of us. But he did! God is a gracious God! Start praising him more!

But before I leave this subject on grace I'd like to talk to the women here for a moment, if you don't mind, I'd like to talk about "Modesty" Ladies, be ladies, how we dress and carry ourselves in public matters, it is very important sisters that we be modest in our dress, let's not go around looking half naked if you are not a prostitute, don't look like one. I know that sound hard, but I use to be that girl, I use think that I could wear anything I wanted to and there was a time, I did, modesty, what's that? But I've changed. I still enjoy clothes and fashion but I'm born again, and God is my friend and I wouldn't want to make him look bad in the end. Ladies we can still be gorgeous and beautiful but we must be modest in our dress. Today lets separate ourselves from the rest.

The Care Plan suggest "Females" women and young girls, Christians and Non- Christians alike, dress upright! God knows you're beautiful, but don't look like the lady of the night! The way we dress matters to God. Also, from a flesh standpoint, it's in our safest and best interest to be modest so that we don't get taken advantage of, and tricked into thinking it's love.

So, ladies, zip up, button up, loosen up, don't become the lustful man's prey. dress modest and practice **'Holiness'** today.

Hear what saith the **LORD!**
"Be Holy for I Am Holy."
1 Peter 1:16

Give Us Grace!

Grace, Grace, Grace and 'More Grace!'

Grace, Grace, Grace and more Grace, it's never too much!

People, Grace is so much more than you know and so much better than you think, that's why it is so necessary and important that we spend as much time with God and his word as possible, me, I tell you the truth, I cannot function without him, his grace abounds, it undo me in all the right places, my dress, my attitude, and the way I live my life, Jesus is love, he has changed my heart, therefore, I cannot go on sinning, but if I did, I know because of his grace and mercy he'd forgive me — God's grace is good like that, but can I tell you something, I don't want to participate in sin, I don't want to live unholy anymore. I don't want to have sex outside of marriage, or be around those who do. I don't want to wear what I want to wear, I want to dress to please God, and I don't want to do what I want to do, not anymore, I want to be led by God. His love and grace has changed my life forever. And I want that so very much for all of you. Don't underestimate the power of grace and what it can do!

Now may "The God of Grace" always live inside of you. **Amen!**

Is Sufficient Enough!

Grace Care Plan

Make These Your Realities Day and Night

- I have the free unmerited favor of God in my life, Grace!
- Let grace have his way all day!
- Grace knows when to speak, when to be quiet!
- Grace erases your past and gives you a future that last!
- God is good, God is grace, never forget that.
- **G**od is the alpha and the omega
- **R**escues the lost
- **A** help in time of need
- **C**arries the load, died on the cross so we could live.
- **E**verlasting life, awaits all those who believe.

May The God of Grace Abound In our Lives!!!!!!!!!!!!!!!!!!

"Lady Grace"

- I am beautiful.
- I am full of grace.
- I like being a born again virgin.
- Although I have made a lot of mistakes, I can still be blessed by God, I can change, I can learn from my mistakes and move on to graceful living.
- I am a single mom, I have decided to give my life to Christ today, and bring my new baby up in righteousness! As for me and my house we shall serve the LORD!
- I am humble, meek, refined, classy and righteous.
- I am so thankful to God, for delivering me from me.
- I realize now, that my body is not my own, it belongs to God, my job is to keep it holy and pure. I shall wait for marriage, while I wait, I will pray and practice self-discipline "PURITY" Matters!

- I am changing into the kind of woman God is calling me to be "Gracefully!"
- I trust God to send me a **Godly man,** one who loves God as much as I do. When I meet that person we both shall:

Get The Care Plan
Open The Care Plan
Do The Care Plan

Is with You!

My Care Plan

From now on, I commit to ______________________________________

I will make necessary changes because ___________________________

I will allow God to ____

I want to be more and more like Jesus in this area because _________

My prayer is ____

Reflection Diary Journal

Date __________

Father God,

Amen.

GRATITUDE

I AM GRATEFUL"—WHEN was the last time you said that? I am grateful. Being thankful for what you have whether it's a little or a lot is very important. Murmuring and complaining will not send blessings your way; being full of Gratitude does!

And for those who are dealing with emotional storms, "Chaos" worry, disorder and confusion, well let me say this to you, I found that gratitude helps a lot, it calms the storms of life, the wind, the rain. I tell you the truth, all one has to do is give Jesus all your problems and pain. Besides he'll be so happy you humbled yourself and called on his holy name. The bible says cast all your cares on him, for he cares for us, remember, **In God We Trust!** I want to share this with all of you too, when I'm dealing with **" The Storms of Life"** hatred, persecution, financial difficulties—and attacks from every side. I no longer hide. I have no pride! Jesus in on my side, I had to get stronger in the word and learn to sit back and enjoy the ride! I remembered Jesus's saying to me, ***Count It All Joy"*** *"you don't belong to this world anymore!"* ***"Count It All Joy"*** and just stay focused on ***"ME"!*** Yelp, ***'Count It All Joy'*** when they hate you, they hated me first! (James 1:2, Matt. 5:11, and Luke 6:22).

Many times, it was not easy to have joy in some of those situations

I'll be honest; I wasn't there yet, **'But'** I was thankful and full of gratitude. I kept saying, "Thank you God, I trust you. Thank you for my house. Thank you for my health. Thank you for my peace that passes all understanding. Thank you for not letting me retaliate. Thank you for teaching me to forgive and love my enemies. Thank you for being with me. Thank you for comforting me. Thank you for helping me to sleep peacefully at night! Thank you for being that guiding light! Father God, strengthen me, help me get stronger and stronger so that I can easily count it all joy. And he did, Look, **"I'm Still Standing!"**

I was sent to help you now, and I say this, if you want to win in life, Gratitude is a must, we must always look at what's good in our lives, not the bad stuff, — God's word promises to help us with all that. Our main focus should be on God and his Son Jesus Christ! **Gratitude is nice, try it sometimes.**

Gratitude Care Plan

Be Thankful! God's Got You in the Palm of His Hand!

Make These Your Realities Day and Night

- Keep counting it all as joy when you are persecuted, disliked, and rejected.
- Count your blessing.
- Wake up thankful.
- Go to bed thankful.
- Show the world you're thankful by your attitude.
- Read the promises of God word every day!
- Meditate on how good God is, think about what he's already done.
- Start singing or dancing, just keep on praising him, for "HE" is worthy to be praised!
- During tough times, say, "God, I know you are going to work it all out in my favor because I trust you," then get your mind and hands off of it. Cast all your cares on him, Jesus doesn't need our help, he knows how to fix it!
- My story, God's glory I find a way to be thankful for everything, including problems, trial and tribulations. I know it's all a test of faith anyway, I don't know about all of you, but I am not going to let nothing keep me down as long as God's around!
- Get strong, grow up, time to eat meat, learn the ways of Christ!
- Gratitude, can handled being used, because it knows God is going to work everything out in its favor, that's why gratitude remains thankful no matter what life throws its way!

Gratitude Prayer!!!!

The Lord is my strength and my shield; my heart trust in him, and he helps me. My heart leaps for joy, and with my song I praise him.

Psalms 28:7

Get The Care Plan
Open The Care Plan
Do The Care Plan

Is with You!

My Care Plan

From now on, I commit to ______________________________

I will make necessary changes because ______________________________

I will allow God to ______________________________

I want to be more and more like Jesus in this area because ______________________________

My prayer is ______________________________

Reflection Diary Journal

Date ___________

Father God,

Amen.

THE CARE PLAN for God's People!

How We Think and Live Matters!

"Knowing these teachings will mean true and good health for you."
Proverbs 4:22

Read Your Bibles Everyday!

HEALER

JESUS SAID IN Matthew 11:28, "Come to me, all you who are weary and burdened and I will give you rest." Christ did not say go to somebody else or use drugs and alcohol, or commit fornication to help relieve your pain and frustration. No, don't do that! That will only make things worse for you, and send you straight to hell too, don't do it! Stop! Haven't you heard, "The wages of sin is death"? All you are doing is hurting yourself, messing your own life up, don't do that anymore.

Choose Christ! Choose Life!

Everybody, Everywhere, hear me clearly, true healing can only come from Jesus — He healed me, He will do the same for you. But you have to be willing to come out of the world and give your life to Christ, He heals troubled minds. Whatever is going on in your life, I don't care what it is, 'Our Healer' can fix it!

Choose Christ, Choose Life!

I tell you the truth, without Christ in our life, we will remain, **Sick**, **Stuck** and **Stupid**, the devil is going to have his way with us. I know that's kind of harsh, but it's true. I was lost, but now I'm found! Those 3 'S's don't apply to me anymore! I got Saved! I got Healed! I got Smart! Hope you will too!

Choose Christ, Choose Life!

And to those of you that won't choose Christ,' you say, 'I am rich; I have acquired wealth and do not need a thing, But you do not realize that you are miserable and poor and blind and naked. Revelation 3:17

How sad, outwardly some of you may have it all, but inside, you are an empty shell, like the bible says, "Blind", can't even tell. I employ all of you, let's not go out like this, — turn your life over to Christ, before it's too late! Everybody, Everywhere, In Jesus name, I lay hands on you "HEAL"! **'YOU'** cannot live for this world and God too, Unfortunately, there are those who will lash out and say, mind your own business, and don't tell me what to do, if this is **"YOU"** still I'll be praying for you. What else can I do? What else can those who care and love you do? We can't save you. Whether you go to heaven or hell the choice is not ours, but on "You". **Y - O -U** and it's sad but true, some people just have to find these things out the hard way; it may even cost them their lives. Don't let that be **YOU**, here's what you do:

Choose Christ! Choose Life!

Today if you are down and out, troubled and have lost your way, wondering where the healer is? Who is he? 'Where he at'?

Well, **The Care Plan** has good news for Everybody Everywhere, we found 'The Healer, his name is' Jesus of Nazareth, yes we found him, Jesus Christ Our Lord and Savior has come to heal the world, He is still very much alive today, He lives, He heals, and His spirit can be found all through **'The Care Plan'** too, he's waiting for you, "jump start your walk with him:

Get The Care Plan
Open The Care Plan
Do The Care Plan

Is with You!

But, — yes there's a but, you have to do the work to receive your healing, you have to first get saved, that means bye, bye world and hello to righteous living. **Next: G**et a bible in your hands, **O**pen it up and get busy reading his word, then **D**o what **GOD** word says.

Get The Care Plan
Open The Care Plan
Do The Care Plan

Is with You!

Tell all your neighbors, friends, relatives, and co-workers too, The Healer Lives' Tell them to: "Tell Everybody, Everywhere to:

Get The Care Plan
Open The Care Plan
Do The Care Plan

Is with You!

Hum! I'm the writer but still, I think it's true, **'The Care Plan'** is just what the doctor ordered! It helped me and it can help you too. This book can help **Everybody, Everywhere!**

Go in peace, says the **LORD**, your faith has made you well!

Luke 7:50, Luke 17:19, Mark 5:34

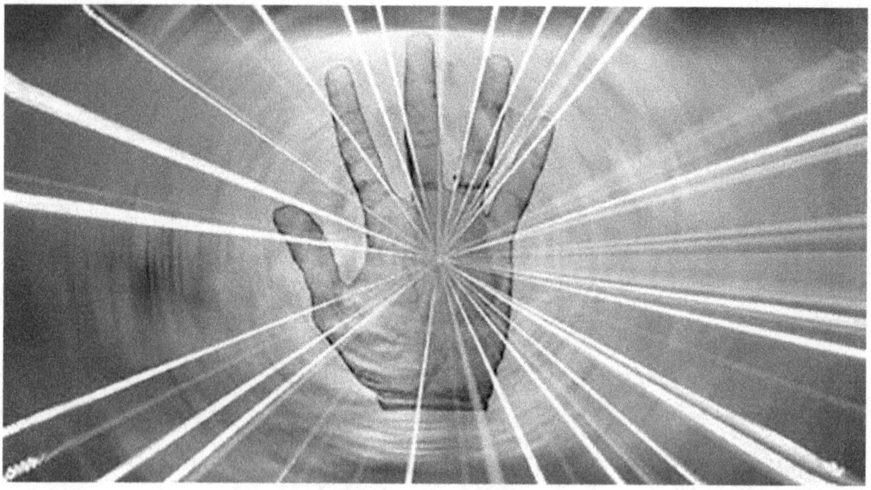

The Care Plan
for
God's People!
How We Think and Live Matters!
HOLY
BIBLE
Miss Asondra StarN'air

Everybody, Everywhere!

'The Care Plan' is giving a call out to all of those who are frustrated, fed up, and have realized you just can not make it without Christ. You have tried everything and it's not working. So many of us are burden down with all kinds of trials and tribulations however, in this world that's to be expected the bible tells us so. We have all kinds of things going on: our health, cancer, addictions, sickness, obesity, joblessness, poverty, drugs and alcohol, loneliness, depression, brokenhearted, divorce, anger, broken homes, homelessness, starvation, a trouble nation, racism, all kinds of stuff going on but we don't have to carry the load by ourselves, in fact , we don't have to deal with any of it at all. Jesus says this: Come to me , all you who are weary and burdened, and I will give you rest. Take my yolk upon you and learn from me, for I am gentle and humbled in heart and you will find rest for your souls. **Matthew 11:28-29** But on the flip side, there is no peace or rest for the sinful man or person who has denied Christ. Satan rules over you now. Some are in bondage to pornography, we have people who have turned into drug dealers, prostitutes, thieves, killers, habitual liars, gamblers, strippers lewd/lascivious entertainment, bullies, animal abusers, wife beaters, cheaters, assassins, bank robbers, greed, mentally confused, womanizers, idol worshipers, rapist, same sex relationships & marriages, bombers, scandals, murders, witchcraft do evil and laugh! You name it, narcissism, it's out there, this world is evil and dark, none of this is from God, none of it. Choose ye this day whom you will server. For those of us who belong to Christ Jesus says, no worries, he overcame the world, we don't have to live in darkness if we don't want to. listen to Jesus now: *"A time is coming and in fact has come when you will be scattered, each to your own home. You will leave me alone. Yet I am not alone, for my Father is with me. I have told you these things, so that in me you may have peace. In this world you will have trouble. But take heart! I have overcome the world"* **John 16:32-33**

'Come All You People', you are at the right place, let's all get saved! If some of you don't want too, the choice is yours, skip this page.

However for all those out there who want too, speak these words right now:

Dear God, heal me, set me free! I know I am a sinner, and I ask today for your forgiveness, Deliver me from me, help me to be all I can be, let your will be done in my life. God recue me, I need a savoir. I do believe your Son Jesus Christ die on the cross for me, suffered greatly too, he die for my sins, yet I am not to go on sinning, I must stop, the wages of sins is death, and I don't want that to happen to me. I want everlasting life now! This is why I am reaching out to you father God today, help me, give me the strength I need to get right with you, heal me of my iniquities, and all my wrong doings, although I cannot take them back, I can repent, change my ways and start all over again, I do hope it is not too late.

Today I want to move forward, I want to make Jesus LORD over my life. I want to live a righteously from now on. No more selfishness, I'm tired of me. I want to be free! So God please hear my cry, hear my plea, and heal me. Make me over! Create in me a clean heart, let me be done with this world, the one Jesus overcame, grant me the same. Right now, right this minute I am asking in Jesus name, give me a fresh start! Only you can heal and save me, I have been lost for a long time and now I want to come home to Christ. From this day forward, I give you my life to you Lord, guide me, instruct me, give me your daily bread, become part of my everyday life. Holy spirit, take over my life now, never give it back to me, I'm your for all Eternity! SAVE ME!

In Jesus name Amen!

If you just deeply and lovely prayed that prayer, without a doubt in my mind or God's **"YOU" Just Got Born Again"!!!** If you must, return to this prayer over and over again until it's deeply rooted in. "Ooh wee", I can still feel the power of that prayer, healing has happened. Many of you just got saved today. Go in peace, you have been forever changed!

Welcome to the house of believer, **"YOU ARE HEALED"!**

Congratulations

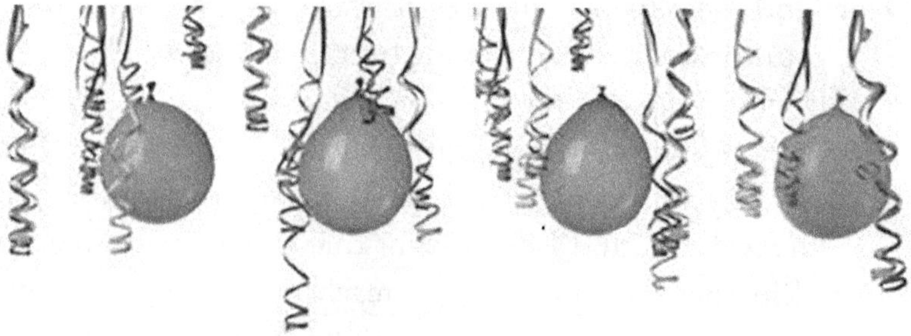

Celebrate!

Tell Everybody, Everywhere, "Today" I just got Born Again!

Name ______________________________ Date __________________________

____

____

____

____

____

____

Take Action, Find a "Church Home"!

Healing Care Plan

First of all if you just prayed that incredible prayer, with all your heart and meant every word you said, you must feel amazing right about now. Congratulations. You have become a New Creature in Christ! 'YOU' are healed, now go in peace and sin no more!!!

Make These Your Realities Day and Night

- I will read my bible daily.
- Tune into Trinity Broadcasting Network, **(TBN)** daily, retire regular TV, watch programs that are pleasing to God, sex filled TV and violent crime shows, must be eliminated from your life period. This is not the Godly way nor the Christian way!
- If you are struggling with something, go to God first then, go find a pastor or trusting friend to talk to. Let people of God pray over you too.
- Stay away from sinning, start hanging around God's people!
- Watch what you watch! Soap operas are poisonous to the soul and spirit. I know some of you are not trying to hear it, but again, you've been warned. Garbage in, garbage out!
- Watch what you listen to, too. Those who have ears let them hear. If God wouldn't entertain it, nor should we.
- Lord echoes, give up on TV, study my word and spend your time with me. **"YOU"** must choose wisely. Guard your eyes and ears!
- Take care of your physical body as well, it belongs to God, don't abuse it with over eating and things that will cause great harm, like drugs and alcohol so now let that be a thing of the past because you have a new life now!
- Remember, God did not create sickness, "WE" did. And in order to be healed, we must start to live for him in every way, and the Bible teaches us how. **'The Bible'** is our "**B**asic **I**nstructions **B**efore **L**eaving **E**arth" book and when we follow these basic

instructions, we do well, we live well too; healing will be a thing of the past. Remember what Jesus said in John 10:10, "The thief comes only to kill and destroy, I have come that they may have life and that they may have it more abundantly." I don't know about you, but I will have what Jesus is offering" Eternal Life!" Live right, don't think twice:

Get The Care Plan
Open The Care Plan
Do The Care Plan

Is with You!

My Care Plan

From now on, I commit to ______________________________

I will make necessary changes because ______________________________

I will allow God to ______________________________

I want to be more and more like Jesus in this area because ______________________________

My prayer is ______________________________

Reflection Diary Journal

Date ___________

Father God,

Amen.

HOLINESS

HOLY, HOLY, HOLY is his name and also something I had to learn to be. For many years, I felt I could do and wear whatever I wanted, — and I did. I was my own woman, nobody was going to control me or tell me what to do, is that you? But all that changed when I got saved, and I'm glad it did. Reading God's word changed my life forever— I am not the same person I use to be, I'm different! I'm born again! I'm a 'New Creature in Christ'! "Wait" didn't I tell everybody that already, I think I did, well I'm telling you again, I love being a Christian!

One day God had to have a little talk with me, he called me to our prayer closet (I have one in my home) and he spoke to me. I listened, he told me I was beautiful, but being beautiful still does not give me the right to wear what I want to wear. Be fashionable, nothing wrong with that, but don't bring shame to my name. Don't dress anymore like a **"Scarlet"**, a lady of the night. *"You belong to me now, not the world"*. Oh, my god, right then and there, I felt convicted in my heart,"Ouch" just throw me on the couch!" Quick, fast, in a hurry I threw those sleazy clothes out! Today, I am more mindful about what I put on. I don't wear high slits, and I avoid plunging neck lines. so far what I wear now seems to be fine, I haven't felt any condemnation, and if I do, I ain't wearing it! I'm sharing this with you because, I come to realize that how we dress matters to God. If we say we belong to him, we can't look like we belong to the streets. We belong to God, we were bought with a price, that price was "CHRIST"! God's Message pertaining to the body is simple ladies "Be Holy Because I Am Holy"! And oh my god, lord have mercy, females, listen especially teenagers, watch what you wear to church! Nothing holy about thigh high heel boots and skin tight jeans! Come on REALLY! Not judging, I'm just sayin'

There is a time and place for everything. We must show more respect to the house of the Lord! Wear that on your own time!

God was blunt and hard on me, so I'm blunt and hard on you, all because I love you too! I do, I want all of us to grow holy together, if you see me with something on, I shouldn't be wearing, if you love and care about me, say something please. Too don't misunderstand God wishes that we be holy, we are females, we can still be gorgeous, fantastic looking and dress sharp too, but, we just have to do it in a more wholesome and God pleasing way. I tell you the truth, friends, I feel more beautiful than ever before without those half naked and alluring clothes. I Feel Holy! I feel marvelous too! "Shout out to God" He saw something unholy looking, He said something! It stung, but I knew, he was right, and I was wrong. I can't just wear what I want to anymore, we just can't. "Our bodies are not our own"! Oh my, how this sister has grown!

Sister's from my ears to yours, here's what saith the Lord, "*how we dress matters to our Father in heaven!*" Here's a song I'm working on **"Get It Together!"**

Listen up Everybody, Everywhere (God Speaks)

"Do you not know that your bodies are temples of the Holy Spirit, who is in you, whom you have received from God? You are not your own, you were brought at a price. Therefore honor God with your bodies."

1 Corinthians 6:19

Can we talk, here's a real problem, the carnal / fleshly man is sick in sin and has no problem burning in hell for it. They will not honor God with their bodies, a lot of these men still think that they can lay hands on as many women as they'd like, like Solomon in biblical times, well they are wrong and so was Solomon and he paid a price for his foolish and lustful behavior in the end too. Yes it's true, at some point in Solomon's life he came to realize that pleasure is meaningless. And too, he said, after he surveyed all that his hands had done, and what he worked to achieved, everything was meaningless, a chasing after the wind. Men, he meant sex too, women cannot replace our first love, God. If you try to make that happen, you will be empty and disappointed just like King Solomon became. He found out and a little too late that nothing and no one can ever take the place of the 'The Almighty GOD'. In a nut shell, We Need "GOD" More Than Life Itself!

Everything else become "Meaningless!"

People I'll leave you with this **1 Corinthians 6:9-11** ready, read:

Or do you not know that the unrighteous will not inherit the kingdom of God? Do not be deceived: neither the sexually immoral, nor idolaters, nor adulterers, nor men who practice homosexuality, nor thieves, nor greedy, nor drunkards, nor revilers, nor swindlers will inherit the kingdom of God. And such were some of you. But you were washed, you were sanctified, you were justified in the name of the Lord Jesus Christ and by the Spirit of our God.

Final Word From God:

You shall be holy, because I am holy.

1 Peter 1:16

Holiness Matters!

Holy Care Plan

Make These Your Realities Day and Night

- Reframe from watching ungodly TV shows, don't be a worldly Christian, be a Kingdom Christian. Choose programs that are pleasing to God and good for your spirit!
- Same when it comes to music, choose positive inspiring material to enjoy.
- Women, girls, stop wearing luring and revealing clothes. Throw them out, get rid of them, cut them up—that's what I did.
- Practice Holiness!
- Ask your lover to leave, don't shack up with that person anymore. If you are good enough to lay with, you are good enough to be that persons spouse.
- Discipline your flesh; don't let it ruin your life anymore, stop having babies out of wedlock. God's Children deserves better than that —Get married first, "Be Holy"!
- Be patient, wait on God to send you your spouse.
- Realize, that sex is only for marriage, not for girlfriend-and-boyfriend relationships. Marriage only (Heb. 13:4). Get away from inhibitors, those who refuse to live for Christ.
- Become born again, become virgins again, become holy like our Father in heaven is again.
- Stop dating if it's going cause temptation, "Don't Date"!
- Read your Bibles, get to know Christ! Get to know what's expected of you.
- Fall in love with Jesus —make him your "Always and Forever", first.
- Embrace the thought of being pure and holy, then do it—it's a beautiful thing. Holiness comes with light and power! It also adds more years to your life—turns back the clock, so to speak! Age in reverse ladies!

- Read scriptures on "Holiness" The Bible is truly the book of life for those who really want change. I want that, and I hope you do as well.
- Pray for self-discipline, if you give in to temptation, "Repent" and work hard not to repeat the behavior, true repentance means you are going to do the work and get the help you need so that you will not do that thing again. Nevertheless, we are humans, and all fall short **"ME TOO"** but, again the more we study God's word, the less we fall back into sinning against God. Therefore, let us stay focus and committed, Purity takes time, but it must happen if "WE" want to see God. Those who do not practice righteous and holy living will not enter God's kingdom. **Romans 14:17, Galatians 5:21, 1 Corinthians 6:9,** and **Revelations 22:15, Ephesians 5 ...**

Lastly—please know I am not judging you—I have been where you all are, and I was miserable. Living for the world puts us outside of God's will and when that happens we become unholy, sick, insecure, and full of fear and doubt, that's why I got out. I wanted something real, and I found it with Jesus. I will serve him for the rest of my days! Jesus came in and changed my life in so many ways, and I want that change to happen for all of you, I want it to happen to **Everybody, Everywhere!** So today, right now, I encourage everyone reading **'The Care Plan'** to get right with God. Stop playing games, get your house in order, undo the things that you know are not pleasing to God and only you and God knows what that is, I'll just exit with this:

God knows and sees everything we can't hide anything from "The King." And if we want to reside with him, "Holiness" is what we must bring, otherwise don't bring him anything!

Get The Care Plan
Open The Care Plan
Do The Care Plan

Is with You!

"Be Holy Because I Am Holy"!

1Peter 1:16

My Care Plan

From now on, I commit to ______________________________

____

____

____

____

____

I will make necessary changes because __________________

____

____

____

____

____

I will allow God to ____________________________________

____

____

____

____

I want to be more and more like Jesus in this area because ________

____

____

____

____

____

My prayer is ____

____

____

____

____

____

Reflection Diary Journal

Date __________

Father God,

Amen.

THE CARE PLAN for God's People!

How We Think and Live Matters!

"Knowing these teachings will mean true and good health for you."
Proverbs 4:22

Read Your Bibles Everyday!

IDOLATRY

"You shall not make for yourself an image in the form of anything in heaven above or on the earth beneath or in the waters below. You shall not bow down to them or worship them; for I, the Lord your God, am a jealous God, punishing the children for the sin of the parents to the third and fourth generation of those who hate me, but showing love to a thousand generations of those who love me and keep my commandments.

—Exodus 20:3–6

But as for the cowardly, the faithless, the detestable, as for murderers, the sexually immoral, sorcerers, idolaters, and all liars, their portion will be in the lake that burns with fire and sulfur, which is the second death."

—Revelation 21:8

IDOLATRY IS A serious offense as you can see, it's woven in with other detestable sins, I tell ya, Idolatry is nothing to play around with. One of the wises ways to look at idolatry, so that you don't get caught up in it, is to look at 'Idolatry', like this, anything or anyone we place before God. Sports, TV shows, fame, entertainers, material things, ourselves, our desires, our gifts and talents, and ministries too; that's right, I said ministries too, leaders must still have a personal relationship with Christ. Can't be all church business, and no real relationship with God. Idolatry is a huge problem today, an epidemic if you will, — so many people have idols or practice idolatry. And many times we are not aware that we're doing it, but we should be. All you have to do is ask yourself, did I spend time with God today? Let's look at males and sports (We have female sports fanatics too) and use that as our example, "Sports Rules"! "Nothing" and no one is going to get in the way of the game, "Nothing!" Not only does God have to take a back seat, but their wives and families do too this my friend is what God considers Idolatry and of course now I can clearly see why. However,"Sportohlics" will beg to differ, but of course they would, "They're HOOKED"! So much so they can tell you all the in's and out's of the game. The do's and don't's, who gets paid what, and whose about to get cut! Yet they know nothing about God's word, and can care less about going to church either. Again, this is a form of Idolatry, in fact it is Idolatry. God hate all forms of idolatry. **Exodus 20:3-6**. Too many men believe this is "A Man's World" and now we have "Women" out there too talkin bout, I rule the world, we rule the world, ladies rule the world, "Please" nobodies ruling anything if you are you're ruling it with Satan. The bible teaches us "Jesus" is to be made Lord over our lives, not us or our desires. There will only be ***"One KING"*** and it's not LeBron James. With all do respect, God has blessed him, "WE" root for him, he plays a brilliant game! But **"Jesus Christ"** is "Not" his name. Nobody reigns, nobody shall rule. Idolatry is for fools. And it's sad, today, people have become their own gods. men and women alike have left their first love. But, I'm here to tell you, there is going to be a penalty for your behavior, some of you may be going through something right now. Oh, but it's not too late to turn around. Let those who have eyes see, you're full of idolatry" Let those who have ears hear, "The fear of the Lord is the beginning of wisdom!"

If you know someone caught up in "Idolatry" talk to them, tell them about the **The Care Plan**, whatever you have to do get this book in their hands! Because they are sinning against GOD, and the wages of sin is.....! So if you care about that person help try to save them, I am only one person, one book, I can't do it alone.

And now before I finish, let me just say this, all those who do enjoy sports, "Have Fun!" Go on, watch sports, go to the game, play sports too— nothing wrong with sports or any other fun activities, I like Karaoke, God does want us to enjoy ourselves while we're here. but that's not an issue or the problem, "Idolatry Is"! Last time, when we put anything before ***"The Mighty King"*** Idolatry rings and says let's do our own thing! At that point, we have turned our backs on GOD once again. Think about that tonight, **"Wake Up Everybody! Repent, Get It Right!"**

Right now, forget the touch down, turn your life around!

Idolatry has a burn in hell sound!

Idolatry Care Plan

Make These Your realities day and night

- Touch down, men, ok, women too — Everybody, Everywhere, — touch down, — turn your life around! No more idols!
- Put God before **NOUNS:** People,Places and Things! **Sports** too.
- Read scriptures on idolatry, so that you don't get caught up in it!
- Spend time with God, listening to the Holy Spirit's guidance. Read your bibles daily, **'Keep God First!"**
- Pick your friends carefully, less you become like them!
- Praise and worship our **'LORD'** daily, for he is worthy to be praised.
- Live for God, not man!
- Stay far away from fornicators and idol worshippers.
- Pray for the the loss person also pray they repent and give their life to Christ.
- Enjoy Your Everyday Life, and always," **KEEP GOD FIRST!"**

Get The Care Plan
Open The Care Plan
Do The Care Plan

Is with You!

My Care Plan

From now on, I commit to ______________________________

____
____
____
____
____

I will make necessary changes because ______________________________

____
____
____
____

____

I will allow God to ______________________________

____
____
____
____

I want to be more and more like Jesus in this area because ______________________________

____
____
____
____
____

My prayer is ______________________________

____
____
____
____
____

Reflection Diary Journal

Date __________

Father God,

____

____

____

____

____

____

____

____

____

____

____

____

____

____

____

Amen.

THE CARE PLAN for God's People!

How We Think and Live Matters!

"Knowing these teachings will mean true and good health for you."
Proverbs 4:22

Read Your Bibles Everyday!

JESUS

GETTING TO KNOW Jesus should be our first priority, but it's not, and because of that, man suffers. Everyone suffers. Jesus is supposed to be our role model; without him, we remain lost. This world's leadership is like the blind leading the blind. Sorry, but it's true.

According to Jesus, no one can get to the Father except through him, which means he is the only way. He must rule "Your World"!

But how can we get to know Jesus and follow his leadership if we don't spend time with him or read the Bible? I don't know why "YOU" think you can bypass that part, — just go to church on Sunday's and listen to the preacher preach — that's good, that's great, because faith comes by hearing the word, but I'm afraid it's not enough! If you think it is, you are sadly mistaken. Going to church is a must, we do need to be around other Christians we really do, — absolutely! However, each individual still must get to know Jesus Christ for themselves. So listen to me when I say this: 'Your pastor and others you look up to, they cannot save you. They can preach to you, — pray for you, love over you too, but they cannot save you PERIOD. There is "Only One Savior, **JESUS"!**

Jesus is Our Savior, Not Man!

Please say this with me until this sinks in:
Jesus is Our Savior, not man!
Jesus is Our Savior, not man!
Jesus is Our Savior, not man!
Jesus is Our Savior, not man!
Jesus is Our Savior, not man!
Jesus is Our Savior, not man!
Last time, Jesus is Our Savior, not man!

Give Your Life To Him, Take His Hand!

Why Don't You Come..

Hey there, Jesus is waiting for you, don't keep putting him off.

Later for the streets, later for all that wild living and partying all the time. Say 'NO" to marijuana, drugs, fornication and drunkenness. "There, I said it"! Aren't you tired, haven't you had enough? "Grow UP!"

Take a "Look" at yourself, (I did) question, why are some of you still so miserable and empty inside? Don't answer, I'll tell you why, Jesus is missing, you have not given your life to him fully. You're still out in the world trying to make things work, yet, you stay hurt, disappointed and confused. Exactly the way Satan wants you to be. I've been there, now I'm with Jesus, "I'm Free!" You're not! You are still on that wide road the bible talks about that leads to destruction; yes, you know I'm telling the truth. **"YOU"** are still living for this world and paying a price for it too — look at you! Your life's in shambles, but you can change all that if you really want it to. And I do hope you want to, because the path you're on leads to destruction. I got off that path, a long time ago and now I've come back for all of you. This is what I had to do, I had to die to self. I had to give me up! Yes, I had to come to the realization that life would never be about me or my vanity. No matter how fine or handsome we think we are, people we're not going that far, without God. And so what you've acquired cars, money and material things and all that bling; "wait", Holy Spirit speaks: "It's garbage, not fit for a King, "vanish," no longer seen". So there you have it, what we accumulate won't mean a thing! To enjoy a more peaceful and joyous life down here we must surrender to the **"KING"**! So, why don't you come...

Jesus is waiting, yes he's waiting for you to come to him. Christ wants to clean you up, help turn your life around. Our Savior wants "YOU" to invite him into your heart, He wants to become a major part of your life now, because without him you won't make it, without Jesus, none of us will. John 14:6 "Look it Up!"

Get on **The Care Plan, Stay on The Care Plan!** Get saved, give all of your life to Christ, not some of it, all of it! Tell those who want to stay in bondage and stuck in the world bye-bye! "See you later alligator, in a while crocodile"! And don't forget to pray for them and smile! Hold on, don't change the dial, this also goes for those close to you too, family members and friends, still **"YOU"** must ***"Stand Up For Christ!"*** Tell'em, hey, if you don't want Jesus in your life, "See ya, wouldn't want to be ya!" If it comes down to that, do that! Jesus must be your "First Love", The First Person You Serve, The First Person You Follow. For no one else can promise you a better tomorrow. Nor can they give you everlasting life; don't get it twisted, **"Get It Right!"** Listen to what Jesus the messiah has to say: *"Anyone who loves their father or mother more than you love me, you are not worthy of being mine; or if you love your son or daughter more than me, you are not worthy of being mine."* **Matt. 10:37**

Are "You" Worthy? Get Worthy

Get The Care Plan
Open The Care Plan
Do The Care Plan

Is with You!

"Take Up Your Cross and Follow Jesus!"

If You're ready "Rock steady"! Time for change, time to leave all foolishness behind, time for a new mind! No more living in this world blind! After we're done, open up your bibles, "go meet Jesus", study the Gospels, **Matthew, Mark, Luke and John,** read those books, get acquainted with Jesus and his teaching, pay very close attention to Jesus ministry, his walk; learn to walk like that. We all can you know, if we really want to, lets want to, I do!

Get yourself acquainted with Christ! It'll be an adventure, there's a lot he wants to share with you through those pages and beyond, I've become fond of it all! Like I said earlier. "I'm Free", this sister's having a ball! Through Christ, I tell you the truth, **"We Can Have It All!** But first we have to die to self, we have to fall. Every knee shall bow, and every tongue shall confess, Jesus is **LORD!**

While your falling, dying out of the world, denying the flesh, no worries, there's help, stop by **Matthew 5** Jesus is there. He speaks, listen to him preach the **'Sermon on the Mount',** — I know that it was preached thousands of years ago, but each time you visit that spot, the pages come alive. There's wonders working power in those pages, you'll see, don't take it from me. Go, hear him preach, Jesus will know you're there, Jesus and the Father feels his children's presence everywhere!

Go, no more worldly excuses! Just do it! Yawl do "Nike" but let me tell you something, those shoes won't save you brothers and sisters.

Do Jesus! And Do Jesus **N.O.W**! Let me tell you what I found, **N**o **O**ne **W**orks, but **JESUS!** Things don't! Money don't! People don't! Fame don't!

No **O**ne **W**orks but **JESUS!** Sister, your man don't, brother, your woman don't! I'll say this again and again and again, **N**o **O**ne **W**orks but **Jesus! N**o **O**ne **W**orks! Not happening **Keep Jesus First!** He is the only one who can set us all free, and get Everybody, Everywhere where we need to be, stay with him all the way from **A to Z.**

If you don't believe me, check this out, let's put an end to your doubt!

Thomas said to him "Lord we do not know where we are going, so how can we know the way? John 14:5

Jesus answered, "I am the way and the truth and the life. No one comes to the father except through me, John 14:6

See, Didn't I tell Ya! So:

Get with Jesus
Obey Jesus
Do the work of Jesus
Is with YOU!

Jesus Care Plan

Make These Your Realities Day and Night

Gather! Everybody, Everywhere, Jesus Speaks, Lets Listen:

- "Come to me all who are weary and burdened and I will give you rest" (Matt. 11:28).
- "Whoever want to be my disciple, pick up your cross and follow me" (Matt. 16:24).
- "Let the spiritually dead bury their own dead, your job is to preach the gospel" (Matt. 8:22).
- "Whoever drinks the water I give them will never thirst again" (John 4:14).
- When you are ready, meet me on the mountainside, I want to teach you "The Beatitudes". (Matt 5-7).
- "Very truly I tell you, whoever believes in me will do the works I have even greater things than these because I am going to the Father." John 14:12
- "Be strong and courageous, I will never leave you" (Deut. 31:6).
- "Walk in obedience to all I have command you that it may go well with you." (Jer. 7:23).
- Honor the Lord with your wealth with the first fruits of all your crops.
- "Praise him constantly and work toward living righteous lives. Don't hand out with evil doers lest you become like them" (Prov. 4:14).
- The wages of sin is death, but the gift of God is eternal life. (Rom 6:23)
- Keep spending quality time with me.
- Don't get off 'The Care Plan' it got you covered from A to Z.
- Learn The Ways of Our LORD, "Get On Board", Stay on Board!

"All Aboard!"

Get The Care Plan
Open The Care Plan
Do The Care Plan

Is with You!

Miss Asondra StarN'air

The Care Plan, just what the doctor ordered!

Get Yours Today!

My Care Plan

From now on, I commit to ____
____
____
____
____
____

I will make necessary changes because ____________________________
____
____
____
____

____
I will allow God to ____
____
____
____
____

I want to be more and more like Jesus in this area because _________
____
____
____
____
____

My prayer is ____
____
____
____
____
____

Reflection Diary Journal

Date ___________

Father God,

____

____

____

____

____

____

____

____

____

____

____

____

____

____

____

Amen.

THE CARE PLAN for God's People!

How We Think and Live Matters!

"Knowing these teachings will mean true and good health for you."
Proverbs 4:22

Read Your Bibles Everyday!

JOY

JOY TO THE world, The Lord has come" let earth receive her king"! Let's Keep joy in our hearts always, Jesus Lives! He Reigns Forever! Jesus is with us right now! He said that, he will never, ever leave us! He will be with us, always. Joy to the world, yes the Lord has come Jesus our Lord and Savior dwells in the lives of those who have made Him Lord over their lives. The joy we have is an everlasting joy. The world didn't give it to us nor can it take it away. "Can I get a witness"? See, for the true believer, we understand that Jesus is not a once-in-a-year holiday treat; a 'Wal-Mart Christmas present' under a tree or a great big old turkey, oh no, he's more than a feast. He's 'The Messiah' The Savior of The World. Hallelujah, **JOY, JOY, JOY!** The Alpha and The Omega! The First and the Last! The only one who can save us and forget our past! "Joy to the world" he's our strength when we are down and out or weak, he's the one who'll help us get back on our feet, that's why we ought to be singing his praises constantly! Joy to the world, the Lord has come, let earth receive her king, let every heart prepare him room, and let heaven and nature sing! Here's my spin on it: Joy to the world, every boy and girl, let Jesus come into your life and do his thing, let every soul, be full of joy, Jesus is not about toys, Jesus is not about toys, Jesus, - is – not –about – toys….if you agree with this make some noise, if you agree with this make some noise, if – you- agree –with – this – make – some – noise. Joy to the world, Jesus is always near, so never have no fear, let every care you have, give it to Jesus and laugh, let your joy be seen, let your joy be seen, let – your – joy – let your joy be seen, we know the king, joy to the world the Lord has come!

Jesus is with us winter, spring, summer, and fall so don't sell him out for the shopping mall! Let every heart prepare him room, did you know, he's coming back soon, yes he's coming back soon, Jesus- is -coming- back- soon. Joy to the world the Lord has come let heaven and nature sing, let him in your life, so He can do his thing, Celebrate all the peace, love and joy **HE** brings!

Everybody, Everywhere, **Sing!**

Joy to the world, The Lord has come! Let earth receive her king!

Let every heart, prepare him room, let heaven and nature sing, and let Jesus come into your life and do his thing! Let Jesus – come – into – your – life –and – do –his thing! Celebrate all the peace, love and joy He brings, celebrate – all- the- peace- love - and- joy- He -brings!

"Now" how about that one? I love it!
"Jesus Is Joy To The World!!!"

Joy Care Plan

Make These Your realities Day and Night

- Rejoice always no matter what's going on, keep praising God.
- When someone throws lemons at you, ask them is that all you got!
- Sing joy to the world, when life tries to beat you down, welcome that sound! Sing it all year around.
- Read all the promises of God, this will help renew your strength and keep you joyous!
- Every day and everywhere you go, no matter what's going on, **'Think Jesus', 'Think Joy!'**
- Think about all the wonderful things Jesus has already done in your life, still doing, and is about to do in your life, Praise him every day, **'Think Jesus, Think Joy!'**
- Do what I do: sing "Joy to the world / The Lord has come." Keep singing it until victory's won. No weapon formed against a child of God will ever prosper, so **'Think Jesus, Think Joy!'**
- Fight for your ***'JOY'*** man did not give it; therefore, don't let people or circumstances take it away **'Think Jesus, Think Joy!'**
- **Pray for Joy, Pursue Joy, Press on in Joy and Prosper in Joy!** Stay Blessed, **"Enjoy!"**
- When despised, Dance like David! Leap up out of your seat, get up on your feet, and dance that dance, dance that dance of joy before the Lord! If you are his and you know it, don't be afraid to show it! Praise and dance with all you might, that's how **"WE"** Christians fight. (2 Sam. 6:14) **"Keep Joy Alive!"**

Get The Care Plan
Open The Care Plan
Do The Care Plan

Is with You!

My Care Plan

From now on, I commit to ______________________________

____

____

____

____

____

I will make necessary changes because ____________________

____

____

____

____

____

I will allow God to _______________________________

____

____

____

____

I want to be more and more like Jesus in this area because ________

____

____

____

____

____

My prayer is ____

____

____

____

____

____

Reflection Diary Journal

Date ___________

Father God,

Amen.

THE CARE PLAN for God's People!

How We Think and Live Matters!

"Knowing these teachings will mean true and good health for you."
Proverbs 4:22

Read Your Bibles Everyday!

KINDNESS

But love your enemies and do good, and lend, expecting nothing in return; and your reward will be great, and you will be sons of the most high, for he is kind to the ungrateful and the evil.

—Luke 6:35

WHAT IS CHRIST saying here? I believe he's saying this, when people disappoint us, hurts us, slander and tell lies about us, use us, throw us away like garbage — mistreat us badly, not only are we to forgive them, we are to still help them if they are in need or in trouble. But let me be clear here, because people will take your heart and kindness for weakness — family too, in fact the scriptures say so, it says 'Your' with a capital Y, Your enemies are right in "YOUR" own household. Matthew 10:36

Don't I know, don't I know, — but don't I **FORGIVE**, don't I **HEAL**, don't I **GROW!** Kindness, is not always easy, especially when you've been wronged, get with Jesus, he'll help you along, he helped me. I am not angry at those who crossed or hurt me, don't you be either. Kindness sets God's people apart from the rest of the world, but like I said it is not always easy to be kind. Because there are times when people of the world will take your kindness for weakness. But still, no matter what, it is very important that we practice kindness. But just as important, especially now with all the evil and darkness that exist out in the world today, we are to still guard our hearts— that means we are not to just sit there and allow people, family members too or the world to trample all over us. Not at all, as God's children —we must protect ourselves and the kingdom too. Oh. Yes, yes, yes, we must fight for our right to be Christians, but we don't' fight the way the world fights, we fight with love and kindness, we fight with faith, we fight with the word of God.

As it is written, 'Real Christians' like us "WE" face death/hatred all day long, we are hated in this world, the bible says "WE" are regarded as sheep to be slathered. Romans 8:36

So for some of you babes in Christ, I'm sure the questions still remains, how in the world can we still be kind when we have enemies on every side? How can we be expected to love these kinds of people, how? I ask God our Father, the same thing, and this is what he said to me, ask Jesus?

So I did, and this was his response, forgive them, for they know not what they do! Now this is what **The Care Plan** is telling all of you, to say and do, Father, forgive them, for they know they do! Luke 23:34

I know it hurts sometimes and don't seem fair saints but Jesus knows more than anybody else how painful it is to be persecuted and hated for being good, but still, Jesus forgave and remain kind hearted all the way to the end. Let me encourage your hearts today to hold on to Christ, hold on to his kindness, because we can't pull this off without him, in our own flesh, we are more likely to take matters in our own hands, and do something rash, kick somebodies — oops, I cannot say that, I' za 'Christian' now! Lord have mercy on me, so glad I got saved! And just in the nick of time!

'Kindness Your Highness' brothers and sisters only in Jesus will we find it! So let's not take matters in our own hands, Jesus has a different plan, want to hear some of them, here they are:

- Be kind and compassionate to one another, forgiving each other, just as God forgave you. Ephesians 4:32
- But the fruit of the Spirit is love, joy, peace, forbearance, kindness, goodness, faithfulness, gentleness and self-control. Against such things there is no law. Galatians 5:22-23
- But love your enemies, do good to them, and lend to them without expecting to get anything back. Then your reward will be great, and you will be children of the Most High, because he is kind to the ungrateful and the wicked. Luke 6:35
- Talk about kindness, look what God did: For God so loved the world that he gave his one and only Son, that whoever believes in him shall not perish but have eternal life. John 3:16

- Do not let kindness and truth leave you; Bind them around your neck, Write them on the tablet of your heart. Proverbs 3:3

So there you have it, it pays to be kind, to be full of love and forgiveness. God will bless you! Be strong and courageous, learn the ways of Christ so when people betray or hurt you, — with kindness in your heart, you too can say, like Jesus ***"Father Forgive Them For They Know Not What They Do."***

Besides kindness will look good on **"YOU"** It certainly looks good on "Me", this ain't vanity!

This is Christianity!

This little light of mine, I'm going to let it shine and be kind and be kind and be kind!

Kindness Care Plan

Make These Your Realities Day and Night

- Smile more! It makes you more kindhearted.
- Kindness loves and gives to others, kindness forgives its sisters and brothers!
- Learn more about how kind and generous Jesus was. He was so kind and generous that he *gave* up his own life for us. Open up your bibles read the four Gospels: **Matthew, Mark, Luke and John**. Hurry!!! "Miracles" "Wisdom", "Kindness" plus more awaits you.
- Do random acts of kindness every day! You'll be surprised, others may follow by example, kindness can go a long way!
- Tithe it's ah beautiful thing! There is nothing like it, plus it's what's expected of us. Kindness says, **"In God We Trust" Kindness** gives God what he ask for and more!
- Volunteer to do something without payment or expecting anything in return. **Giving People are Free People!** Therefore be kindhearted, **"Live To Give!"**
- Forgive and love no matter what — love does not depend on others, just you!
- Hang out with loving and forgiving individuals, people who have no time for bitterness or hatred.
- To singles especially, be kind to yourself —Love yourself like God loves the church, you don't have to wait for a spouse to do it, you do it! When was the last time you bought yourself some f lowers or took yourself out to dinner? Do it! Have dinner with Jesus!
- Help People Out! —**Help Everybody, Everywhere!**
- Keep, **"KINDNESS"** in your heart!

Kindness comes in so many forms, through words, service, when we smile and when we help others when they are down.

Get The Care Plan
Open The Care Plan
Do The Care Plan

Is with You!

My Care Plan

From now on, I commit to ______________________________

____

____

____

____

____

I will make necessary changes because ______________________________

____

____

____

____

____

I will allow God to ______________________________

____

____

____

____

I want to be more and more like Jesus in this area because __________

____

____

____

____

____

My prayer is ______________________________

____

____

____

____

____

Reflection Diary Journal

Date ___________

Father God,

____

____

____

____

____

____

____

____

____

____

____

____

____

____

____

Amen.

THE CARE PLAN for God's People!

How We Think and Live Matters!

"Knowing these teachings will mean true and good health for you."
Proverbs 4:22

Read Your Bibles Everyday!

LOVE

SO "WE" THINK we know what love is — **"WE"** don't! Only God and his son Jesus knows what love is and what love is not. My story, God's Glory, I met God at the tender age of seven, on a roof top. My heart stopped, my head dropped, that roof top became a holy spot! The love I encounter there could never ever be described. That day, I died —*He* came alive. Yes, I met love, I talked with love, I let go and surrendered to love. After that, I was never the same — I can no longer live for me" what's there to gain? "Nothing" Jesus reign!

So **"YOU"** think you know what love is, **"YOU"** don't! The world's kind of love is treacherous! All kinds of things are required, and if you don't meet those requirements than, there's a price to pay. Jesus found that out, one dark and cruel day. But Love brought him back away.

Love, loves Everybody, Everywhere! Whether you're black or white, crooked or not right, **"Love loves"** it never leaves that position! Love, does not hurt or bully others, it's not Jealous and conniving. Oh no, on the contrary, people, love's always arriving!!! And **Love** is always there when we need it, "relax", close your eyes, sit back and breathe it. **L.O.V.E** "World We Need It!"

"Whoever lives in love, lives in God, and God in them."
1 John 4:16

JESUS IS LOVE and he thinks love! And if we say we love him, "WE' should think love too. What do I mean by **"Think Love"?** I learned this from Christ a long time ago, If you love someone because they love you, we are not loving at all. We love, when we love our enemies, — we love, sisters and brothers when we are hated, —we love, when we are not loved back. —That's when we truly love.

Moving forward, **'Think Love'**! If you do, you'll be free as a dove!

Right now Jesus wants to challenge you, give you something to think about, while you 'think love' ponder this, *"If you love only those who love you, why should you get credit for that? Even sinners love those who love them."* **Luke 6:32** what ah scripture, now that's love, so from now on **"Think Like Love"**

Jesus and I have become one, join us on our mission,

Stay In the Love Position!

Love Position

It is written that in this world we are going to have trials and tribulation, and be mistreated too. So here's want you do my sisters and brothers, get full of his word and suit up, wear the full Amor of God, "WE" are going to need it, even in the love position. We still are going to have to fight for our right to be Christians.

- If you are hated, or despised, same thing, stay in the love position.
- If you lose your job no that, God shall still provide for his children **Stay In the Love Position!**
- If you've been betrayed by someone very close to you, Jesus too, me too, forgive them, and heal, but stay in the love position.
- If your good name got dragged down to the mud, Jesus too, me too, **'Think Love'** focus on forgiveness'
- If you were schemed on, lied about, and had to deal with financial losses because of it, don't hate nor retaliate, "Vengeance is mines, says the Lord," Their foot shall slip in due time.. **Deut.32:35, Rom.12:17**
- And lastly, If you feel abandon, all alone, like nobody's there, nobody cares, Jesus too, (My God, My God why hast thou forsaken me? **Matthew 27:46,Mark15:34)** Me too, (Why am I so misunderstood and hated for doing good?). Christian, we must remember that in this dark and evil world, we are like sheep to be slaughtered. **Stay In the Love Position** let that be our life long mission!

Love Will Bring Us Back!

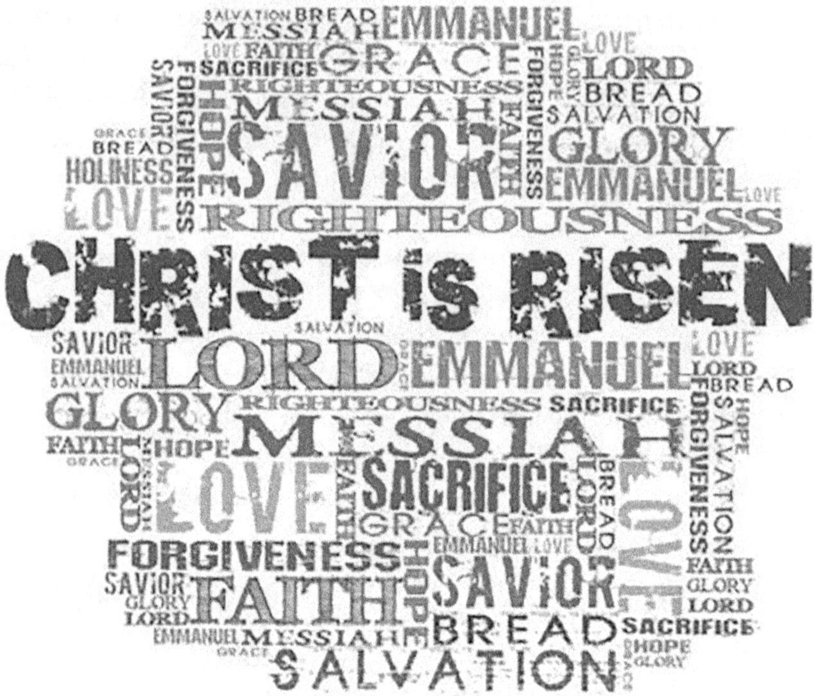

Stay With Love, Stay In The Love Position!

Hold On To Your Love!

Ephesians 4:2 "Be completely humble and gentle; Be patient, bearing with one another in love."

Peter 4:8 "Above all, love each other deeply because love covers a multitude of sins."

John 15:12 "My command is this: Love each other as I have loved you."

Fly High on Jesus, "He's Love!"

Get The Care Plan
Open The Care Plan
Do The Care Plan

Is with You!

Love Care Plan

Make These Your Realities Day and Night

- Stay in the love position, Period! Don't leave it for bitterness, Unforgiveness, or anything. Love conquers all. Never forget that!
- Read your bibles! Go to 1 Corinthians 13:4–8 find out what loves all about. Print it out and post it on your nightstand—that's what I did. Let's read it every day and every night until we get it right!
- Pray daily! Ask the Holy Spirit to show you what love is and what love is not. People, don't be gullible please find this out, — especially women, many times our enemies are right in our own households. Matthew 10:36
- Be humble and think of others as better than yourself (Phil. 2:3).
- Love the way Jesus loves, **"Think Love"!**
- Fall in Love with love, before man! Only those who eat the meat of the word understands.
- Help people, love your enemies, let them see Christ in you, every day, I know it's hard sometimes, pray!
- "Give", love gives and keeps on giving.
- Listen to positive recording and watch positive and uplifting things. Don't be a soap opera queen! If you say you are a Christian, don't do such things!
- Love is God, God is Love, Accept This Gift From Above.
- Stay focus on "LOVE" — Love is all that matters!
- Jesus speaks, "Anyone who loves me will obey my teaching." John 14:23
- Love is patient, love is kind, love forgives a thousand times!

LOVE

1 Corinthians 13

If I speak in the tongues of men or of angels, but do not have love, I am only a resounding gong or a clanging cymbal. If I have the gift of prophecy and can fathom all mysteries and all knowledge, and if I have a faith that can move mountains, but do not have love, I am nothing. If I give all I possess to the poor and give over my body to hardship that I may boast, but do not have love, I gain nothing.

Love is patient, love is kind. It does not envy, it does not boast, it is not proud. It does not dishonor others, it is not self-seeking, it is not easily angered, it keeps no record of wrongs. Love does not delight in evil but rejoices with the truth. It always protects, always trusts, always hopes, always perseveres.

Love never fails. But where there are prophecies, they will cease; where there are tongues, they will be stilled; where there is knowledge, it will pass away. For we know in part and we prophesy in part, but when completeness comes, what is in part disappears. When I was a child, I talked like a child, I thought like a child, I reasoned like a child. When I became a man, I put the ways of childhood behind me. For now we see only a reflection as in a mirror; then we shall see face to face. Now I know in part; then I shall know fully, even as I am fully known.

And now these three remain: faith, hope and love. But the greatest of these is love.

Get The Care Plan
Open The Care Plan
Do The Care Plan

Is with You!

My Care Plan

From now on, I commit to ______________________________

I will make necessary changes because ______________________________

I will allow God to ______________________________

I want to be more and more like Jesus in this area because __________

My prayer is ______________________________

Reflection Diary Journal

Date __________

Father God,

Amen.

LONELINESS

LIVING THE CHISTIAN LIFE here on planet earth can be lonely and depressing at times. We have very few friends, if any at all. We are wonderful individuals but hated too—rejected because of our walk with Christ. We are in the world but not of it, and it shows. Therefore, a lot of people hate us and reject the love and kindness we have to offer, they don't connect with us and they don't want us around. It feels as if we are abandoned, and we are—abandoned by the world at large and perhaps by love ones too, "Me Too" **"WE"** are different, and it shows, we don't live like the world does, or share its beliefs. The people of the world believes that we only live once. Therefore, "just do it" party like its 1999, go for it! All of it! Sex, drugs and rock and roll baby! Live life, the way you want to, do whatever feels good and right to you! A ain't nobody's business kinda world, lust, Sodom and Gomorrah, filled with both females and males prostitutes and whores. But that is not the Christian way, those of us who really love Christ and respects God's authority over our lives, — we don't think like that, we don't live like that either. We might have in the past gone along with that kind of foolishness and stupidity, but we've changed. We grew up, and became 'New Creatures in Christ'— born again, we don't practice sin and unclean living anymore. And gossip and strife, we want no parts of, so we hang out by ourselves a lot, at least I do, and many times it gets lonely, very lonely. But we *must* press on people of God, and realize this is what's meant by **"Pick Up Your Cross And Follow Me"**. — 'Live Righteously'! And because we do that, we're outcasted. Jesus already warned us in his word, he said, you will be hated by everyone because of me, **Matthew 10:22**

But not only hated, rejected too.

Therefore, being a Christan can be quite lonely.

We must also realize that loneliness is part of life it happens to Everybody, Everywhere, people get lonely. And for various reasons too, breakups, loss of a loved one, loss of a pet, loss of something, or if you're single like I am, loneliness can be a problem, especially around the holidays, but me, I'm okay, I'm lonely in a special way! I long for my Lord, so I pray! Nevertheless, life goes on, Christ was born! So if there's anybody out there struggling with loneliness, **"Choose Christ"** living for him is nice! Be strong and courageous, fight! Don't let loneliness get you down. Pull out your bibles and go to the book of Psalms and read, read and keep reading until that loneliness is gone. Google scriptures on loneliness, — I still do. If you can't read, then get on your knees and pray, — invite Jesus in, again, loneliness and broken hearts do mend. I am not only a writer, but I'm also a Certified Nurse Assistant and let me tell you I have seen a lot of loneliness and depression in my lifetime and let me tell you, loneliness is no good for anybody — especially if it hangs around too long, and here's why I say this: Loneliness can lead to fornication, over eating, medication, and drug and alcohol abuse. It can also lead to suicidal thoughts and attempts. In other words, loneliness if not dealt with can be very dangerous to your mind, body, and soul. There's no telling what Satan will have you do. Therefore if you are lonely, do something positive about it quick, get into the Lord's word. Don't go searching for love in all the wrong places. Don't take to the streets, not caring who you sleep with or meet; that kind of loneliness is going to hurt you, it can lead to unplanned pregnancy —prostitution — sexual diseases — anger— disappointments, — assault — rape — kidnapping — porn — and other evils the bible talks about. Now as you can see, loneliness can wreck your life from terribly. And it gets worse, loneliness can make you become corrupt, if you don't give it up! next thing you know, you are in bondage to all kind of things. Next comes hopelessness and despair. Be strong and courageous, fight against loneliness, Jesus cares and ***He*** promises to always be there! **Deut.31:16** Do something about loneliness. Don't wait until it's too late, not often, but when you get a chance, take a look at what's going on in the news these days; people are lonely depressed and dying. And check out **"Hollywood"** too — stars have dropped dead, overdosed, hung themselves, committed suicide. Loneliness is nothing to play around with period, it can cost you your life. See, **"Loneliness"** is no respecter of persons, not at all, oh no, this thing called **"Loneliness"** it will come after anyone, rich, poor, black, white, young, old, everybody, everywhere. **"Loneliness"** robs steals and kills if you let it. It's like a thief in the night, just waiting for us to get depressed, "cave in", give up or end our lives, **"DON"T DO IT"!** Get up, don't just keep lying around crying all day, get with God, get with Christ, let him wipe those tears away, give your life to him today. He is the only way we can defeat this world, take back the life God meant for us to have. And another thing, this goes out to the ladies, when you feel lonely or your heart is breaking, stop playing all those sad love songs, or somebody done me wrong songs instead get with Jesus, read his word get strong and move on. Jesus says ***"Come to me all who are weary and carry heavy burdens, and I will give you rest."*** Matthew 11:28

Throw all your anxieties (bills, problems, heartbreaks, mistakes, loneliness, unpleasantness, depression, car problems, job problems, health problems, relationship problems, family problems) —you name it, cast it all on him, because he cares for us. 1 Peter 5:7

But there is something each one of you have to do too, because faith without you doing some work to help make things better for yourself is dead, you have to get off your butt and do something, you have to make up your mind, who you're going to live for, Man(this world) or Christ? If it's going to be Christ, then get busy, **"Clean House"** Keep worldly folks out!

Listen everybody, if you want to defeat loneliness,"I have", then you have to work with Christ, He is not going to do all the work for you, while you sit back and keep feeling sorry for yourself, get up, enough is enough!

Listen up, Jesus said, if my people, who are called by my name, will humble themselves and pray and seek my face and turn from their wicked ways, then I will hear from heaven, and I will forgive their sins and I will heal their land. Some of you have brought the pain of loneliness on yourself, you can't continue blaming others for that, you are not living right and you know it, — In order for some of that loneliness and pain to go away, you have to get right with God. Just Do it! Do what that scripture just said, turn from your wicked ways, —people sex outside of marriage is wrong — that's just one example the Lord had me to throw out there! Unclean living in any shape or form, is not good, no good things is going to come out of it.

We must give up this world and say good-bye to our worldly ways, then God will heal us, we'll live, we'll be okay. However, no one is going to force you or make you choose, if you win, you win, if you lose, you just lose! But why stay lonely, depressed, in bondage and used? Why don't you get your life cleaned up and help me spread the good news.

Jesus Christ has a better life for YOU!

Lastly, whether you are going through something hard that you don't think anyones else understands or you are facing a change in life, or perhaps you just got some bad news and you feel all alone and just don't know what to do. Turn to God and his word, let him comfort, strengthen and guide you out of the world and into His. You don't have to be scared, depressed or lonely find your peace with him, make him your one and only.

Come to Christ, He's still waiting...

"Peace I leave with you, my peace I give you. I do not give as the world gives. Do not let your heart be troubled and do not be afraid. **John 14:24**

"I am with you and I will protect you wherever you go ...I will not leave you until I have finished giving you everything I have promised you. **Genesis 28:15**

For I know the plans I have for you, declares the LORD, "plans to prosper you and not harm you, plans to give you hope and a future. **Jeremiah 29:11**

Turn to me and be gracious to me, for I am lonely and afflicted. **Psalms 25:16**

So do not fear, for I am with you; do not be dismayed, for I am your God. I will strengthen you and help you; I will uphold you with my righteous right hand. **Isaiah 41:10**

Loneliness Care Plan

Make These Your Realities Day and Night

- Read the book of Psalms.
- Come out of the world and stay out.
- Get plenty of sleep and watch what you eat.
- Remember, there is power—wonder-working power in the name of Jesus. He will heal you and help take away your loneliness, let Him!
- Pray for wholeness!
- Keep loving and forgiving those who have hurt you.
- If you are single, stay holy, stay pure, reframe from having sex outside of marriage, — don't do it! Otherwise, you jeopardizes everything, your body, your future and all your blessing too. Men this goes for you too. re-frame from sexual intercourse until you are married. We don't want a "Man's World", We want a **GOD'S** World!
- If any of you are experiencing any kind of loneliness treat yourself to a nice time, go out and do something fun, treat yourself wonderfully, Buy chocolate and flowers for yourself once a month. Take candle -light baths make that a normal routine, do something! Don't let loneliness keep you down.
- Read your bibles daily — guard your hearts and minds — Take every thought captive — Keep living for Christ — Keep fighting the good fight of faith— and remember nothing can separate us from the love of God that is in Jesus Christ Our Lord and Savior, **"Nothing!"**
- Now, repeat after me: "I don't believe in loneliness. I am so very loved by God, I can heal from anything, I know ***"The King"*** and all the happiness He brings, who wants to hook-up with loneliness, not me, I want to be happy and free. **Loneliness is *not* living with me, Christ is!**

- Be strong, be courageous, be ready, be on guard, because **Loneliness** gets lonely without people, it will try to overtake you, don't let it!
- Loneliness is not your friend, don't let loneliness in! Don't do it! Instead do Christ! Get with Him, Stay with Him.

Get The Care Plan
Open The Care Plan
Do The Care Plan

Is with You!

Loneliness Oh, "NO" I'm Not Having It!

My Care Plan

From now on, I commit to ____
____
____
____
____
____

I will make necessary changes because ___________________________
____
____
____
____

____
I will allow God to ____
____
____
____
____

I want to be more and more like Jesus in this area because ________
____
____
____
____
____

My prayer is ____
____
____
____
____
____

Reflection Diary Journal

Date __________

Father God,

____

____

____

____

____

____

____

____

____

____

____

____

____

____

____

In Jesus's name. Amen!

LIGHT

"Be Light"!

THIS LITTLE LIGHT of mine I'm gonna let it shine, this little light of mine, I'm gonna let it shine, let it shine, let it shine, let it shine, everywhere I go, I'm gonna let it shine, everywhere I go, I'm going to let it shine, let it shine, let it shine let it shine!"

We must do this "**Let Our Light Shine"** we must not let the world defeat us Christians, light is stronger and more powerful than darkness.

> *"Let your light shine before man in such a way that they may see your good works, and glorify your Father who is in Heaven"* (Matt. 5:16).

This is God's request to all those walking in love and truth. You are full of his light! So what if the world hates us? We must not let that stop us from shining. Because we are Jesus's followers we are needed, we light up in places that are dark. Christ puts it like this:" You are the light of the world, A city on a hilltop that cannot be hidden! Matthew 5:14

How cool is that! Here's more...

> *"Arise, shine, for your light has come, and the glory of the LORD has risen upon you"* (Isaiah 60:1).

We are the crème de la crème, the salt of the earth; we make everything wonderful and delightful, we make the world a better place to be in my friend! Keep your head up!

To Everybody, Everywhere, **Be Light!**

Let Your Light Shine!

- Christians
- Church Leaders and Pastors
- Young and Old
- Single Parents
- Husbands and Wives
- Singles
- Students
- Teachers
- Artist /Entertainers
- Professionals
- Soul Searchers
- Caregivers
- The Incarcerated and Rehabilitated
- Addict and Substance Abusers
- The Brokenhearted and Lonely
- All Races and Colors
- For the Lost and Found
- For you, For me

The harvest is plentiful but the laborers are few; Matthew9:37

Let the Christ in "US" Shine Everywhere We Go!

- **Christians**, Everybody, Everywhere is watching us, we are to be the examples of righteous living, and a heart that's always giving. We are 'The Light of Jesus Christ', we are the change that the world needs to see, **Be Love — Be light!**

- **To the Young and Old:** Makes no difference, Choose Christ! **Be Love —Be Light!**

- **Husbands and Wives:** Be Jesus kind to each other, let his light in you produce love and peace in your home. **Be Love — Be Light!**

- **Students:** Make reading your bibles top priority, go to school too, but don't forget to take Christ with you. **Be Love —Be Light!**

- **Artist and Entertainers:** They say, "Ain't No Business Like Show Business" — no I say world, Ain't No Business Like God's Business"! Put him first or be cursed! Watch what you do or rehearse. consider the mind of God first, **Be Love — Be Light!**

- **Soul Searchers:** Search no more, Jesus is here waiting — walk through the door, everything you tried doesn't work anymore, why wrestle with unrest, or be confused about whose philosophies are wrong or right, come to Christ, **Be Love —Be Light!**

- **The Incarcerated and Rehabilitated:** Just because you messed up, God said, **"Tell The People I Love'em, Tell The People I'm Here"** So I say, use this moment right now as a perfect time to get right with God, to learn and grow from all the mistakes you've made. Today's a new day! A chance to start all over again — for Christ is the only one who can wipe all our sins away — remember them no more. It's time to walk through a different door, a door that leads to eternal life. God's mercy and kindness keeps on forgiving, please forgive yourself too, come join us —Live right **—Be right — Be Love —Be Light!**

- **The Brokenhearted and Lonely:** Be patient my child, this too shall pass, there is someone closer than a brother, closer than a mother too, that is always with you, you don't have to be lonely, God is with you, Jesus Christ he's our comforter! Our healer The lifter of our head, the only one who can make everything all right. So don't worry, be happy, Dry your tears, don't cry, look to him, cast all your cares on him, because he cares for you. Put your life in Christ hands, you'll be more than alright. **Be Love — Be Light!**

- **The Lost and Found:** Each has a role to play, **The Lost** — God has his angels out searching for you, it's time to come home! It's time to lean on God, it's time to be strong. "Come Home" fight! **Be Love —Be Light!** To **'The Found',** come on, take action, help spread 'The Gospels' of **—Matthew — Mark —Luke —**and **John**. Help point the way to Jesus, win souls for Christ! **Be Love —Be Light!**

- **Church Leaders and Pastors:** Practice what you preach! And remember this too, to whom much is given, much will be required. And to whom people have committed much, of that person, they will ask more. That's what leadership is for, God bless you, — We love and appreciate all of you. — **Be Blessed — Be Love — Be Light!**

- **Single Parents:** God's word will get you through the toughest times —the ups and downs, He will be a helper in time of need. Don't worry about what you will wear or eat, he will always put food on the table and shoes on your child's feet! —Lean on God, have faith and stay strong in the **LORD,** you'll be more than alright.— **Be Love— Be Light!**

- **Singles:** Singleness is a gift from God! It's a simpler life in many ways, out attention is not so divided, we can give God 100% of us, and be used full time without any guilt or compromise, and bypass all the worldly drama and upsets relationships can bring. But if you cannot manage your desires, wait for God to send you a spouse. Sex is for marriage only. Don't follow this world's mindset, we are to remain pure until we marry. If you already messed up in that department, 'Me Too" but, I repented made all the necessary changes and got back on a righteous path... and so must you. This message goes out to men too. — Good things comes to those who wait! Trust God to send you your soul mate! Stay pure, wait, **Be Love —Be Light!**

- **Teachers:** Keep on teaching, Preachers, keep on preaching! Teachers make great students and good people out of all of us! Jesus was a teacher, Jesus was a preacher too! — If there were no teachers we'd all stay lost! Teachers we appreciate you! Keep doing what you do. **Be Love —Be Light!**

Professionals and Politicians: Both are positions of power, and know that ***"God Is Watching"*** yes He is watching ever second, every minute and every hour! Therefore, watch what **"YOU"** do with that trusted power? **—Be Fair, don't devour — Be Love — Be Light Do What's Fair and Right!**

- **Caregivers:** O' how beautiful you are, you are God's shining stars you help care for the sick, you help care for the poor, you even wash feet and mop up f loors, you are someone very, very special, someone God adores! Although many times over-looked, over-worked, and under-paid too, — like the late great 'Donna Summer' found out **"We Work Hard For The Money" "So hard for it honey"!** And God sees, trust me, He does and He's going to reward you! Keep on serving. **Be patient — but be expecting** too, He's going to take good care of you. — **Be Love — Care for the people right — Be Light!**

- **Addicts and the Substance Abusers:** There is no substitute for Love and Peace, you tried them all, nothing working and nothing ever will. Christ is the only way! Without Christ in your life, I tell you the truth, you will perish, along with all the lude parties, sexual sins, drugs and drunkenness, wicked friends, workers of iniquity, dark secrets, pornography, idolatry, drug and evil money, pride, greed and whatever else people are into these days, — Well stop the madness, and get into gladness! There is a much better way to live than that. Stop doing what your friends do and do you. You were made for greatness, you were made to succeed. You don't need to drink , do drugs or smoke weed. Why can't you see, that the path you are on is wrong, it's destroying your life and hurting all those who love you. Right away today, right now, let's change all that, okay, don't be afraid to start living for Christ, you are not alone, God is with you! Hear me, you cannot do this or handle your problems on your own, we need a savoir, you need Christ and you need him now. **Seek HELP** now don't wait, today, tomorrow, this week, find or call a local church in your areas, or turn to TBN, Trinity Broadcasting Network it's Christian Television you can call them 24 hours a day, seven days a week and they have prayer lines too, pick up the phone and call, it's Toll Free, **1-888-731-1000** in the united states or **1-714-731-1000** seek help as soon as possible, but most importantly, don't wait anymore, give your life to Christ, ask him to remove all impurities out of your system, ask him to clean you up **N.O.W** tell him that you want a new life and that you want it with him. If you do what I am asking you to do then your life will be spared, you will be saved and on your way to recovery. The care plan for right now is for you to keep reading and working **The Care Plan!** — Over and over again from **A to Z!** — This book will help strengthen you — help get where you you need to be and that's with Jesus, then His Holy spirit will take it from there… in the meantime, stay away from that environment you were in and far away from those so called friends, they are not your friends, they are friends who are into destroy each other and they are destroying you. It is written that a man of too many companions may come to ruin. But there's a friend that I have come to know who sticks closer to you than a brother. He won't sit and watch you take drugs and drink your life away. Nor will he let you have anything to do with this dark and crazy world. He will love and stick with you like glue, because he loves and wants the best for you. All of you out there should already know his name by now, you made it all the way to letter **L**. His name is light, and his burden is too, let him now take good care of you. Here's what you do, "today", get into Jesus word, and do what Christ tells you to do especially if you want to get out of the hell you're in. But, let me caution you, one of Jesus's biggest complaints about people was this, wait, hold on, I'll let him tell you: "Why do you call me LORD, LORD, and not do what I tell you?" Luke 6:46 How many of us are guilty of this, all of us are, so stop it! From now on, God wants you to stay clean and holy, free from drugs and drunkenness, free from all things that are not pleasing to him, He wants all of us to live for him and him alone. **Substance Abuse/Addiction:** in Jesus name, "BE GONE". **Be Love —Be Light!**

- **All races and color:** Billy Graham the evangelist said it best, God belongs to the **"Whole World"** black, white, Jews and gentiles alike, he is color blind when it comes to people! Let's all come together and help make this world a better place, "I Pledge allegiance to the Flag of the United States of America and to the Republic for which it stands, one nation, ***"Under God"*** (thank God President Eisenhower encouraged congress to include our creator, place him above all things and everyone)indivisible, with liberty and justice for all." So, can we please get back ***"Under God"?*** Because this world has gone wild, it's out of control, family are being destroyed, people are dying in the streets, we are becoming a world on drugs, living with hatred, violence and thugs. I tell you the truth, a world without Christ is doomed, our forefathers knew that, that's why they insisted on adding under God to the pledged of allegiance, they thought like one of God's worriers and leader Joshua, when he said to his troops as for me and my house we shall serve the Lord! We as a people, must find our way back home, right now we are lost, Everybody, Everywhere is lost if they are not under God. Get under God, otherwise we have no real protection!

Without God, There Is No Love, There Is No Light!

Then I heard a voice of the Lord saying, "Whom shall I send? And who will go for us? And I said, "Here am I, (Me, Miss Asondra StarN'air) Send Me!" Isaiah 6:8. I'll be the voice, shouting "Read Your Bibles Every day, Do His Care Plan" "Live for Christ" **Be Love —Be Light!**

Jesus is Love, Jesus is Light!

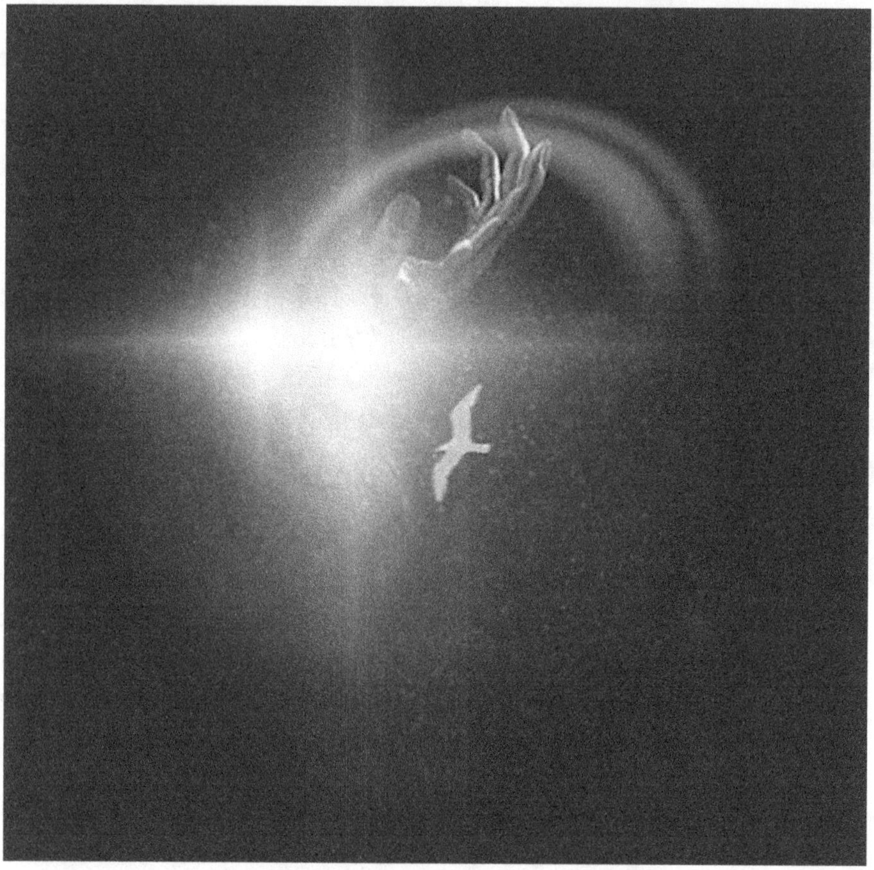

God is Love, Be a Dove, "Fly" Go for Everlasting Life!

Light Care Plan

Make These Your Realities Day and Night

- Let your confidence be in the Lord.
- Keep spending time with God so his light will shine all over you.
- Be love, give love and expect nothing in return.
- Keep your body holy, you cannot 'Be Light' — if you're not living right, Repent!
- Pray for this world. Be light!
- Live for Christ, do what he tells you, Be Light!
- Smile and say hello to Everybody, Everywhere, why? Because Jesus says, we should love one another like sisters and brothers, so let's start by saying hello!
- If you want to Be Love —Be light, then, do what God says in his word, live righteously, seek his Kingdom first!
- Pursue love and peace at all cost, make Jesus light the boss!
- If you want Jesus Light', come from amongst them, get out of the world and stay out!
- People of light, they give, they tithe, and go beyond the call of duty. What's your excuse? Don't have anymore, Be Light!
- Be Excellent and be prefect just like our Father in heaven is.
- Dress well, look good, and celebrate your inner and outer beauty but be holy!
- Men, be good godly leaders, marry a godly woman. Be faithful and true, she's a gift from God to you. treat her right, Be Love, Be Light!
- Keep loving and forgiving those who have wronged you.
- You cannot be light if you don't forgive your enemies.
- Lastly, dance like David (2 Sam. 6:14) with everything you have in you! Dance the joy and light of Jesus, Celebrate the light of God in your life, give him all the praise and glory —For He is worthy to be praised, without him there is no LIGHT!

Get The Care Plan
Open The Care Plan
Do The Care Plan

Is with You!

My Care Plan

From now on, I commit to ______________________________

I will make necessary changes because ______________________________

I will allow God to ______________________________

I want to be more and more like Jesus in this area because ______________________________

My prayer is ______________________________

Reflection Diary Journal

Date __________

Father God,

____

____

____

____

____

____

____

____

____

____

____

____

____

____

____

In Jesus's name. Amen!

THE CARE PLAN for God's People!

How We Think and Live Matters!

"Knowing these teachings will mean true and good health for you."
Proverbs 4:22

Read Your Bibles Everyday!

MEN

MEN, BE MEN of God, or you are not a real man. A real man follows Christ. All through history, the Bible reveals that real men who served God turned out to be excellent providers and leaders; those who were not died defeated and ruined. Look what happened to all the pharaohs and others who created idols or tried to build their own cities, worlds, or selves, God destroyed them, set them on the shelves! Life is about Christ, nobody else! Men, that's right, you heard me correctly, you ain't it nor am I, life is not about **YOU** or your resumes, degrees, money or financial status. And if you are a sport star or entertainer, you are not the messiah, you are not the one who gives life. And you are certainly not the one who brings everlasting peace, love and joy to the world — Christ is the only real Star to follow, this ★ will help make a real man out of men —not your friends, or idols. In fact God hates idols, so if you have them get rid of them. It is written that, God will have no other gods before him, so that means God must come first in your life. Not sports, women or entertainment. If God is not first in your life but other things are, then you are caught up in what is known as 'Modern Day Idolatry 'and what that means is you worship and love todays created things over the Creator, 'GOD'. For example, your cars, sport, money, video games, TV, celebrity personalities, and so on ...you get the picture! Again, if those things are coming before your walk with Christ that means you have idols! Just get rid of them that all, sometimes we have them but don't realize it, but the best way to ensure we don't have them, again, **'Put God First!', 'And Keep God First!'** So from now on, now that you know what idolatry is, — get busy, get your house in order. Start with your mind, give up your ways, and learn the ways of Christ! Each day, first thing first in the morning go spend time with God, sit, pray and talk with the holy spirit of Jesus Christ, get to really know him, he certainly wants to be with you, he's been waiting a long time for you men, but unfortunately and sad too other things have gotten in the way, but it's okay because you are about to change all that now, "right"! Gemmy a "high five!" And from a woman's prospective, men it's time, and especially for the black man to take back his power. Right now today, we need all the brothers to step up, we need men of God, **"YOU"** to help take back our communities, and help rebuild our homes again. Our young black children need their fathers in the home and we need you too, **"Come Back!"** All in all, the truth is, men of all colors, **"YOU"** are the leaders God chose to care for this earth, it's time to take back that responsibly if you call yourself a real man. Real men don't abandon their own children! Real men don't cheat on their wives, real men who cannot control their sexual urges, finds themselves a godly woman and get married, they don't take to the streets like male prostitutes laying with one woman after another, no, a 'Godly Man 'settles down they don't cheat or sleep around. Like I said, real men "Follow Christ!"

AS AN ORACLE of the Lord, I have been called to tell it like it is and I'm not going to hold back any punches. So I don't care if some of you don't like what I'm about to say, **"Let's Box!"** Often times, the truth stings, hurt too, but here it is, too many of **YOU** are still stuck on **YOU** and not **GOD**, our creator. You're in the world and loving every minute of it, the sex, the drugs, the violence, the porn, and every evil and filthy thing that turns **YOU** on **"It's A Man's World"** you say, but mightiest well call it truth, **"It's Satan's World"** especially for the carnal man, who entertains filth, pornography, lust , violence and deception along with all kinds of evil in his heart. And not to mention other things like money, pride, and greed, a lot of men have self-destructed. You have become your own god and that is not good, no, not good at all, the bible says all that and pride goes before destruction and a haughty spirit (arrogance, big attitude, swaggering, and obnoxious) before a fall. **Prov. 16:18** You are not making God number one like you should. Can I share this with you, Christ has been waiting and waiting for so many men to humble themselves and come to him, but yawl won't — women come, no problem, men you tend to think as long as the woman you are with, she goes, everything is fine, "WRONG"! wrong, wrong, wrong, each individual has to come to Christ on their own, another person can't save you; Yes for the sake of arguments, it is true and also indicated in the pages of the holy bible, that the other persons love for God and the way they devote their lives to him, can help change you, make you see the light, so that you will want to be saved., **1 Corinthians 7:14** For the unbelieving husband is made holy because of his wife. And vice versa! But brother man, cool daddy, big poppa, slick rick, whatever you call yourself these days, you still have to come on your own to Christ, you have to develop your own personal walk with him, your spouse can't do that for you. And this shacking up stuff, what's up? Are you the one the bible warns women about in **2 Timothy 3:6**, have you wormed your way in? **"Sin!"** "Why buy the milk when you can get the cow for free," take a look in the mirror, is that **"Me"** As a writer for the Lord, I don't know how else to say it! I already wrestled with God, about my style, like Moses, I said, Lord choose somebody else to write, I am not eloquent, and my speech is limited, but then God persisted, I was the one he wanted. Again and again I pleaded with him, I said LORD, LORD, now you know, how I am, I am not going to write what folks want to hear, I am going to be courageous, blunt and bold! Perhaps that's exactly why he chose me for **The Care Plan**. Brother man, I tell you the truth and no lie, you are going to have to choose Christ, not your lover, (which is already a death sentence of some kind, for it is written forever, that the wages of sin is death) if she's not your wife! So, come on stop your foolishness, make that change, start doing things right. Hey don't you want to be set free from all the pain,disappointments and misery? If your answer is yes, then get serious, discipline thyself and stay devoted to Christ and start living right! Get off of **"YOU"** and out of the streets, and from up under the sheets, stop laying with every chick you meet.

Stop being a liar and a cheat! Warning, if "YOU" don't get right with God or make that life style change; don't find it strange when your bodies in pain and your life down the drain. They'll be no memory of you, not even your name, but you would have done it to yourself, for the wages of sin is still death, there's no one to blame.

Men, don't go out that way, Get born again, STAY!

Now before we end this conversation there are a few more things I need to say, then God himself will speak. As Godly men, or men who are moving toward the light of God, you must honor God always, especially in those late night hours, besides, you're supposed to be sleeping, not peaking **"Hello"!** Know this, and hear this too, sin is often the result of lust or wrong selfish desires, You can't be watching half naked women on the screen and you know porn is out of the question don't you? Don't even go there or think about indulging in something so addictive and dangerous to your soul, — please I beg you, my husband died young, because of what he was doing in the dark. Guard your life, guard your heart. Men, I'm warning you, choose your downtime wisely, Satan the tempter wants to rob and destroy you. Please listen, don't go there, don't do what Jesus wouldn't do, stay faithful, holy and true. I hope this book is really ministering to you I really, really do. I'm trying hard to help save you. My husband is now dead and gone and he died so young. Now I'm like a robot for Christ, a flashing light, **"WARNING, WARNING"** don't join the world in sinning against God.

Unholy and unrighteous activities, will cost you something in the end. And men, when you give into those fleshly desires, you are not being strong men at all, you are being a weak men, you are opening the doors for the devil to run havoc in your life, and break down everything you worked for, destroying any chance of any real happiness. So think before you act, be strong and courageous, 'Don't do **"YOU"** anymore, Do Christ!' Men, the bible says this "Put to death, therefore, whatever belongs to your earthy nature: sexual immortality, impurity, lust, evil desires and greed, which is idolatry. Colossians 3:5

Psalms 119:133 says this, brother each time you pray, say this: Direct my footsteps according to your word; let no sin rule over me.

The Care Plan, has no gender, it speaks to men too, so take action.

Open it up, read it from A to Z, make this book too, an important priority! The end results should be, YOU want to commit to change!

YOU also want to become a real man and not of the flesh, but a man of the true living God. Along with that, you want that light, that other godly men have, you want to join them in becoming the change this world needs to see. Listen. I do hope you know I love you and am only trying to help save your soul, accept this wisdom, it's **"Gold".**

If this book has changed your life like it has done for so many others, then take Jesus up on his offer, ***"Come Follow Me and "I Will Make You Fishers of Men"!*** Matthew 4:19

"Answer The Call" To all brothers black, white and in-between, hang out with Christ and embrace the change. Today welcome Jesus into your life, **"Live For Christ"** "Don't Gamble with Your Life"!

Come Into God's Marvelous Light!

Before we part, Men, I put together a top priorities list that I believe God would be very pleased with, something that will help keep you strong and focus on living the best life possible. In my heart I believe that Everybody, Everywhere men and women alike should live life in this order: **God First — Family Second — Job/Career Third** and so on… we can't go wrong if we do this, God would smile, He'd be proud to call us his own, I just know

it! I do hope men that you take **'The Care Plan'** serious and reprioritize some things and that this book has helped open your eyes, — that you come to realize you have to change, you can't stay the same, if you want what Christ is offering, if you want that peace that passes all understanding, if you want eternal life, then brother fight, put on those boxing gloves, knock Satan, and this world out, get with Jesus, man, for once in your life, live right!

And for all you fools out there, saying man, you believe in that Jesus crap, he ain't real, you a __________ pay no attention to that person, God's work and power speaks for itself, but don't take it from me, I'm just a woman right, what do I know, oh but please don't challenge me Miss StarN'air about Christ, don't even go there!

He is the beginning, the end, the alpha and the omega dude! I'm starting to get worked up, let me at some of these unbelievers Jesus, let me at them, "give me the boxing gloves, I'll make those fools float like a butterfly, sting like a bee, Lord, give me the moves of **"Muhammad Ali"** man what you talkin' bout, **"Jesus Is REAL!"** And He's is the world's greatest, greatest, everything, boxer and all. Know ones better than HE. He defeated Satan and this world, talk'en that crap to me! Of course Jesus is real, fool! Again brother, don't listen to that crap, listen to God, without further ado,

The Lord Speaks

"Who is this that obscures my plans
with words without knowledge?
Brace yourself like a man; (let's see how bad you are now!)
I will question you, (talkin that talk, like a fool!)
and you shall answer me.

"Where were you when I laid the earth's foundation? (Bam!)
Tell me, if you understand.
Who marked off its dimensions? Surely you know! (Nope, he don't know!)

Who stretched a measuring line across it?
On what were its footings set,
or who laid its cornerstone—
while the morning stars sang together
and all the angels shouted for joy?
"Who shut up the sea behind doors
when it burst forth from the womb,

when I made the clouds its garment
and wrapped it in thick darkness,
when I fixed limits for it
and set its doors and bars in place,
when I said, 'This far you may come and no farther;
here is where your proud waves halt'?
"Have you ever given orders to the morning,
or shown the dawn its place,
that it might take the earth by the edges
and shake the wicked out of it?

Bam! no man ain't
got it going on like that!

The earth takes shape like clay under a seal;
its features stand out like those of a garment.
The wicked are denied their light,
and their upraised arm is broken.
Have you journeyed to the springs of the sea
or walked in the recesses of the deep?
Have the gates of death been shown to you?
Have you seen the gates of the deepest darkness?
Have you comprehended the vast expanses of the earth?
Tell me, if you know all this. (Bam) Another blow!
What is the way to the abode of light?
And where does darkness reside?

Can you take them to their places? (Nope!) brother that's why we keep GOD, first!
Do you know the paths to their dwellings?
Surely you know, for you were already born!
You have lived so many years!
Have you entered the storehouses of the snow
or seen the storehouses of the hail,
which I reserve for times of trouble,
for days of war and battle?
What is the way to the place where the lightning is dispersed,
or the place where the east winds are scattered over the earth?
Who cuts a channel for the torrents of rain,
and a path for the thunderstorm,
to water a land where no one lives,
an uninhabited desert,

brother bout to go down!

to satisfy a desolate wasteland
and make it sprout with grass?
Does the rain have a father?

Who fathers the drops of dew?
From whose womb comes the ice?
Who gives birth to the frost from the heavens
when the waters become hard as stone,
when the surface of the deep is frozen?
Can you bind the chains of the Pleiades?
Can you loosen Orion's belt?

Oh my, somebody ring the bell!
Brother man bout to hit the ground

Can you bring forth the constellations in their seasons
or lead out the Bear with its cubs?
Do you know the laws of the heavens?
Can you set up God's dominion over
the earth?
Can you raise your voice to the clouds
and cover yourself with a f lood of water?
Do you send the lightning bolts on their way?
Do they report to you, 'Here we are'?
Who gives the ibis wisdom
or gives the rooster understanding?

too late, he's down!!!!!
1,2,3,4,5,6,7,8.9,10
he's out! Knocked out cold!!!!
That'll teach men like that, not to
question or mess with my GOD!

Who has the wisdom to count the clouds?
Who can tip over the water jars of the heavens
when the dust becomes hard
and the clods of earth stick together?
"Do you hunt the prey for the lioness
and satisfy the hunger of the lions
when they crouch in their dens
or lie in wait in a thicket?
Who provides food for the raven
when its young cry out to God
and wander about for lack of food?

Thinking out loud and for crying out loud, "I don't get it?" Why in the world do men think that they can figure life out on their own, you're wrong! And that you can just push Jesus aside and act like he never existed at all. For far too long, many of you haven't given him the time of day, yet when it comes to sports, you bow down and worship a false god. You know every move those players make, yet you nothing about Christ, nor want to. Oh well, all I can say right here in this spot is **"Oops" there goes another Knock Out!**

Every Knee Shall Bow And Every Tongue Shall Confess

"I Am Lord!"

Bottom line fellas is this, each will have to give an account, for brushing God and Jesus off but you can change man, you can began anew. A few minutes ago, God spoke to you, and I do hope you took what he said to heart and now ready to make a fresh start, I really do, I'm sure those close to you do too. Here's the thing, women are tired of losers! I most certainly am! We want Godly men! We want to see the God in you because the fleshly man will no longer do.

And here's why, For you are going to be far more greater and wonderful, to the planet and your family hanging out with Christ. And I'm sure God likes sports too, but first things first! Seek the kingdom and his righteousness and all else shall be given In closing, **Men Be Blessed, Be Champions of Christ, Come Out of the World.** Don't gamble with your life. Get saved, don't get **"Zapped"** I'm done now, **That's ah Rap!**

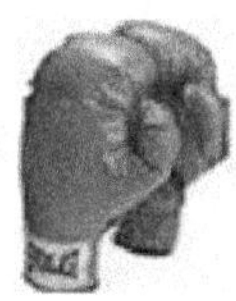

Men Care Plan

Make These Your Realities Day and Night

- Put God first, keep God first!
- Remember, **"Real Men"** follow Christ!
- Real men don't cheat on their wives!
- Spend time with God every day, don't stop!
- Watch who you hang out with, or else you become like them. Don't be around fools or whorish men, that prostitutes themselves day and night! And if you are single and cannot manage your urges, get married —find a godly wife!
- Throw away your idols, get rid of them all, never love anything or anyone more than God, ever!
- Read your bibles every day —Be men of God, not of the world, men of the flesh will perish, but You man of God, will have everlasting life.
- **Choose Christ, Choose Life!**
- Take care of your responsibility, if you make a baby, take care of the baby, it's your own flesh and blood, a good man leaves an inheritance for his children's children says the Lord! Proverb 13:22
- Remember too brother, your body does not belong to you, it belongs to the Lord. Sex is for marriage. Keep thyself holy!
- Find a godly wife and build a strong family life! Later for the streets!
- Get to know Jesus! Learn from his teaching, grow into the kind of man God wants you to be.
- For Christ, man, you got to discipline thyself, control your fleshly desires and learn how to float like a butterfly, sting like a bee, put Satan in his place, knock him out! "Bam" 1-2-3 send his back where he needs to be.

Get The Care Plan
Open The Care Plan
Do The Care Plan

Is with You!

Fight For Christ!

Knock Satan Out, Go For Eternal Life!

My Care Plan

From now on, I commit to ______________________________

I will make necessary changes because ______________________________

I will allow God to ______________________________

I want to be more and more like Jesus in this area because __________

My prayer is ______________________________

Reflection Diary Journal

Date __________

Father God,

Amen.

MONEY

FOR THE LOVE of money, people will do anything! "Money, money, money, some people got to have it, some people really need it . . . do things, do things, do bad things with it . . ." People of God ain't that the worldly truth! This was a popular hit song back in the early 70's by The O'Jays' an R&B group from Canton Ohio, it was a hit song because it hit so close to home, people were out there in the world without Christ in their lives robbing and killing each other, women were selling their precious bodies for money, and there was a lot of people hungry and living on the streets back then too, Has that changed? Are we better off now? Think about it for a minute, because the bible says things are going to keep on getting worse and worse until Christ returns. **2 Timothy 3:1-7**

> But mark this: There will be terrible times in the last days. People will be lovers of themselves, lovers of money, boastful, proud, abusive, disobedient to their parents, ungrateful, unholy, without love, unforgiving, slanderous, without self-control, brutal, not lovers of the good, treacherous, rash, conceited, lovers of pleasure rather than lovers of God—having a form of godliness but denying its power. Have nothing to do with such people.
>
> They are the kind who worm their way into homes and gain control over gullible women, who are loaded down with sins and are swayed by all kinds of evil desires, always learning but never able to come to a knowledge of the truth. Just as Jannes and Jambres opposed Moses, so also these teachers oppose the truth. They are men of depraved minds, who, as far as the faith is concerned, are rejected. But they will not get very far because, as in the case of those men, their folly will be clear to everyone.

Okay, so I'll ask you all one more time, are we better off since that song, money, money, money? **Of Course Not!**

In fact things are worse than ever before, No doubt about it, The OJay's, hit it right on the nail with that song — people will lie and they will cheat. Be careful, be wise, we must watch were we plant out feet!

Now let's talk money! "For the love of money is the root of **all kinds** of evil. It is through this craving that some have wandered away from the faith and pierced themselves with many pangs" 1 Timothy 6:10 Then In Matthew 6:24, it goes on to say this: "No one can serve two masters, for either you will hate one and love the other, or he will be devoted to one and despise the other."

I'm with Jesus, I'm with God, and he shall supply all my needs, and he knows what each one of us need and how much. And many times it is not money, its Faith! People we cannot serve Money and God —you cannot do it! — No way! No how! You got to choose one or the other. Besides, money will never make us happy or complete anyway — only God can do that, and he will if we let him, let him. Be smart, don't choose money, money, and more money over God, don't do it!

Open your eye, just look at what's happening to the rich and famous all over the world today who don't serve and live for God, they may be rich, but in God's eyes, they are poor. The bible puts it this way: "You say, 'I am rich; I have acquired wealth and do not need a thing.' But you do not realize that you are wretched, pitiful, poor, blind and naked." Revelation 3:17

Nevertheless, still there are so many people that think the grass is greener on the other side and wish that they had the lifestyles of the rich and famous, **'MONEY'** but, I tell you the truth, without God it's a disaster waiting to happen. How many more superstars do we have to lose before people realize life doesn't work without Christ? How many, listen there is nothing wrong with being rich and famous, I plan to be, except I desire to be rich and famous in God! No other way will work, or give me eternally life, Miss Asondra StarN'air, me, I **"Choose Christ"** no amount of money will ever do, hey, take a look at this scripture too,

"Again I tell you the truth, it is easier for a camel to squeeze through the eyes of a needle than for a rich person to get into the Kingdom of God." **Matthew 19:24**

Lastly, before we move on to our next letter, let's end money on a more positive and uplifting musical note. Money is indeed good for us it's very, very good, looks good, taste good too, money is not bad, it's good to have plenty of money, live in beautiful homes, have lots of nice things, look good and drive nice cars, feast, eat out at fabulous restaurants and enjoy the wholesome desires of our hearts along with much success. He wants his children to live good and have the best. And God, wants to give that kind of abundance to everybody, everywhere, we don't have to be a star to be in God's show!

But we have to live right, do right by others. And most importantly, we must obey, (read his word daily) love and serve God with all our heart, mind, body, soul and spirit! Hope I didn't leave anything out, oops I did, we are to tithe, and be givers too. If we can rock and roll like that, we are blessed! Go ahead live like kings and queens, "money ain't nothin' but a thang!" Seriously, when we put God first and not money, God will give us that and so much more, God said in his word, **John 14:13,** you many ask me anything in my name and I will do it. In fact it's repeated throughout the gospels, **Matthew, Mark, Luke** and **John**, go read it for yourself, don't just take my word for it. Get close to those prosperous pages, let the word of God penetrate your every need and desires, let him take you higher, not money. God's word and will for your life promises to bring you good tides, you'll be blessed beyond your wildest dreams.

Ooh, and woe to the world of fools, those that just got to have that money, for them, like an addict, they will do just about anything for it, sell their souls to the devil do whatever, but **'The Care Plan'** the one you have in your hands, wants to help make your life better, don't choose money, chose the latter, 'GOD', — Choose Christ! Money, money, money, some people got to have it, some people really need it, do bad things with it, but not us, right? And let all of God's people say "RIGHT"! We're taking a different flight!

In God We Trust!

Not Man or Money!

Walk in his word, and you will have all you'll ever need!

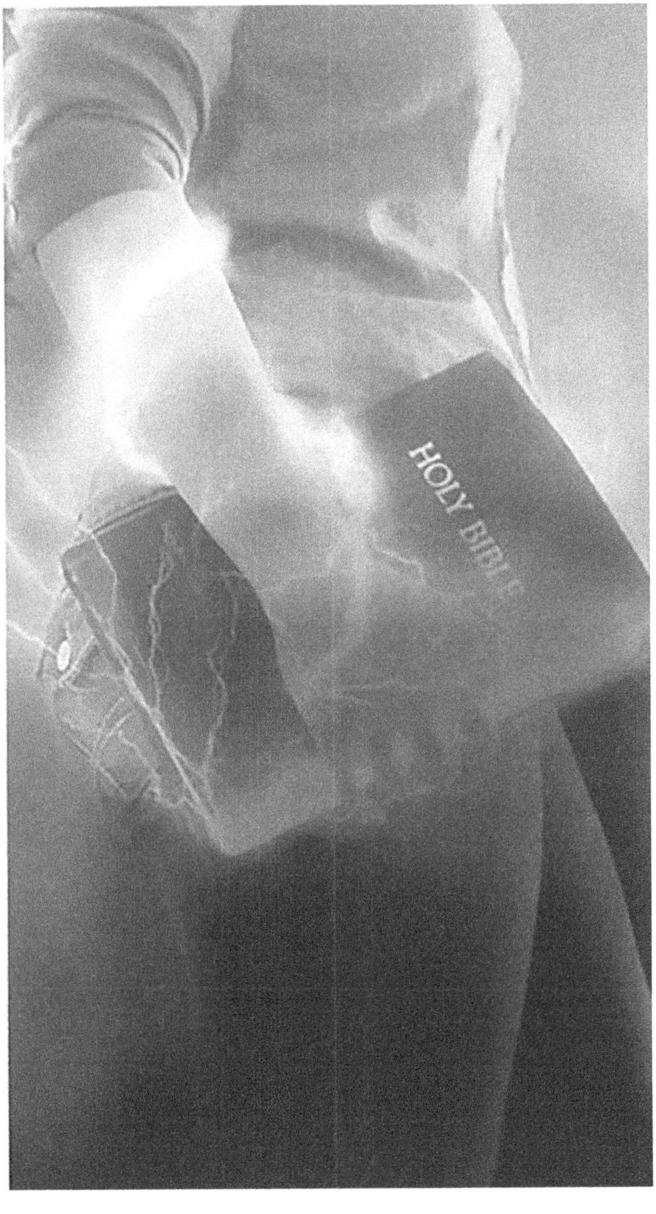

Money, Money, Money, 'Do Godly Things' With It!

tithing
sharing
GIFT
GIVE
BLESSING
sharing
FAITH
GIVING
SHARE
BLESSING
OFFERING
growing
GIFT
GIVE
sharing
GIFT
FAITH
sharing
OFFERING
growing
FAITH
GIVING
GIVE
GIVING
BLESSING
growing
SHARE
sharing
OFFERING
OFFERING
GIFT
BLESSING
growing
GIVE
FAITH
FAITH
sharing
GIFT
BLESSING
GIVING
SHARE

Money Care Plan

Make These Your Realities Day and Night

- Love God not money, there is a difference!
- Put money in its place, not in your heart.
- Tithe, so there will be food in God's storehouse
- Open a giving account, start a ministry, use those funds to help others.
- Make godly plans for those funds, donate.
- Help somebody for free.
- Don't friend up with money lovers, don't eat with them either!
- Keep it all balanced—your mind and your money.
- Pardon me, but I gotta' add this one, because I am music, here's to the music man, If you are going to rap, Don't say I got my mind on my money and my money on my mind, instead say this, I got my God on my mind and my mind on my God! Yeah, now that's a real rap! 'I'm feelin' that!'
- Sing and praise God for he is worthy to be praised, do that and we'll see better days.
- Get with God, pay off all your debt as fast as you can.
- Go from a thirty-year mortgage to a fifteen-year one, or if you can pay the whole mortgage off completely, be done with it!
- Read scripture on money, keep you mind on God first, find out what he wants you to do with your money, then do it, stop shopping so much! Discipline thyself or you will stay in debt — no money left! So don't do that! Stop spending money you don't have.
- Remember to leave an inheritance for your children and your children's children.
- Ask God, not people for all the desires of your heart, but remember to give away the overflow, leave some behind! Lev. 23:22
- Don't be like that song, money, money, money, got to have it, get it and do bad things with it anymore, don't practice sin, or

live like Sodom and Gomorrah! Don't do it! Ladies don't strip, don't take your clothes off anymore — God has a better life in store.

- Lastly, stop wanting, more and more and more, learn to be happy with what you got!

If your eyes is pure, there will be sunshine in your soul. But if your eye is clouded with evil thoughts and desires, you are in deep spiritual darkness. And oh, how deep that darkness can be! You cannot serve two masters: God and money. For you will love one and hate the other, or else the other way around.

Matthew 6:22-24

Everybody, Everywhere "Choose Christ"

Get The Care Plan
Open The Care Plan
Do The Care Plan

Is with You!

Break Free!
Don't Let The Love Of Money Chain You!

Last Warning

For the love of money it's the root of all kinds of evils.
1 Timothy 6:10

My Care Plan

From now on, I commit to ____
____
____
____
____
____

I will make necessary changes because ______________________
____
____
____
____

____
I will allow God to ______________________________________
____
____
____
____

I want to be more and more like Jesus in this area because ________
____
____
____
____
____

My prayer is ____
____
____
____
____
____

Reflection Diary Journal

Date __________

Father God,

____

____

____

____

____

____

____

____

____

____

____

____

____

____

____

Amen.

THE CARE PLAN for God's People!

How We Think and Live Matters!

"Knowing these teachings will mean true and good health for you."
Proverbs 4:22

Read Your Bibles Everyday!

NOW

QUESTION, WHAT ARE you doing right now in your life? And are you being all you can be? Are you happy?

These are just a few questions I have for you, because some of you have given up on yourself and your dreams too. You feel useless and defeated, but you not!

You look at your life right now and don't see how you can ever get things up and going again because you've made so many mistakes and bad decisions, but the **The Care Plan,** the one you have in your hands right now, says **"So What"**! That's right you heard and read correctly **"So What"**! I say this because we've all been foolish and have made bad decisions — all of us, your mother, your father, your sisters, your brothers, your cousins, nieces, nephews, friends, bosses and co-workers too, ministers, teaches, preachers alike, people of color, black and white, **Everybody, Everywhere,** we have all struggled and messed up, made mistakes, again **"So What"!** Now you have to fight! — It's all part of growing up! We are human, we screw up. Plus too, we can hit a rough patch in our lives, that makes it difficult to see straight — It happen to me, it can happen to you, but here's the thing, it's how you deal with this situation that make you who you are. You are not a loser, so don't act like one. Just start over! Many times, life has to teach us painful lessons, knocks us down a time or two, but a winner learns from their mistakes and get back up again.

Scripture says this, so listen, "No discipline seems pleasant at the time, but painful. Later on, however, it produces a harvest of righteousness and peace for those who have been trained by it. Hebrews 12:1. But like I was saying, winners, they don't quit, or lay around feeling sorry for themselves. No they choose again, they learn from their mistakes, and work to change their circumstances; they also ask themselves, how can I take the lemons in my life and make the best lemonade, the world has ever tasted? Next, they get up and get busy, they rebuild! So, sisters and brothers, Everybody, Everywhere I have an announcement to make:

NOW is the time to win again! So get up out of that bed, or off that coach and on your feet — **"Grow"! Get Dress, Get Ready, Get Set, Go........**

Yes, you heard me, "GO", yes go and take back the life God intended for you to have, it still have your name on it! **You Can Do It! You Must Do It!**

And to those out there who have lost their will to even try, because of loneliness, depression and hopelessness, **The Care Plan** is just what the doctor ordered, let me pray for you right NOW, now in the name of Jesus, take all the pressure off of those who:

Got the blues!
Overjoy them, with laughter, because you know the devil is a liar.
Do for them right now, what they are unable to do for themselves.

Is with You!

O' Righteous God and Holy Father, let this be a sign to you, that they are ready to give their life to you NOW

They have come to know O' Lord, Father God that they just can't make it without you anymore, they need a savior, your son Jesus Christ to help heal and guide them. Lord strengthen them too, Lord I am asking in Jesus name, pull this person and others that are reading **The Care Plan** right now, pull each and every one of them out of the darkness, give them faith and dry up their tears, take away all their worries, pain, sufferings and fears. Lord bring them unto you, into your marvelous forgiving and comforting light. Son of God, teach people your ways, how to live right. Without delay Lord, don't let the weary hearts out there go another day without your perfect peace, heal them ***"Now"*** Okay, pause right where you are at for a minute, **"People"** feel His presence, can you feel Him? I feel him moving all over your soul, there is wonder working power in the name and blood of Jesus, Father God, heal them right now, all of you, be still and know He is God, in the mighty name of Jesus, strengthen them, don't let them give up, take away all hopelessness and despair, **"Right Now"** father God, reach out through these pages, let them know you are there, Lord, bring them unto you and heal their weary souls. **"Right Now"** give them what they need to move on, **"Make Them Whole"** Please do it for those on this **'Care Plan'** Jesus we know you got the whole world in your hands, if anybody can heal and help rebuild their lives, **LORD** we know you can.

Now touch his hand, you are healed, go in peace!

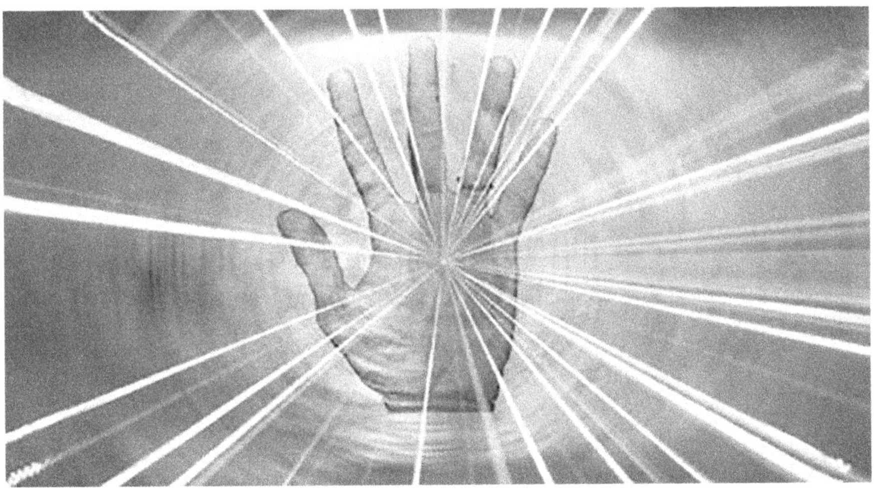

Your faith has made you well!
Mark 5:3, Luke 17:19

Loved ones, if you just received that powerful prayer, then hurt and worry no more! It is finished! It is over! Jesus Christ our Lord and Savior, and our Healer too, has forgiven you and he wants to live inside you "N.O.W". Right now it's time to look ahead and start anew.

People before you go, I have something that I want to leave with you, all of you and I want you to remember this always, never let this part from you heart or mouth, carry this **NOW** everywhere you go moving forward,

No
One
Works your life out, better than Christ!

Now is the time to choose whom this day you will serve. Join Joshua and me when we say, as for me and my house we shall server the Lord. Get on board! Always remember this:

No

One

Works But **Jesus!**

N.O.W Care Plan

Make These Your Realities Day and Night

- Today I'm giving my life to Christ.
- I will stop feeling sorry for myself, I will correct my mistakes now and move on to a better life.
- I will choose my friends wisely this time around.
- I will get my body back in shape.
- I will make no more excuses, I will exercise and eat right. "Good Food In, junk Food Out"!
- Now I will bless the Lord at all times, I will keep my focus on pleasing him, not man.
- Today I will go back after my goals and dreams.
- No more negative behavior, I will straight up and fly right, straighten up and be right!
- No more trying to fit in with fools, and haters.
- No more drunken days and nights.
- No more lovers, — I'll wait on God to send me my life mate.
- No more drama!
- No more living like the world does, I have to be holy. Simply put, I gotta' live right!
- I must read the bible, I cannot get set free and stay free if I don't make reading his word a top priority.
- I will dress more appropriately, more respectfully!
- Today I'm going to do the work, and grow stronger and stronger in the lord. Now I know it won't happen overnight, but I know Jesus is the only one that's going to give me a better life, I want that **"N.O.W."**, "Right Now"!
- Today, is a new day for me and I hope for other too, I have changed, I live for Christ **Now!** My future is bright! **N**o **O**ne **W**orks my life out better than ***Christ!***

N.O.W

- God's back in control of my life, I'm going to keep it that way from now on.
- I am getting my priorities straight, I'm going to find a good bible teaching church to attend regularly.
- I am ending all relationships that are not pleasing to God, sex outside of marriage is wrong. 1 Corinthians 7:2, Genesis 2:24 and there's plenty more... sex is for marriage— Fornication don't come hanging around my door, your lover don't live here anymore! Fornication, don't come nowhere near me, I'm free!
- I will celebrate, go out and enjoy myself, God wants me to have fun, but not act and behave like I use too, I chose my locations carefully. And make sure I'm with other Christians to help keep me accountable. I like my new life with Christ!
- I'm getting my life back in order I feel brand new, and God it's all because of you.
- I'm serving you Lord for the rest of my days.
- I'm a new creature in Christ, throw the rice!
- I'm trusting God more than ever before.
- I'm following Jesus, becoming one with him, we are becoming friends, best of friends until the end!
- I'm committed to reading **The Bible** and doing **The Care Plan** always, these books are not one time reads. These books feed souls in need!
- I have come to realize, repetition changes our condition, and puts us in position to carry out God's mission! This is why I must study God's word and being on **'The Care Plan'** helps, I'm staying on it!
- Bottom line is, I am changing, I'm better than before, I'm not afraid of living for Christ anymore!

N.O.W I'm On A Roll!

- I am on my way to living the life, I was meant to live, forgetting what's behind, I made my bed, but I don't have to lie in it anymore, because God has forgiven me. Today I'm moving on now and pressing on to what lies ahead, my past is ***"DEAD"***.

With **The Holy Bible** and **The Care Plan** by my side now I know for sure, that I can do all things in Christ who strengthens me, in Jesus name **Amen!**

Welcome into the house of believers, brace yourself, get ready to be transformed into love, after all, isn't that what we've been dreaming of? I have! **N.O.W** for the next 90 days read all those affirmation three times a day, four times if you can. Do those each morning, noon, evening and night! If you do, I promise you, everyone will know there is something very different about you, your friends and family will too! Do share, tell them to:

Get The Care Plan
Open The Care Plan
Do The Care Plan

Is with You!

No **O**ne **W**orks **B**ut **Jesus!**

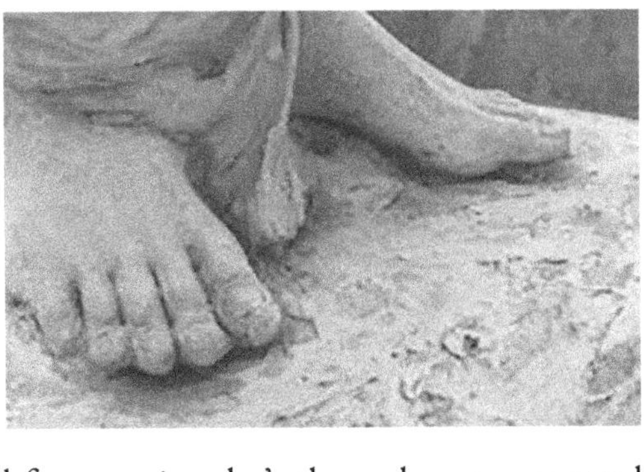

Jesus died for our sins, he's the only way we can live again!

My Care Plan

From now on, I commit to ______________________________

I will make necessary changes because ______________________________

I will allow God to ______________________________

I want to be more and more like Jesus in this area because ____________

My prayer is ______________________________

Reflection Diary Journal

Date __________

Father God,

____

____

____

____

____

____

____

____

____

____

____

____

____

____

____

Amen.

THE CARE PLAN for God's People!

How We Think and Live Matters!

"Knowing these teachings will mean true and good health for you."
Proverbs 4:22

Read Your Bibles Everyday!

OBEDIENCE

> *Children, obey your parents in the Lord for this is right. "Honor your father and mother" — which is the first commandment with a promise — "so that it may go well with you and that you may enjoy long life on the earth".*
>
> —Ephesians 6:1–3

BUT SAME GOES for adults, we have a heavenly Father to answer too as well, we are his children. Obedience to God is important for Everybody, Everywhere that claim to love him, just like we expect our earthly children to honor and obey us, our God expects the same from grown folks, so let's not be hypocrites. Children learn by our example, if we don't practice obedience why should they? Look at your life today, are you being a good example? Are you obeying the Father in heaven? Or are you out there like so many others, — living for the world, caught up in drama, — living a soap opera life, man after man, — don't want to be nobody's wife? Or are you a man out there, still believing, that "This is a Man's World", a world where you can live for your flesh, and consider nobody else? Well you are wrong, dead wrong, Why don't you learn to be a godly fearing man, a real man — how many more babies will you make, abandon, escape? Why don't you grow up and realize that the way you think and live is wrong. Wait a minute,"Rappers",why not put those lyrics in a song! Hey, lets not stop here, lets keep the music playing, say "dead beat dads, no more, be gone!" Tell the females "hey" if the man won't marry you, say good-bye, so long! Or is this message too strong. Light came into the world and man rejected it says the lord,"the people of the world. like doing wrong! **John: 3:19** Be that as it may, both male and female each one of us will have to give an account for how we lived our lives. We "All" reap what we sow! Obedience to the words of God, determines which way we go!

> I'm done rapping and speaking Jesus is up next, he has a question: **"Why do you call me 'Lord, Lord and not do what I tell you?"** Luke 6:46,
>
> **"If You Love Me Keep My Commandments".** John 14:15

THE COMMANDMENTS OF JESUS

Jesus, in the Gospels, laid down the great foundational principles and laws to govern the children of God during the entire church age – "even unto the end of the world," as we see from His great commission as recorded in Matt; 28:18-20. Our great duty and privilege is to do as He said, **"Follow Me."**

We see the practical results which followed the keeping of His commandments in the great revivals as recorded in the book of Acts. Further explanations and application of the commandments of Jesus are given by the Lord through the writers of the epistles, but the foundational principles and the final authority rests in the words of Jesus Himself. In the book of Revelation Jesus gives His final warnings, reproofs, instructions and encouragements to the Church.

An outline of the Commandments of Jesus, under twenty-one principles, is given below. Examine yourself by these. Read over these words of our Lord and take an inventory often. See if you are, in truth, pleasing God, or if you are deceiving yourself. God, the heavenly Father, loved you so much that He gave His Son, Jesus, to die for you (see John 3:16). He will help you if you humble yourself, are willing to follow Jesus, and will earnestly seek HIM.

Ask God to help you understand the teachings of Jesus, and to live them out in your life. Salvation and the true Christian life is a gigantic love affair. It is not by merely keeping the letter of the Word that we will please God; we must keep the spirit of the two great commandments all through our lives, and remember that these two great principles are given to guide us in knowing just how God would have us apply the teachings of His Holy Word. Here are the two great foundational commandments: "Jesus said…Thou shalt love the Lord they God with all thy heart, and with all thy soul, and with all thy mind. This is the first and great commandment. And the second is like unto it, Thou shalt love thy neighbor as thyself. On these two commandments hang all the law and the prophets." **Matt.22:37- 40**

Read

THE COMMANDMENTS OF JESUS

I.

REPENTANCE

1.	"Repent"	Matt. 4:17; Rev. 2:5
2.	"Come unto Me"	Matt. 11:28
3.	"Seek first God and His righteousness"	Matt. 6:33
4.	"Forgive if ye have ought against any"	Mark 11:25
5.	"Deny Yourself"	Matt. 16:24
6.	"Ask…seek…knock"	Matt. 7:7
7.	"Strive to enter in at the strait gate"	Luke 13:24

II.
BELIEF

1.	"Believe the Gospel"	Mark. 1:15
2.	"Ye believe in God, believe also in Me"	John 14:1
3.	"Believe on Him who He (God) hath sent"	John 6:28-29
4.	"Believe Me that I am in the Father and the Father in Me"	John 14:11
5.	"Believe the works…I do"	John 10:37-38
6.	"While ye have light believe in the light"	John 12:36
7.	"Believe that ye receive"	Mark 11:24

III.
THE NEW BIRTH

1.	"Ye must be born again"	John 3:7
2.	"Cleanse first that which is within"	Matt. 23:26
3.	"Make the tree good, and his fruit good"	Matt. 12:33
4.	"Abide in Me and I in you"	John 15:4
5.	"Have salt in yourselves"	Mark 9:50
6.	"Labor…for that meat which endureth unto everlasting life"	John 6:27
7.	"Rejoice, because your names are written in heaven"	Luke 10:20

IV.
RECEIVING THE HOLY SPIRIT

1.	"Receive ye the Holy Ghost"	John 20:23
2.	"Let the children first be filled"	Mark 7:27
3.	"If any man thirst, let him come unto Me and drink"	John 7:37-39
4.	"Keep my commandments and…the Father…shall give you another comforter"	John 14:15-17
5.	"Ask…with importunity"	John 16:24; Luke11:5-13
6.	"Tarry…until ye be endued with power from on high"	Luke 24:49
7.	"When the comforter is come…He shall testify of Me: and ye also shall bear witness"	John 15:26-27

V.
FOLLOWING JESUS

1.	"Follow Me"	John 12:26
2.	"Be baptized"	Matt. 3:13-15; Matt. 28:19
3.	"Take this...(communion) in remembrance of Me"	Luke 22:17-19
4.	"Ye also ought to wash one another's feet"	John 13:14-15
5.	"If any man will come after Me...let him take up his cross daily"	Luke 9:23
6.	"Learn of Me"	Matt. 11:29
7.	"Continue ye in My love"	John 15:9

VI.
PR AYER

1.	"Pray always"	Luke 21:36
2.	"Pray that ye enter not into temptation"	Luke 22:40, 46
3.	"Pray...the Lord of the harvest, that He would send forth labourers"	Luke 10:2
4.	"Pray for them which despitefully use you"	Luke 6:28
5.	"Pray to the Father...in my name"	Matt.6:6; John16:24, 26
6.	"After this manner therefore pray ye : our Father, which art in heaven..."	Matt. 6:9-13
7.	"When ye pray, use not vain repetitions"	Matt. 6:7-8

VII.
FAITH

1.	"Have faith in God"	Mark 11:22
2.	"Be not faithless"	John 20:27
3.	"Neither be ye of doubtful mind"	Luke 12:29
4.	"Take no thought for your life"	Matt. 6:25-34
5.	"Let not your heart be troubled"	John 14:1,27
6.	"Be of good cheer"	Matt. 14:27
7.	"Be not afraid"	Mark 5:36: Luke 12:4-7

VIII.
SEARCHING THE SCRIPTURES

1.	"Search the scriptures"	John 5:39
2.	"Remember the word that I said"	John 15:20
3.	"Let these sayings sink down into your ears"	Luke 9:44
4.	"Take heed therefore how ye hear"	Luke 8:18
5.	"Take heed what ye hear"	Mark 4:24
6.	"Beware of the leaven (doctrine) of the Pharisees"	Matt. 16:6, 12
7.	"Beware of false prophets"	Matt. 7:15-17

IX.
LETTING YOUR LIGHT SHINE

1.	"Let your light so shine before men, that they may see your good works"	Matt. 5:16
2.	"Take heed therefore that the light which is in thee be not darkness"	Luke 11:35
3.	"Go and bring forth fruit, and …bear much fruit"	John 15:16, 8
4.	"Be ye therefore merciful, as your Father"	Luke 6:36
5.	"Tell…how great things the Lord hath done for thee"	Mark 5:19
6.	"Lift up you eyes, and look on the fields"	John 4:35
7.	"Walk while you have the light"	John 12:35

X.
THE SECOND COMING OF CHRIST

1.	"Hold fast till I come"	Rev. 2:25; Rev. 3:2-3
2.	"Be ye therefore ready also: for the Son of man cometh"	Luke 12:40
3.	"Let your loins be girded about, and your lights burning; and ye yourselves like unto men that wait for their Lord"	Luke 12:35-36
4.	"Take heed…lest…your hearts be overcharged with surfeiting, and drunkenness, and cares of this life"	Luke 21:34
5.	"Remember Lot's wife"	Luke 17:31-32
6.	"Take heed that ye be not deceived"	Luke 21:8; Mark 13:5-6
7.	"Watch"	Mark 13:34-37

XI.
SUPREME LOVE TO GOD

1.	"Thou shalt love the Lord thy God with all thy heart...soul...mind...strength"	Mark 12:30
2.	"God, and Him only shalt thou serve"	Matt. 4:10
3.	"Worship the Father in spirit and in truth"	John 4:23-24
4.	"Call no man your father upon the Earth"	Matt. 23:9
5.	"Thou shalt not tempt the Lord thy God"	Matt. 4:7
6.	"Fear Him (God) which...hath power to cast into hell"	Luke 12:5
7.	"All men should honor the Son"	John 5:22-23

XII.
OUR DUTY TO GOD AND MAN

1.	"Render to Caesar the things that are caesar's, and to God the things that are God's"	Mark 12:17
2.	"Swear not at all"	Matt.5:34-37; Mark 4:22
3.	"What therefore God hath joined together, let not man put asunder"	Matt. 19:5-6
4.	"Agree with thine adversary quickly"	Matt. 5:25
5.	"We saw one casting out devils in thy name...Forbid him not"	Mark 9:38-40
6.	"Eat such things as are set before you"	Luke 10:8
7.	"Gather up the fragments that remain, that nothing be lost"	John 6:12

XIII.
OUR DUTY TO OUR NEIGHBOR

1.	"Thou shalt love thy neighbor as thyself"	Matt. 19:17-19
2.	"Thou shalt do no murder"	Matt. 19:18
3.	"Thou shalt not commit adultery"	Matt. 19:18
4.	"Thou shalt not steal"	Matt. 19:18
5.	"Thou shalt not bear false witness"	Matt. 19:18
6.	"Honor thy father and thy mother"	Matt. 19:19
7.	"As ye would that men should do to you, do ye also to them likewise"	Luke 6:31

XIV.
COVETOUSNESS

1.	"Take heed and beware of covetousness"	Luke 12:15
2.	"Lay not up for yourselves treasures upon earth…but lay up for yourselves treasures in heaven"	Matt. 6:19-20
3.	"Ye pay tithe…and not leave (them) undone"	Matt.23:23
4.	"Give to him that asketh thee, and from him that would borrow of thee turn not thou away"	Matt. 5:42
5.	"Give alms of such things as ye have"	Luke 11:41
6.	"When thou makest a dinner..call not thy friends, nor thy brethren…but….call the poor"	Luke 14:12-13
7.	"Make yourselves friends of the mammon…"	Luke 16:9

XV.
HYPOCRISY

1.	"Beware ye of the leaven of the Pharisees, which is hypocrisy"	Luke 12:1
2.	"Beware of the scribes, which desire to walk in long robes"	Luke 20:46-47
3.	"do not ye after their works"	Matt. 23:2-3
4.	"Make not My Father's house an house of merchandise"	John 2:16
5.	"do not your alms before men, to be seen of them"	Matt.6:1-4
6.	"When thou prayest thou shalt not be as the hypocrites…to be seen of men…enter into thy closet and pray in secret"	Matt. 6:5-6
7.	"When thou fastest, anoint thine head, and wash thy face; that thou appear not unto men to fast"	Matt. 6:16-18

XVI.
MEEKNESS

1.	"Take my yoke upon you…for I am meek and lowly in heart"	Matt. 11:29
2.	"The princes of the Gentiles exercise dominion over them…but it shall not be so among you"	Matt. 20:25-26
3.	"Whosoever of you will be the chiefest, shall be servant of all"	Mark 10:43-44
4.	"Be not ye called rabbi"	Matt. 23:8
5.	"Sit not down in the highest room"	Luke 14:8-11

6.	"Rejoice not, that the spirits are subject unto you"	Luke 10:20
7.	"Say, we are unprofitable servants"	Luke 17:10

XVII.
OUR LOVE TO THE BRETHREN

1.	"Love one another as I have loved you"	John 15:12
2.	"Despise not one of these little ones"	Matt. 18:10-14
3.	"Have peace one with another ... and be reconciled to thy brother"	Mark 9:50; Matt. 5:23-24
4.	"If thy brother...trespass against thee go and tell him his fault between thee and him alone"	Matt. 18:15-17
5.	"If thy brother trespass against thee seven times a day...thou shalt forgive him"	Luke 17:3-4; Matt. 18:21-22
6.	"Judge not according to appearance... first cast the beam out of thine own eye"	John 7:24; Matt. 7:1-5
7.	"Condemn not"	Luke 6:37

XVIII.
PERFECT LOVE

1.	"Be ye therefore perfect"	Matt. 5:48
2.	"Sell that ye have and give alms"	Matt. 19:21; Luke 12:32-33
3.	"Love your enemies"	Matt. 5:44; Matt. 26:52
4.	"Do good to them which hate you"	Luke 6:27-28
5.	"Lend, hoping for nothing again"	Luke 6:35
6.	"Resist not evil"	Matt. 5:39-41
7.	"In your patience posses ye your souls"	Luke 21:19

XIX.
FAITHFUL UNTO DEATH

1.	"Be thou faithful unto death"	Rev. 2:10
2.	"Hold that fast which thou hast"	Rev. 3:11
3.	"When men shall revile you, and persecute you,... rejoice, and be exceeding glad"	Matt.5:11-12 Luke 6:23
4.	"When they persecute you in this city, flee ye into another"	Matt. 10:23

5.	"When they deliver you up, take no thought how or what you shall spek"	Matt. 10:19
6.	"Murmur not among yourselves"	John 6:41-43
7.	"Look up and lift up your hands"	Luke 21:28

XX.
PREACHING THE GOSPEL

1.	"Preach the gospel to every creature"	Mark. 16:15; Matt. 10:7
2.	"Repentance and remission of sins should be preached in His (christ's) name"	Luke 24:46-47
3.	"Baptize disciples, in the name of the Father, and of the Son, and the Holy Ghost"	Matt. 28:19
4.	"Teach them to observe all things whatsoever I have commanded"	Matt. 28:20
5.	"What I tell you ... that speak"	Matt. 10:27; Mark 4:22
6.	"Feed my sheep"	John 21:15-17
7.	"Heal the sick"	Matt. 10:8

XXI.
WISDOM

1.	"Be ye therefore wise as serpents, and harmless as doves"	Matt. 10:16
2.	"Beware of men"	Matt. 10:17
3.	"Let (the blind leaders) alone"	Matt. 15:12-14
4.	"Give not that which is holy unto the dogs, neither cast ye your pearls before swine"	Matt. 7:6
5.	"consider the lilies... how they grow"	Matt. 6:28
6.	"Whatsoever city ... ye shall enter, inquire who is worthy; and there abide ... Go not from house to house"	Matt. 10:11-13; Luke 10:5-7
7.	"Whosoever will not receive you ... shake off the very dust from your feet for a testimony against them"	Luke 9:5; Luke 10:10-11

"IF A MAN LOVE ME, HE WILL KEEP MY WORDS."
John 14:23

I do believe that obedience is a must for adults and children alike. That means **"We All"** must live right!

Be warned: The Lord is not slow about his promise, (to deal with those who practice sinful behavior and won't stop) as some people think. Rather, he is patient for your sake. He's Just being patient, He's merciful like that, He's giving each one of us a chance to repent, but don't take our God for granted, don't be stupid, better get right with God before your time is up. 2 Peter3:9

The fear of the LORD is the beginning of wisdom (Prov. 1:7) Stop listening to your fake friends or those fools out there who have no respect or fear of our creator. Check yourself before your wreck yourself! Now let's get back to the children, what about the children, for they are a gift from god, he's placed them in our care, so be there! Please re-consider your life, ask yourself, especially if you are a parent, am I setting a good example for my child, am I living righteously? If you don't have children then fine, still, obedience matters! We are his children, it matters to God how we carry on and live our lives down here. This is why he put together commandments and orchestrated every word in the bible, to be used as a manual, **B**asic **I**nstructions **B**efore **L**eaving **E**arth **'BOOK"** Open it, it's a gift from God and it holds key to eternal life! It's beautiful too, ital make you cry. God wishes no one to perish! nor do I, I don't want to die. Nevertheless, and don't ask me why, some folks believe all this Jesus stuff, heaven and hell is all made up, a lie.

Well this is what I say to them, I'll take my chances, to this world and unbelievers **GOOD-BYE!** Moving right along, here's something to get excited about, Jesus said this, his sheep hears his voice, and it's true, I'm a witness. He called me when I was seven years old. So whether you believe or not, there's hope for the children. And because there is, children listen up, kids and teenagers alike, **"Obedience Matters"!** Honor your parents, one, because the bible says so and two, they are your parents. Forgive us when we mess up, **Parents Aren't Perfect,** "reverse", **Perfect Aren't Parents! "WE"** make mistakes, **"ME TOO"** but we make up for it in other ways too, so don't be so hard on us, we love you. Children and teenagers too, hear me on this, listen to your mom and dad, do what they ask and God says, all will go well for you and your future. Go to school, focus on getting great grades, finish school. **"Don't Drop Out, Work It Out"!** Go beyond high school, go to college or trade school, just don't waste your life or hang around with fools — now that not cool!

If you have a problem and don't feel comfortable talking to your parents or anyone, start early, talk to Jesus, he will lead and guide you, I tell you the truth, and I know this for sure, **N**o **O**ne **W**orks but **Jesus,** remember, He's the answer to everything.

> *Again, Children, obey your parents in the Lord for this is right. "Honor your father and mother" — which is the first commandment with a promise — "so that it may go well with you and that you may enjoy long life on the earth".*
>
> —Ephesians 6:1–3

> *"I tell all of you with certainty, unless you change and become like little children, you will never get into the kingdom of heaven.*
>
> —Matthew 18:3

Obey God and his word, don't say you haven't heard! One more time **"Obedience Matters"!** Get to Know Christ Better. **Straight Up To The Letter!**

"Bless His holy Name!"

"Become Like Little Children!"

"Then he said, "I tell all of you with certainty, unless you change and become like little children, you will never get into the kingdom of heaven. Matthew 18:3

Obedience Care Plan

Make These Your Realities Day and Night!

Say this ten times a day for 21 days and before you go to sleep at night:

I'll read and obey God's Word.

I'll read and obey God's Word.
I'll read and obey God's Word.
I'll read and obey God's Word.
I'll read and obey God's Word.
I'll read and obey God's Word.
I'll read and obey God's Word.
I'll read and obey God's Word.
I'll read and obey God's Word.
I'll read and obey God's Word.

Next I Will:

Get The Care Plan
Open The Care Plan
Do The Care Plan

Is with You!

My Care Plan

From now on, I commit to ______________________________________
____
____
____
____
____

I will make necessary changes because ____________________________
____
____
____
____

____

I will allow God to ____
____
____
____
____

I want to be more and more like Jesus in this area because __________
____
____
____
____
____

My prayer is ____
____
____
____
____
____

Reflection Diary Journal

Date ____________

Father God,

____

____

____

____

____

____

____

____

____

____

____

____

____

____

____

Amen.

THE CARE PLAN for God's People!

How We Think and Live Matters!

"Knowing these teachings will mean true and good health for you."
Proverbs 4:22

Read Your Bibles Everyday!

PRAYER

Lord Teach Us To Pray!

—Luke 11:1

The Lord's Prayer

Our Father which art in heaven, Hallowed be thy name.
Thy kingdom come,
Thy will be done in earth, as it is in heaven.
Give us this day our daily bread.
And forgive us our debts, as we forgive our debtors.
And lead us not into temptation,
but deliver us from evil: For thine is the kingdom,
and the power, and the glory, forever. Amen.

—Matthew 6:9–13, King James Version (KJ

Hello Everybody!

POP, POP, POP!

"Power **O**f **P**rayer**"**

"Power **O**f **P**ractice",
"Power **O**f **P**atience"

POP, POP, POP, "Don't Stop!"

PRAYER

PRAYER IS AN opportunity for "Everybody, Everywhere" to spend quality time with God. To really understand the heart of God and his will for our lives, we need to pray!

Prayer is simply spending intimate time with God just you and
Him. And talking to him about everything that's going on in
your life, your hurts, your disappointments, your goals and
dreams, your struggles, your good news, your bad news, your
heartbreaks, your loneliness, your stress, school, "that math test",
your joys, your sorrows, your fears of tomorrow — whatever!
These kinds of conversations are a form of prayer too,
we need to share it all with God in prayer — all of it!
'The Good, The Bad, The Ugly'
We need God ***Every Day*** and in ***Every Way,*** that's why we **"Pray!"**

Cast all your cares on me says the **LORD!**
1Peter 5:7, Psalms 55:22

When we spend time with God, things get resolved God's way, which is the best way, by the way! He'll guide us and tell us what to do and say. This is why it's so important that we pray. I don't know about you, I can't do this life on my own. No, I don't need all the drama and the problems of the world slowing me down anymore — stagnating me, no, not at all, my focus is on my father's business and the promise land. Keep prayer in practice, hold on to it as tight as you can! Stop trusting in man! Don't do that, if we do, we're going down like quicksand! **Trust God Only! Devote Your Life To Christ, Keep A Prayer Life!**

Otherwise, people you'll struggle more than you have too, without a prayer life, you'll feel the burden, like every things on you. But can I ask yawl this, why should we keep carrying loads that were never meant for us to carry? Stop it! StarN'air's not doing that anymore! No I am not! I suggest you all do what Jesus said, "Cast all your cares onto me"! I do, and now I see, stress can't touch me!

Listen, prayer works for those who take the time out to pray, those who take the time out to stay in God's word. Never stop praying, never stop saying, Christ I need you!

Here's to all those out there with a prayer life, those who have come to know the power of prayer, and have the life that proves prayer does work! Well this scripture is for us, you and me and all the ones who believe — Jesus want us to know, "I no longer call you servants, because a servant does not know his masters business. Instead, I have called you friends. John 15:15

Pray, People!

But when you pray, go into your room, close the door and pray to your Father, who is unseen. Then your Father, who sees what is done in secret, will reward you. Matthew 6:6

Rejoice always, pray without ceasing, and give thanks in all circumstances, for this is the will of God in Christ Jesus for you.
Thessalonians 5:16

Prayer Care Plan

Make These Your Realities Day and Night

- Find a quiet place to spend time with God.
- Find a special location, a prayer room or closet.
- Keep a notebook and pen handy. God gives excellent ideas and know-hows.
- **'Begin Your day With God'!** Go to him first thing in the morning and again before you go to sleep. **'End Your day With God!'**
- Keep your **'Bibles'** with you at all times, take one to work, keep a pockets size one in your purse ladies. Men you too, keep one with you as well, put one in your vehicle, never know when we need a scripture, or a word from God to help save the day, or have to pray for someone.
- Read Your Bibles Daily!
- Pray daily, Be still and know He is God and that he answers the prayers of the faithful ones.
- When you pray, listen too, don't do all the talking.
- Pray and Praise! Soon you'll see, when the praises goes up the blessings come down.
- Remember too, prayer time is also the perfect time to cast all your cares on him. Jesus is a caregiver you know, not only is he the greatest love of all, he's the greatest caregiver of all too, especially during difficult times. Jesus will help make a way out of no way, another reason why we pray!
- Pray for others, pray for the loss, pray for your boss, love and forgive, no matter the cost!
- Grow in the word of God, become a prayer worrier, find a church, find out how you can minister to others.
- Pray for spiritual guidance, and pray too, for peace on earth!
- No matter your circumstances, or what life throws at you, just pray, just pray, just pray; I know, if you're with Jesus, you'll all be Okay! Always spend time with him **"PRAY"!**

Oops, Sticky note for your heart: almost forgot this one, Prayer time too, is for everybody, everywhere that do not know God, heard about him, but have not experienced him, or given their life to Christ, do this, go to Him in prayer, N.O.W! I'm a witness, **N**o **O**ne **W**orks but Jesus!

Get down on your knees pray and repent, come clean with God, and start over, make a U -Turn— New Life, New Direction!

Hear me, God loves you, don't play with his affection, — get serious about living right. Stop playing games with your life. Grow up! **Choose Christ, Choose Life!**

Now this is my prayer, may the grace and peace of God be forever present in your life always as "WE" become united as one with Christ in prayer. Remember we are never alone, Christ is there!

Amen!

Get The Care Plan
Open The Care Plan
Do The Care Plan

Is with You!

My Care Plan

From now on, I commit to ______________________________________

____

____

____

____

____

I will make necessary changes because __________________________

____

____

____

____

____

I will allow God to ____

____

____

____

____

I want to be more and more like Jesus in this area because _________

____

____

____

____

____

My prayer is ____

____

____

____

____

____

Reflection Diary Journal

Date ___________

Father God,

____

____

____

____

____

____

____

____

____

____

____

____

____

____

____

Amen.

PROMISES OF GOD

And because of his glory and excellence,
he has given us great and precious promises.
These are the promises that enable you to share his divine nature
and escape the world's corruption caused by human desires.
—2 Peter1:4

IN OUR BIBLES, there are thousands of promises God has made to his children, but a lot of us have no idea what they are because we don't read the Bible.

Today, so many of us are weighed down by the cares and pressures of this world. Life has become a drag, hard, but it doesn't have to be that way. God promised that he will be a help in time of need to all those who call on him; God doesn't want us to worry, tomorrow's problems will take care of itself says the Lord. God promise to take care of his children and work everything out in our favor too, — and he will! All we have to do is trust and believe, our God is not a God who would lie! (Matt. 6:25–34).

Trusting and believing to some is easier said than done, but I tell you the truth from my own experience, not trusting God, makes things a whole lot worst. He put all those promise in the bible for a reason so that we would know he's got our backs, he will not abandon us in time of difficulty. Our Father says, to his children don't be afraid, for I am with you; don't be discouraged, for I am your God I will strengthen you and help you. I will uphold you with my righteous hand. Isaiah 41:10

I take that to mean, He will protects us, nothing will get in the way of his plans for our lives, nothing. No job loss, no relationship gone bad, no health issues, you are not going anywhere before your time, God can heal you. Like He said, "I will uphold you with my righteous hand". And world you'd better believe He can. What an awesome God we serve! And how great is this, there are 5,467 promises from God in our bibles maybe a few more, who's counting. Brothers and sisters these promises of God does reveal his particular and eternal purposes to which he is unchangeable committed and upon which believers can totally depend and rely on. These promises are however, conditional, if we want all these blessing, and the peace of knowing that God is with us then we must live righteously! Be Christ focused, we must conduct ourselves like faithful and devoted Christians, we cannot blend in with the world.

And for all those who don't belong to God, the ones who love this world, and refuse to give God the time of day, don't pray, — won't take his word seriously, well you folks are pretty much on your own! Those 5467 promises you can kiss goodbye, you will not be blessed by them until you wake up, change your mind, change directions, come out of the world and start to live for Christ! Like Joshua told his crew, if serving the Lord seems undesirable to you, then choose you this day whom you will server... and he said some other things too, and I'm pretty much saying the same thing too, because like Joshua, as for me and my house we shall server the ***LORD! Joshua 24:15*** All those promises belong to us, God's people. If you want them, **"Choose Christ, Live For Christ!"**

Now back to those who do live for him, we are blessed! We are blessed in the city we are blessed in the field, we are blessed when we come and when we go, we cast down ever strong hold, when problems come, and they come, so what, still the devil is defeated, **"We Are Blessed!**

So if there's anybody out there that belong to God and is in need of reassurance, in any area of your life, whether it be your finances, your health, your marriage, your goals and dreams, if you are going through a crisis, heartbreak, a loss of any kind, cancer, depression, you name it. — God is with you, like **'The Care Plan'** He's got you covered from A to Z and more than me, He's got you covered eternally! I tell you the truth, 'The Almighty God' has promises for everything you could think of or imagine. He is faithful in keeping those promise too, all you have to do is open up your bible and just pick one of those promises that fits your need. Yes indeed, all these promises can be found in The Holy Bible, the best 'Care Plan' ever known to man!

So next time you're in a situation and you don't know what to do or where to go, remember this promise to you from God, *Don't be afraid, for I am with you; Don't be discouraged, for I am your God I will strengthen you and help you. I will uphold you with my righteous hand.* Isaiah 41:10

Question, **N.O.W,** can the world or man make those kind of promises to you? Of course not! **N**o **O**ne **W**orks but ***Jesus!***

Now may the God of Abraham, Isaac and Jacob, be with us all!
In Jesus name **Amen!**

The Holy Bible is the ultimate source for truth and God is faithful to fulfill every last one of his promises.

For no matter how many promises God has made, they are "YES" in Christ, And so through him the "AMEN" is spoken by us to the glory of God.
2 Corinthians 1:20

Ten Scriptures, Chosen Just For YOU!

2 Peter 1:4

1. Through these he has given us his very great and precious promises, so that through them you may participate in the divine nature, having escaped the corruption in the world caused by evil desires.

Matthew 11:28-29

2. "Come to me, all you who are weary and burdened, and I will give you rest. Take my yoke upon you and learn from me, for I am gentle and humble in heart, and you will find rest for your souls.

Philippians 4:19

3. And my God will meet all your needs according to the riches of his glory in Christ Jesus.

Jeremiah 29:11

4. For I know the plans I have for you," declares the lord, "plans to prosper you and not to harm you, plans to give you hope and a future.

Proverbs 1:33

5. but whoever listens to me will live in safety and be at ease, without fear of harm."

Romans 10:9

6. [9] If you declare with your mouth, "Jesus is Lord," and believe in your heart that God raised him from the dead, you will be saved.

Isaiah 40:29-31

7. He gives strength to the weary and increases the power of the weak. Even youths grow tired and weary, and young men stumble and fall; but those who hope in the Lord will renew their strength. They will soar on wings like eagles; they will run and not grow weary, they will walk and not be faint.

Romans 6:23

8. For the wages of sin is death, but the gift of God is eternal life in Christ Jesus our Lord.

Luke 11:13

9. If you then, though you are evil, know how to give good gifts to your children, how much more will your Father in heaven give the Holy Spirit to those who ask him!"

Matthew 6:31-34

10. So do not worry, saying, 'What shall we eat?' or 'What shall we drink?' or 'What shall we wear?' For the pagans run after all these things, and your heavenly Father knows that you need them. But seek first his kingdom and his righteousness, and all these things will be given to you as well. Therefore do not worry about tomorrow, for tomorrow will worry about itself. Each day has enough trouble of its own.

If You Don't Believe God's Promises, Sorry Then, You're On Your Own!

Promise Care Plan

Make These Your Realities Day and Night

- Trust and believe in the promises of God.
- Have faith that God will do what he said he would do.
- Celebrate the promises of God.
- Go after the promises of God.
- Don't let sinful living rob you of your blessing. Get right with God, Stay right with God!
- Tell others about the promises of God.
- Look in the mirror, Make that change, and leave this world behind!
- Start relying on the promises of God—not man, for he will fail you every time.
- Read your bibles., if you don't have one, get one. All the promises are in there just waiting for you to embraced, and take a hold of.
- Hold on to the promises of God for dear life. Never let them go.
- Live as people of promise!

Get The Care Plan
Open The Care Plan
Do The Care Plan

Is with You!

My Care Plan

From now on, I commit to ______________________________

I will make necessary changes because ______________________________

I will allow God to ______________________________

I want to be more and more like Jesus in this area because __________

My prayer is ______________________________

Reflection Diary Journal

Date ___________

Father God,

Amen.

PRAISE AND WORSHIP

Ha la le jah, ha la le jah, ha la le jah to the King of kings Ha la le jah, ha la le jah, ha la le jah is the song I sing

Hallelujah!
Ha la le jah, ha la le jah, ha la le jah to the King of kings Ha la le jah, ha la le jah, ha la le jah is the song I sing

Worthy, worthy, worthy
Worthy, worthy, worthy to the King of kings!
Ha la le jah, ha la le jah, ha la le jah is the song I sing.

Praise and worship is more than singing songs in church — so much more than that! Praise and worship go together it's what we do daily to show God how much we love and adore him. Plus, and it is a plus, Praise and Worship also keeps us close to God, and it shows God exactly where our treasure truly is, it's with him!

Praise is a good thing! It is pleasant, valuable and morally excellent, just like our God. The book of Psalms is the praise book of the bible, and it gives us hundreds of reasons why praise is important, Read for yourself all the beautiful ways one can give praise.

O' hear me Everybody, Everywhere, "Praise Him "Everyday lift him up, exalt, honor, and glorify his 'Holy' name! Once you have him in your life, you'll never, ever be the same!

For He is Worthy to Be Praised!

Make Praise and Worship a part of your Everyday Life!

Keep Praise and Worship alive! Thank God constantly for his goodness and mercy is new every morning. Here is a simple and easy song you can sing each day, personalize it, and add your own words of praise to it, Remember, when the praises goes up, the blessings come down! (Ps. 67:3)

Ha la le jah, ha la le jah, ha la le jah to the King of kings Ha la le jah, ha la le jah, ha la le jah is the song I sing

Hallelujah!
Ha la le jah, ha la le jah, ha la le jah to the King of kings Ha la le jah, ha la le jah, ha la le jah creator, dreams of dreams

Worthy, worthy, worthy
Worthy, worthy, worthy to the King of kings!
Ha la le jah, ha la le jah, ha la le jah is the song I sing!

Praise and Worship Care Plan

Make These Your Realities Day and Night

- Praise him in the morning, praise him in the noontime, and praise him in the evening, and at bedtime too! Praise him all day long! Come up with your own song!
- Remember what I said, praise and worship is not just for church services, it's not meant to be a show either, it's our hearts reaching out, showing God how much we love and adore him. He's up on a throne, we're down on the ground, don't get it twisted, He doesn't need us, we need him around! — **"Praise Him"** make a wonderful sound, a **"Joyful Sound!"**
- Join a praise and worship ministry, *"For where two or three is gather in my name, there I am with them"*. Matthew 18:20
- Praise Christ by the way you live everyone should see his light in you.
- Praise him at home and on your jobs too, be a great co-worker!
- Praise God both, in the good times and the bad times too.
- Praise him!
- When you worship, worship him in spirit and truth **'Be All HEART!'**
- Psalms is the praise book of the holy bible, open it, explore it, enjoy it, praise and worship is good for the soul!
- **"Read Your Bible Daily"** stay strong and rooted in Christ!
- Teach your family to praise him too, have fun! Celebrate what Christ is doing in your life.
- Christians, **Everybody, Everywhere,** make a joyful noise unto the lord, for he is worthy to be praised. Not just during Sundays or the holidays but always.
- Go to some Christian events, Invite a neighbor, — invite me!
- Be very selective in your music choices and what you watch on TV — don't pollute your ears, eyes and mind with degrading and unholy material, guard your ears, eyes, mind and heart — live for Christ, don't get caught up in the dark!

- Praise him publicly, tell people what God has done for you, help others too!
- Make it a daily lifelong practice to bless the **Lord** at all times, let his praise continually be in your mouth!
- Sing with me, this Godly light of mine, I'm going to let it shine, let it shine, let it shine, let it shine go on…praise him — keep singing yawl, everywhere I go, I'm going to let him shine, let him shine, let him shine, let him shine.., Don't stop … add your own words, keep singing … record yourself, make a CD, let the world hear your praise! O' happy days, praise can be done in so many ways!

Be exalted, O God, above the heaven, let your glory be over all the earth.

Psalms 75:11

The Praise and Worship Prayer

Sing to the **LORD**, all the earth; proclaim his salvation day after day. Declare his glory among the nations (and in your heart) his marvelous deeds among all peoples. For great is the **LORD** and most worthy to be praise; he is to be feared above all gods. (Fear no man, or circumstances God will help you.) For all the gods of the nations are idols, but the **LORD** made the heavens. Splendor and majesty are before him; strength and joy are his dwelling place. Ascribe to the **LORD**, (denounce obsessions with sports, drugs, alcohol, sex, lust and fornication, fighting, bullying, gossip and wild living, glorify our God instead, live only for him,) all you families of nations, ascribe to the **LORD** glory and strength. (Leaders, politicians, commander and chief, seal this inside your hearts **"In God We Trust"!)** Ascribe to the **LORD** the glory due his name; bring an offering and come before him (with joy and from the heart, Everybody, Everywhere start tithing a tenth of your income no matter how big or small, **"Tithe",** trust God, he will bless and reward us) Worship the lord in the spender of his holiness. Tremble before him, all the earth! (Read his word, do what it says) the world is firmly established; it cannot be moved. (God owns it all, he decide who wins or lose) let the heavens rejoice, let the earth be glad; let them say among the nations (in your heart when you praise him) "The **LORD** reigns!" **1 Chronicles 16:23-31**

N.O.W. (No **O**ne **W**orks but ***Jesus)*** and forevermore, please say this with me: All the glory and praise goes to our **LORD** Jesus Christ to him who is able to do immeasurably more than we ask or imagine, according to his power that is at work in us. **Ephesians 3:20**

Lift him up always, praise him, keep him first in your life, why? Because like I said,

No **O**ne **W**orks Your life out better than **Jesus!**

If you agree, say Amen, **Amen!**

Now to help keep you disciplined and focused
on living for Christ, this is what you do:

Get The Care Plan
Open The Care Plan
Do The Care Plan

Is with You!

Praise Him, Hallelujah!

When the Praises Goes up, The Blessing Comes Down!

Pray, Sing, Dance, Never Stop Glorifying 'GOD' for He is Worthy to Be Praised!

My Care Plan

From now on, I commit to ______________________________

I will make necessary changes because ____________________

I will allow God to ______________________________

I want to be more and more like Jesus in this area because __________

My prayer is ______________________________

Reflection Diary Journal

Date ___________

Father God,

____

____

____

____

____

____

____

____

____

____

____

____

____

____

____

Amen.

PEACE

The thief comes ONLY to steal and kill and destroy,
I came that they may have life and have it more abundantly.
—John 10:10

WHERE THERE IS no God, there's no peace. I don't care what you accomplished in life. Just look at "Hollywood" the headlines are full of misery, substance abuse, and suicide.

The entire world has become hospitalized by sin and corruption. Men have become sick, wicked and manipulative, lovers of themselves, yet still miserable. Women who get with these kinds of men they themselves become insanely jealous and insecure, (where I come from, I can't walk down the street without being hated by another woman) you become what you lay with, hang around with too. See, when people don't live and honor God, it shows in just about everything we say and do. Peace, where is it? **2 Timothy** is on point, **"Correct"**, people have become lovers of themselves, ***"Brotherly and Sisterly Love"*** I beg your pardon, **"What's That"?** We rejected peace a long time ago remember! Now look at what it has cost us. Today, all around the world there's corruption and hatred everywhere. Killings, and violence in the streets, homes broken down, women still getting raped and beat. "Every thing's out of whack!" Each day, has it's own troubles and the people of God must wear the full armor of God and watch their backs. And it's sad that we have to live like that, but we do and so do you. No one is safe out their anymore. But the truth remains, A world without Christ is doom, but the good news is **"PEACE"** is coming back soon! Yes the prince, not the "purple rain", people sing about prince, I'm talking about the prince of peace, his name is **Jesus of Nazareth**, born in Bethlehem, **"That Man"** He's coming back soon! No More Gloom! stay with **The Care Plan**, help spread the **"Good News"!**

Peace I leave with you; my peace I give you. I do not give to you as the world gives. Do not let your hearts be troubled and do not be afraid. John 14:27-31

Come Now, Let's Leave!

> "You heard me say, 'I am going away and I am coming back to you.' If you loved me, you would be glad that I am going to the Father, for the Father is greater than I. I have told you now before it happens, so that when it does happen you will believe. I will not say much more to you, for the prince (Satan, principalities, rulers in high places) of this world is coming. He has no hold over me, (Jesus would not allow himself to be tempted by the flesh or turn into a sex driven person, nor be tempted by lots of cash, fame and fortune, only a weak person would go for that and they often do.) but he comes so that the world may learn that I love the Father and do **Exactly** what my Father has commanded me.
>
> "Come now; let us leave.

I don't know about all of you, but I am following Jesus, I'm leaving with him!

Sorry, I could not write about peace, when it is plain to see, there is none until he comes!

"Come Out From Among Them and Be Separate, says the Lord."
2 Corinthians 6:17

This World Hates God, Sinful Hearts Will Never Accept Peace!

KJ21

“Think not that I am come to send peace on earth. I came not to send peace, but a sword.

ASV

Think not that I came to send peace on the earth: I came not to send peace, but a sword.

AMP

“Do not think that I have come to bring peace on the earth; I have not come to bring peace, but a sword [of division between belief and unbelief].

AMPC

Do not think that I have come to bring peace upon the earth; I have not come to bring peace, but a sword.

BRG

Think not that I am come to send peace on earth: I came not to send peace, but a sword.

CSB

Don’t assume that I came to bring peace on the earth. I did not come to bring peace, but a sword.

CEB

“Don’t think that I’ve come to bring peace to the earth. I haven’t come to bring peace but a sword.

CJB

“Don’t suppose that I have come to bring peace to the Land. It is not peace I have come to bring, but a sword!

CEV

Don’t think that I came to bring peace to the earth! I came to bring trouble, not peace.

DARBY

Do not think that I have come to send peace upon the earth: I have not come to send peace, but a sword.

DLNT

Do not suppose that I came to cast peace over the earth. I did not come to cast peace, but *a* sword.

DRA

Do not think that I came to send peace upon earth: I came not to send peace, but the sword.

ERV

"Do not think that I have come to bring peace to the earth. I did not come to bring peace. I came to bring trouble.

ESV

"Do not think that I have come to bring peace to the earth. I have not come to bring peace, but a sword.

ESVUK

"Do not think that I have come to bring peace to the earth. I have not come to bring peace, but a sword.

EXB

"Don't think [suppose] that I came to bring peace to the earth. I did not come to bring peace, but a sword.

GNV

Think not that I am come to send peace into the earth, but the sword.

GW

"Don't think that I came to bring peace to earth. I didn't come to bring peace but conf lict.

GNT

"Do not think that I have come to bring peace to the world. No, I did not come to bring peace, but a sword.

HCSB

Don't assume that I came to bring peace on the earth. I did not come to bring peace, but a sword.

ICB

"Don't think that I have come to bring peace to the earth. I did not come to bring peace, but a sword.

ISV

"Do not think that I came to bring peace on earth. I did not come to bring peace but a sword!

PHILLIPS

"Never think I have come to bring peace upon the earth. No, I have not come to bring peace but a sword! For I have come to set a man against his own father, a daughter against her own mother, and a daughter-in-law against her mother-in-law. A man's enemies will be those who live in his own house.

JUB

Think not that I have come to introduce peace into the land; I came not to introduce peace, but a sword.

KJV

Think not that I am come to send peace on earth: I came not to send peace, but a sword.

AKJV

Think not that I am come to send peace on earth: I came not to send peace, but a sword.

LEB

"Do not think that I have come to bring peace on the earth! I have not come to bring peace, but a sword.

TLB

"Don't imagine that I came to bring peace to the earth! No, rather, a sword.

MSG

"Don't think I've come to make life cozy. I've come to cut—make a sharp knife-cut between son and father, daughter and mother, bride and mother-in-law—cut through these cozy domestic arrangements and free you for God. Well-meaning family members can be your worst enemies. If you prefer father or mother over me, you don't deserve me. If you prefer son or daughter over me, you don't deserve me.

MEV

"Do not think that I have come to bring peace on earth. I did not come to bring peace, but a sword.

MOUNCE

"Do not think that I have come to bring peace to the earth. I did not come to bring peace, but a sword.

NOG

"Don't think that I came to bring peace to earth. I didn't come to bring peace but conf lict.

NABRE

"Do not think that I have come to bring peace upon the earth. I have come to bring not peace but the sword.

NASB

"Do not think that I came to bring peace on the earth; I did not come to bring peace, but a sword.

NCV

"Don't think that I came to bring peace to the earth. I did not come to bring peace, but a sword.

NET

"Do not think that I have come to bring peace to the earth. I have not come to bring peace but a sword.

NIRV

“Do not think that I came to bring peace to the earth. I didn’t come to bring peace. I came to bring a sword.

NIV

“Do not suppose that I have come to bring peace to the earth. I did not come to bring peace, but a sword.

NIVUK

‘Do not suppose that I have come to bring peace to the earth. I did not come to bring peace, but a sword.

NKJV

“Do not think that I came to bring peace on earth. I did not come to bring peace but a sword.

NLV

“Do not think I came to bring peace on the earth. I did not come to bring peace, but a sword.

NLT

“Don’t imagine that I came to bring peace to the earth! I came not to bring peace, but a sword.

NRSV

“Do not think that I have come to bring peace to the earth; I have not come to bring peace, but a sword.

NRSVA

‘Do not think that I have come to bring peace to the earth; I have not come to bring peace, but a sword.

NRSVACE

‘Do not think that I have come to bring peace to the earth; I have not come to bring peace, but a sword.

NRSVCE

“Do not think that I have come to bring peace to the earth; I have not come to bring peace, but a sword.

NTE

'Don't think it's my job to bring peace on the earth. I didn't come to bring peace – I came to bring a sword!

OJB

Do not think that I have come to bring shalom al haaretz (peace on the earth); I have not come to bring shalom but a cherev (sword).

RSV

"Do not think that I have come to bring peace on earth; I have not come to bring peace, but a sword.

RSVCE

"Do not think that I have come to bring peace on earth; I have not come to bring peace, but a sword.

TLV

"Do not think that I came to bring *shalom* on the earth; I did not come to bring *shalom*, but a sword.

VOICE

Do not imagine that I have come to bring peace to the earth. I did not come to bring peace, but a sword.

WEB

"Don't think that I came to send peace on the earth. I didn't come to send peace, but a sword.

WE

'Do not think that I came to bring peace on the earth. I did not come to bring peace, but war.

WYC

Do not ye deem, that I came to send peace into earth [Do not ye deem, that I came to send peace into the earth]; I came not to send peace, but sword.

YLT

'Ye may not suppose that I came to put peace on the earth; I did not come to put peace, but a sword;

Bottom line, if you love Jesus like you say you do, prove it, get on the boat! If you have to, leave everything behind, don't worry about time ….

"Let the Dead bury their own Dead" Matthew 8:22

Remember the fish and the bread and all the people Jesus fed!

Matthew14:13

Peace Care Plan

Make These Your Realities Day and Night

- Choose your life partner wisely. Be a fruit inspector!
- If you are in danger, plead the blood of Jesus; call for help.
- Read the Bible; it's your sword.
- Remember, if you are in Christ, Christ is in you! You should know peace!
- Don't waste your life on worldly living, fornication, drugs and alcohol, no, stay focus on what Jesus was focused on, his father in heaven.
- **N.O.W** say this: **N**o **O**ne **W**orks but Jesus! Relax, here's some peace for ya' For I know the plans I have for you, "declares the **LORD**, "plans to prosper you and not to harm you, plans to give you hope and a future. Jeremiah 29:11, how peaceful it that, so don't worry, be happy! Our future outside of the world is "Bright" but it won't be if we don't live right!
- Own this truth: **'Where There Is No God, There Is No Peace!'** Tie this around your neck as a reminder, **No God, No Peace!** Just like in the bible, write this wisdom on the tablet of your heart! Please don't live like a fool, live smart!
- Pursue peace at all times, don't argue with people, be humble, or just walk away! Try very hard to be at peace with all men.
- Create a peaceful environment for yourself and your family.
- Make up your mind to follow Christ and then do it!
- **N**o **O**ne **W**orks but Jesus, so don't try to avoid him and his teaching.

Don't like saying this but it's true, today our world is so full of hatred and violence, and our daily lives can be marred by conflict, confusion, and turmoil, if we are not rooted in Christ, peace won't prevail. Peace is for those who put their trust in God. Peace, the world doesn't have it, we do, but if we are not careful, sinning against God, will surely take that peace away, don't let that happen, be strong, pray. Fight for peace, like Jesus, rebuke the devil, say get behind me Satan, you can't have my peace, no way! Now tell those you know and love to:

Get The Care Plan
Open The Care Plan
Do The Care Plan

Is with You!

Peace I leave with you; my peace I give you. I don't give to you as the world gives. Do not let your heart be troubled and do not be afraid. John 14:27

My Care Plan

From now on, I commit to ______________________________

____

____

____

____

____

I will make necessary changes because ______________________________

____

____

____

____

____

I will allow God to ______________________________

____

____

____

____

I want to be more and more like Jesus in this area because __________

____

____

____

____

____

My prayer is ______________________________

____

____

____

____

____

Reflection Diary Journal

Date ___________

Father God,

____

____

____

____

____

____

____

____

____

____

____

____

____

____

____

Amen.

PROSPERITY

The LORD will command the blessings upon you in your barns and in all that you put your hands to and he will bless you in the land which the LORD your God gives you.

—Deuteronomy 28:8

YES, THE HARVEST is good. The harvest is very good for those who are in right standing with God! **"We Are Blessed!"**

We're blessed in the city
We're blessed in the field
We're blessed when we come and when we go.
We cast down every stronghold
Sickness and poverty must cease
For the devil is defeated
We are blessed!
(Fred Hammond)

My story, God's glory, this is personal, but I think the world should know, I have been persecuted and abandon a lot, because of my love for Christ, but No matter what I go through, I trust God to supply all my needs, and he does each and every time. I am blessed! I can't make it without him, I don't dare try! I can't began to tell you how much he has done for me, if he doesn't do another thing, he's already done enough.

I love my life with Christ, I'm so proud to be a Christian and I hope you are too.

I look at my life today, and after all I've been (walked) through Jesus never left me, he's always been right by my side. And because He has, this lady still has it going on. I'm beautiful black and strong — been through the fire! Hallelujah!!!! My story God's glory! Jesus came and took me higher, he held me up with his right hand, heck, when he rescued me there was no smell of smoke! **"My God Is Real"** He's no joke! **"Wow!!!"** How amazing is that, listen, no matter what this world tries to do to you, if you are with God, God is with you. "He's got our backs; so, Satan, and Haters, **"Deal With That!"**

Prosperity Belongs To Us, In God We Trust!

Live the Good Life!

'Prosperity' is a matter of trusting and believing that you can do all thing in Christ. People I'm living proof so believe me when I tell you, you can get out of debt, you can own your own home, you can open up a business, you can go back to school, you can do whatever your heart desires, just let Jesus, lead you and **Lift "YOU" Up Higher!** He will open doors **no** man, **no** job lost, **no** haters, **no** debt collectors can close, **no** broken hearts or loneliness, **no** I have too many kids, **no** fake friends, **no** low self-esteem, **no** I'm too over weight, **no** I'm too old, **no** I'm not smart enough, **no** I just got a divorce and whatever else we may come up with can close. **"Prosperity Is For Believers and Achievers"** not for wimps or crybabies. No matter what going on in your life Jesus has a solution to it all, Jesus will pick us right back up, if we fall! I tell you the truth, it's hard to keep a devoted faithful Christian down, **"We Win!"** with Christ around! He will open doors none of that stuff can close, man or obstacles won't stop prosperity, it's ours for the taking. Faith of a mustard seed and good works, sisters and brothers that's all we need and of course, we got to believe. **"READ"! Matt.17-20 & Eph. 2.2**

Some People Want It All!

When it comes to prosperity, it's true, **"Some People Want It All"** just like the singer and song writer Alicia Keys sang about in her song entitled "If I Ain't Got You" The money, material things, billboards that light up their names, "FAME"!!!! But, like Miss Keys, "by the way she's awesome"

I don't care about all that, **I Want Jesus!"**

I know the tragedy of fame. **"No Thank You!"** I want to proclaim his holy name, **"Forget Fame"**

What About **"YOU"?** What's **"Your"** story? Is God **"Your"** Glory? Tell Us, Who Are **"YOU"** living for? Stop aways wanting more , more and more!

Everybody, Everywhere, God sees and knows what goes on behind closed doors!

Stop Wanting, More, More, More!

The righteous has enough to satisfy his appetite.
But the stomach of the wicked is in need.
Proverbs 13:25

Prosperity "Live Clearly"!

How you make your loot, I suppose the choice is yours! But mind you, God can undo it all, I'm sure you heard about those who were on top, then suddenly lost it all. **Prosperity "Live Clearly"!** God gives and he also takes away. Unrighteous gains eventually doesn't pay! If you really want it all, do it God's way!

Okay, let me try to bring it all home for yah' as best I can, as you see, when it comes to Christ I can go on and on, like a Michael Jackson song, to the **"Break of Dawn"** Except my lyrics would go something like this: Feel Jesus touch, he loves his children so much, he wants to provide for us, but in him, we must learn to trust, to the Break of dawn, don't sale your soul, or let them bribe you or twist your arm! If you don't know what else to do, be still and rely on the only one that's true, to the break of dawn, prosperity says, I'll provide for you, I'll be there, I'll never leave nor forsake you, I'll protect you, hold you up too, with my right arm! How's that, for the **"Break of Dawn"?** Ooh wee, I like it, I love it!

I think it's time for me, **Miss Asondra StarN'air** to get back into the studio, so that I can keep my f low! Ha, ha seriously, I just want us all to grow. **Prosperity "Live Clearly"!**

This, One's for "You" Signed Sealed Delivered!

"Stay Faithful and True and Prosperity Will come After You!"

From, Miss Asondra StarN'air

No Worries!

"Can any one of you by worrying add a single hour to your life? "Therefore do not worry about tomorrow. For tomorrow will worry about itself. Each day has enough troubles of its own" Matthews 6:27, 6:34

Therefore I tell you, do not worry about your life, what you will eat or drink; or about your body, what you will wear. Is not life more than food, and the body more than clothes? Look at the birds of the air: They do not sow or reap or gather into barns—and yet your Heavenly Father feeds them. Are you not much more valuable than they? Yes Lord!

Prosperity, Prosperity, Prosperity!

Prosperity Promised

Genesis 15:5

And He took him outside and said, "Now look toward the heavens, and count the stars, if you are able to count them" And He said to him, "So shall your descendants be."

Rejoicing In Prosperity

Psalm 127:5

How blessed is the man whose quiver is full of them; They will not be ashamed When they speak with their enemies in the gate.

3 John 1:2

Beloved, I pray that in all respects you may prosper and be in good health, just as your soul prospers.

Prosperity is our if we really want it!

Psalm 1:3

He will be like a tree firmly planted by streams of water, Which yields its fruit in its season And its leaf does not wither; And in whatever he does, he prospers.

Proverbs 28:13

He who conceals his transgressions will not prosper, But he who confesses and forsakes them will find compassion.

Psalm 35:27

Let them shout for joy and rejoice, who favor my vindication; And let them say continually, "The LORD be magnified, Who delights in the prosperity of His servant."

Luke 6:38: For those who want 'Explosive Prosperity' this is what you do,

Give, and it will be given unto you. A good measure, pressed down, shaken together and running over, will be poured into your lap. For with the measure you use, it will be measured to you. **Luke 6:38**

Get The Care Plan
Open The Care Plan
Do The Care Plan

Is with You!

Prosperity Care Plan

Make These Your Realities Day and Night

- Sit with God, find out what his plan is for your life, and then act.
- Be ready to do want God ask you to do.
- Be patient but wise, don't move too fast.
- Be thankful for what you already have, don't want too much!
- Be stubborn and persistent about your dreams, don't let "NO WAY' get in the way or haters. Stay around positive God fearing people. Whatever you do, don't quit. Prosperity Is "YOU"!
- Stay focused, work toward excellence in all that you do, remember that if God is for you, who can be against you? Nobody! Remember this also, One with God is a majority! Press on...keep going! 'Read Your Bibles Daily' — those pages are full of what you need to succeed!
- Read scriptures on patience if you want prosperity.
- Help the poor and those in need, that's another way God prospers us, give and it shall be given unto you.
- Loving and forgiving your enemies, now that's prosperous too, plus, something we were told to do. Matthew 5:44 'coming right back at you!' Hate and retaliations gets us nowhere, God will not prosper us, we will not have favor with God, we must do what his word says, *"love your enemies", do good to those who hate you, bless those who curse you, pray for those who mistreat you.* Luke 6:27-28. Obey God's word, and prosper, be blessed!
- Children, Honor your mom and dad, and all will go well with you. Ephesians 6:2 And I say this to all the grownups out there and to the teenagers who think they're grown: Everybody, Everywhere, children and adults alike, Honor God and his Son Jesus Christ by reading his word, and doing what it says and all will go well with you too. Be Prosperous, Not Pitiful!
- Keep your eye on the cross, not on money, the love of money instead of Christ is the root to all kinds of evils, seek his

Kingdom first and prosperity will chase you down, not the other way around!

- Pray for patience, life stuff still happens, master your 'Everyday Life' with Christ! That's how you stay ahead, that's how you prosper too. Let Jesus wisdom guide you all the way to the promise land. That means children of God, we have to be strong and courageous in the Lord, when things get tough or bills fall behind, don't give up on the promise land! Remember too, you've got **The Bible** and **The Care Plan** in your hands!
- Thank God for prospering you right now. Just reading this book may help turn things around.
- Say, **"I Am Blessed And Highly Favored"** 'Prosperous too'!
- Praise him constantly because when the praises goes up, get ready yawl, the blessing comes down, always remember that! If you want **'Great Big Prosperity'** give your all in all to God, Tithed too, bring to his house (the church) a tenth of your earnings, — all the earning, not just some of them "ALL" so that there will be enough food in my Father's house. Do this people and this is what God promises *"I will pour out a blessing so great you won't have room to take it in."* Put me to the test, says the **LORD** of host! **Malachi 3:10**
- Wow! Talk about ***"Prosperity!"*** That's incredible, another "Explosive Prosperity," in the making, don't you think?, I think so! I don't know about the rest of you, but, I'm going for it! Like A Champion, I"m **ALL-IN!** And I'm so, so excited, this is ah "Me Too" moment, I'm going to:

Get The Care Plan
Open The Care Plan
Do The Care Plan

Is with You!

My Care Plan

From now on, I commit to ______________________________

I will make necessary changes because ______________________________

I will allow God to ______________________________

I want to be more and more like Jesus in this area because ______________________________

My prayer is ______________________________

Reflection Diary Journal

Date __________

Father God,

Amen.

PATIENCE

NOW, LET'S TALK about Patience, because we all need it at times don't we? Everybody, Everywhere, could use some of that! I can and I bet you could too. Patience, patience, patience, my dear loved ones, is a mental state and a discipline we all should master if we want peace. Patience is a virtue, not meant to deny or hurt you.

All of us need to learn how to be still and know that God is God, things will happen in his time, not ours.

Another truth, my story, God's Glory, I have waited on God all my life since age seven. "When God when," I cried? "Please show and tell"? "What's my calling? Lord, If I make a mistake, will you catch me when I'm falling? Tell me right now! (ooooowee tantrum child) What am I supposed to down here? Decades and decades later HE Spoke, "Write for Me"! I could not believe my ears, never in a million years would I think, God thought I had what it took to write for him. Me, I'm still not sure, but I'm in love with Christ, I don't care. These are his books, and "His Call" on my life. I'm just the vessel and not about to wrestle, with the call, if I fail, I fall, I just love him, that's all! But can I tell the world this, as I got older, say fifteen, I started dreaming of becoming a global recording artist, I sing. Perhaps that's his plan too, I hope so. Nevertheless, I'll do whatever he ask me to, he has the final say, I trust his will for my life completely, all the way! My message is this today, "Patients is a virtue never meant to deny or hurt you! Be still, Wait On God!

Wait on God! But oh no, some of you are not trying to hear that, we live in ah 'I Want It Now World'! Patience, **"What's That"?** Oh no, patience, you mean I have to wait, and for how long? It could be months, maybe even years, you mean I have to deal with all these disappointments and tears; um, I don't think so! Today people want things **"Quick,"** fast and in ah hurry!

"Fast Foods", 'Fast Cars', Fast Money", and believe it or not, **"Fast Honey"**. I kid you not, some are even going on the superhighway

(Internet) to hurry love. People are taking matters in their own hands. They are not being patient at all. They are not waiting on God! Who has the patience to wait anymore, my hands are up, "I do"! What about you? Say you do too! Oh please say you do, God will bless you! Remember this always: **Patience Is A Virtue Not Meant To Deny Or Hurt You!**

Patience allow us to persevere and make more wiser decisions which leads to greater success, and more importantly, Our Father knows best!

Be Patient, People, Wait On God!

God is "Almighty" He's The Alpha and The Omega who knows everything.

Our beginnings to our end, including who we will marry and how many children we will carry. To all those who have ears, listen, wait on God! Right now he says this to you: "If my people, which are called by my name, shall humble themselves, pray (first) and seek my face and turn from their wicked ways, (be done with this world) then I will hear from heaven and I will heal their land(prosper and bless you greatly in all you do). **2 Chronicles 7:14** For all those who want what you just read, bow your heads and ask for the gift of obedience and pray for patience, it's a virtue never meant to deny or hurt you!

Patience Care Plan

Make These Your Realities Day and Night

- Be Patient, Be Patient, Everybody, Everywhere, say it with me "Be Patient"!
- Wait on God, Wait on God, Wait on God!
- Be calm cool and collected while you wait.
- Be ready, when it's your time to shine.
- Learn to wait, love is patient, love is kind! 1 Corinthians 13:4-5
- Be kind and patient with yourself too, it's going to happen, God is working everything out, just keep the faith!
- Practice patience, don't move before GOD!
- Be patient, Stay focused, on all the promises of God
- Read your Bibles daily and do what it says.
- If you want to learn how to be patience, be still!
- Read scriptures on patience.
  Say this over and over again, **"Patients Is A Virtue Not Meant To Deny Or Hurt You!"**
- Remember, where we are weak, God is strong, ask God to work with you on patience.
- Pray for patience every day,
- Be patient, yet still go after your goals and dreams; but do check in with God often, make sure your plans line up with his.
- Patience everyone, be anxious for nothing! Philippians 4:68
- Praise him for giving you the gift of patience, teach others how to be patient too.
- Lastly, reward yourself for being patient. It's a beautiful attribute!

Get The Care Plan
Open The Care Plan
Do The Care Plan

Is with You!

My Care Plan

From now on, I commit to ______________________________

____

____

____

____

____

I will make necessary changes because __________________

____

____

____

____

____

I will allow God to ____________________________________

____

____

____

____

I want to be more and more like Jesus in this area because ________

____

____

____

____

____

My prayer is ____

____

____

____

____

____

Reflection Diary Journal

Date __________

Father God,

Amen.

PRIDE

WHAT IS PRIDE?, It is egotism, obsessions, vanity, vainglory, all over one's own appearance or status in life. Pride from a prejudice standpoint is white skin over black skin — superiority in its ugliest form, enslavement —slavery. However, **"Pride"** in the most ruthless form, **E**tches **G**od **O**ut of everything! Pride rides off Ego and Ego's are damaging the world, and breaking up homes. Ego's hate God, they say "I'm going to do what I wanna to do, **"Leave Me Alone"**. Meanwhile the devil roams. This is why **"We"** Christians are to be in the world but not of it. Roman 12:12

The world loves to promote sin, it's not about to let God in. Lovers of this world loves pride, they're not about to hide. For them the Kingdom is "Denied!"

Pride

Etches

God

Out.

Pride etches God out, so no wonder God hates pride. Pride takes on many different forms and can be seen just about everywhere; in the workplace, among neighbors and family members, athletes, entertainers, the rich and famous, white people, black people, all folks, and believe it or not, church folks too, including some pastors of all people, you name it, pride is everywhere today. People are fueling up on pride, they don't even want God in their ride. Prideful folks want to **E**tch **G**od **O**ut of everything until they find themselves in trouble. But the Lord says be sure of this: They will not go unpunished. Pride goes before destruction, a haughty spirit before the fall. **Proverbs 11:2**

God hates pride! He hates it because he loves people and pride prevents people from receiving help from God (Prov. 8:13).

In fact, the Bible goes so far as to warn us that pride is a sin in his eyes, and he will discipline the proud. Not only does he hate pride, God also hates a proud look. God's loathing of pride is unalterable, "for every one that is proud in heart is an abomination to the **LORD**" (Prov. 16:5).

Again, there are those who have absolutely no fear of the Lord Our God, or that scripture, they don't care at all, they are going to carry on the way they always have. Pride says, "My Way", "Party Like It's Nineteen Ninety Nine," "We Rule the World", girls "This is a Man's World" "Ain't Nobody's Business If I Do", "It's Your Thing, Do What You Want to Do". Well I got some news, "Pride" is going to lose! Warning, warning you'd better open your eyes, and be done with pride. God will not be mocked, so, I suggest we take this message to heart!

Characteristic of Pride

A proud person does not read the bible often or at all, they don't want to live for God, these individuals wants to live for themselves period. Proud people make their own way, education, money in the bank, cars, nice homes, personality , charm you name it they got it! They don't want someone like God telling them, sex outside of marriage is wrong, — ooh is that too strong?

'Proud People' want to decide for themselves, what's right and what's wrong. They love themselves and their idols too, no one's going to make them do what they don't want to do, not even God.

If this is you, **"STOP THE MADNESS!", "GET Right With GOD!"** Besides, let me ask you something, who gave you your incredible brain and talents anyway? Mr. (misses)"Big Stuff, who do you think you are Mr. Big Stuff? God needs to have a word with you right now, please sit down! *"Who is this that obscures my plans with words without knowledge?*

Brace yourself like a man; (or woman) *I will question you, and you shall answer me. "Where were you when I laid the earth's foundation? Tell me, if you understand. Who marked off its dimensions? Surely you know! Who stretched a measuring line across it? On what were its footings set, or who laid its cornerstone— while the morning stars sang together and all the angels shouted for joy? "Who shut up the sea behind doors when it burst forth from the womb, when I made the clouds its garment and wrapped it in thick darkness, when I fixed limits for it and set its doors and bars in place, when I said, 'This far you may come and no farther; here is where your proud waves halt' ? "Have you ever given orders to the morning, or shown the dawn its place, that it might take the earth by the edges and shake the wicked out of it?*

The earth takes shape like clay under a seal; its features stand out like those of a garment. The wicked are denied their light, and their upraised arm is broken.

"Have you journeyed to the springs of the sea or walked in the recesses of the deep? Have the gates of death been shown to you? Have you seen the

gates of the deepest darkness? Have you comprehended the vast expanses of the earth? Tell me, if you know all this.

What do you have to say now, Mr. (Ms) Big Stuff? Who do you think you are? God is not done speaking yet! Can you answer these...? *"What is the way to the abode of light? And where does darkness reside?*

Can you take them to their places? Do you know the paths to their dwellings?

Surely you know, for you were already born! You have lived so many years!

"Have you entered the storehouses of the snow or seen the storehouses of the hail, which I reserve for times of trouble, for days of war and battle? What is the way to the place where the lightning is dispersed, or the place where the east winds are scattered over the earth? Who cuts a channel for the torrents of rain, and a path for the thunderstorm, to water a land where no one lives, an uninhabited desert, to satisfy a desolate wasteland and make it sprout with grass? Does the rain have a father? Who fathers the drops of dew? From whose womb comes the ice? Who gives birth to the frost from the heavens when the waters become hard as stone, when the surface of the deep is frozen? "Can you bind the chains of the Pleiades? Can you loosen Orion's belt? Can you bring forth the constellations in their seasonsor lead out the Bear with its cubs? Do you know the laws of the heavens? Can you set up God's dominion over the earth? "Can you raise your voice to the clouds and cover yourself with a flood of water?

Do you send the lightning bolts on their way? Do they report to you, 'Here we are'? Who gives the ibis wisdomor gives the rooster understanding?

Who has the wisdom to count the clouds? Who can tip over the water jars of the heavens when the dust becomes hard and the clods of earth stick together?

"Do you hunt the prey for the lioness and satisfy the hunger of the lions when they crouch in their dens or lie in wait in a thicket? Who provides food for the raven when its young cry out to God and wander about for lack of food?

Job 38:2-41

With all of that being said, tell me this, how can a person , country or the world ever think they don't need God? It baffles me to think, people actually believe this but, I'm afraid it's true. People live for themselves now, in this world pride is the way to go, —it seems successful but it's not! Like God said, "Pride" goes before destruction, and a haughty spirit before a fall. Proverbs 16:18

Forget about pride, no matter what, we do need God. "For God so loved the world, that he gave his only begotten Son, that whosoever believeth in him should not perish, but have everlasting life" (John 3:16.)

Those of you holding on to pride, don't be a fool, let it go, or you'll regret it, and you'll never inherit the kingdom of God. Furthermore, it is written in ***Proverbs 16:18*** that pride goes before destruction and haughtiness before a fall. So don't be stupid or test God and say, ha ha "that's all". Think twice, the fall can cost you your life. Pride in God's eyes is huge, not small. So stop in the name of love, don't get caught up in "Pride" don't let the devil ever tell you, **"You've Arrived!"** No, don't ever think that, cross over to the other side, **"Denounce Pride"** Don't **E**tch **G**od **O**ut, Don't be an EGo, eventually they die out, they reap what they sow. Go for ***"Everlasting Life"*** Don't join them below!

Get The Care Plan
Open The Care Plan
Do The Care Plan

Is with You!

God Does Not Wish That Anyone Perish.

"Throw Away Your Foolish Pride"

Come inside,be done with *Pride!*

When Pride comes, then comes disgrace, but with the humble is wisdom.
Proverbs 11:2

Pride Care Plan

Make These Your Realities Day and Night

- Start putting God first in your life, not you. Tithed too!
- Repent and tell God you have sinned against him. Ask God to forgive you.
- Make all the necessary changes. Only you know what they are.
- Start reading the bible every day from now on and keep doing **The Care Plan**, repetition is the key to learning and growing in the LORD!
- Humble yourself, and start serving others. When was the last time *you* washed someone's feet?
- Thank God he's removing pride out of your life today, because there is a better way!
- You can still be successful and rich, I believe that's a good thing, God wants us to be prosperous, be the head and not the tail. He's just removing all the pride, making you into the kind of loving and humbled person he wants his children to be. So you don't have to compromise your high quality life style, I'm sure many of you have worked very hard at your achievements. But still, don't get high and mighty, or flighty, those are signs of pride creeping in, which is a sin, and worst it's against God. He hates that kind of worldly success, in fact, he says you are wretched and miserable and poor and blind and naked. Rev. 3:17 So, **"Be Wise"** be wise, don't fake it! For what good is it to gain the whole world and lose your own soul? Mark 8:36
- Trust the Holy Spirit to get you where you need to be with God. It's a process; it will not happen overnight. Be patient and stay away from pride, humble yourself, tell God you need him every day and in every way; tell him you'll be lost without him.
- If you ever get rich or buy a fancy car, don't ride with pride! Ride with God on your side.

To Those Who Just Won't Listen

- Some of you may be financially secure but bankrupt in other areas—for example,
  - * Money, but no love, peace or happiness.
  - * Nice house, but a house is not a home.
  - * Cars and material things, but they rust, and turn to dust!
  - * Lots of friends, until you find out, not one, you can trust.

- Jesus once said, "it is easier for a camel to go through the eye of a needle, than for the rich person to enter the kingdom of God" Matthew 19:24
- Humble yourselves before the Lord, and he will lift you up. James 4:10
- If you don't, "The LORD Almighty has a day in store for all the proud and lofty, for all that is exalted(and they will be humble)". Brought low! Isaiah 2:12

God or Pride, You Decide!

Get The Care Plan
Open The Care Plan
Do The Care Plan

Is with You!

My Care Plan

From now on, I commit to ______________________________

____

____

____

____

____

I will make necessary changes because ____________________

____

____

____

____

____

I will allow God to __________________________________

____

____

____

____

I want to be more and more like Jesus in this area because ________

____

____

____

____

____

My prayer is ____

____

____

____

____

____

Reflection Diary Journal

Date __________

Father God,

____

____

____

____

____

____

____

____

____

____

____

____

____

____

____

Amen.

THE CARE PLAN for God's People!

How We Think and Live Matters!

But the fruit of the spirit is love, joy, peace, patience, kindness, goodness, faithfulness, gentleness, self- control, against such things there is no law. And those who belong to Christ Jesus have crucified the flesh with its passions and desires, **Galatians 5:22-25**

Read Your Bibles Everyday!

QUALITIES OF A CHRISTIAN

THE BIBLE SAYS you will know them by their fruits (Matt. 7:15–20). But I have learned also that you will know them by a few other things too, for example, their lifestyles—the way that person live their lives, what they watch on television, the kind of music they listen to and by what comes out of their mouths.

The two main qualities I think God looks for in Christians, are discipline and obedience. Along with many other things of course, and I will list some shortly, but I'm sure, lifestyle and what comes out of our mouths are at the top of his list as well. As followers of Jesus Christ, we should have a clear understanding of what is expected of us. The Holy Bible provides all this and more to the believer.

Therefore, Christians have no excuse to be unholy and full of folly, scriptures are very clear on how we should conduct ourselves until his returns. God says, we are to be,

In the world, but Not of it! 1 John 2:15, John 15:19

In the world, "Yes", because that's what we are here for, we are here to help make this world a better place for Everybody, Everywhere. Also we are here to help save those who are lost. But we are not to be Of the world, "No", we are not to go along with this world at all, — do whatever feels good. We are not to live like Sodom and Gomorrah — cities filled with Prostitutes and whores. Drunks, druggies, fornicators, slanderers and haters, and ("Shacking") two people who live together unmarried,orgies, and one night stands, homosexuality(woman and woman, man and man), vanity, lust, idol worshipers, gossipers, murderers, molesters and rapist, lovers of money, pride, haughty eyes, liars, false witness, or hand around those that are quick to run to evil and god knows what else people do, These behaviors and traits should never be found in Christians that claims to love God and his son Jesus, ever! Separate yourself, come from among them.

Don't be in the world living like that anymore, those are the attributes of those who hate God. The world we live in right now says, **"GO FOR IT"!** The more souls the world can destroy, the better! This world hates God and Christians too.

The Qualities of a Christian, is something one needs to look at in depth. Because evil people are everywhere, Satan has more followers down here than God. That's why we are not to belong to this world. But, saints while we're here we need to ask God for the gift of discernment, we must get good at being able to tell whose who, there are a lot of fake people in the world.

But here's a problem too, and it's a serious one, today, it's becoming harder and harder to tell a person of the world and a Christian apart. People have become clever like Satan at disguising themselves. The bible calls this 'The Angel of Light', and says, even 'Satan' disguises himself as an angel of light. So it is no surprise if his servants, also disguise themselves too. Hear, hear, God sees and knows who you are, "shame on you"!

2 Corinthians 11:14-15

A lot of folks wear camouflage, it's true, so sad to say, some are at church, they look nice, but inside their hearts are full of jealousy and believe it or not, pride. A lot of these angels of light carry bibles, but they don't read it, some preach too, but they don't practice what they preach. These people are smart, 'sharp as a tack', but inside, they are, wicked and rotten to the core. **"Warning This Is A War"** read your bible, get wisdom, that's what it's for. Recognize these fakes quickly! God does, he cannot be fooled. In fact, he's getting ready to take you back to school, **Listen**:

> *I know some of your deeds that you are neither cold nor hot. I wish you were either one or the other! So because you are lukewarm—neither cold nor hot—I am about to spit you out of my mouth. You say, "I am rich. I have acquired wealth and do not need a thing. But you do not realize that you are wretched, pitiful, poor, blind, and naked."* (Rev. 3:16)

Not everyone that says to me, 'Lord, Lord', shall enter the kingdom of heaven; but only the ones who does the will of my Father who is in heaven.

Many will say to me in that day, 'Lord, Lord', did we not prophesied in Your name, and in Your name driver out demons and in Your name preform many miracles? Then I will tell them plainly, 'I never knew you'. Away from me, you evildoers! Matthew 7:21-23

The Qualities of a Christian must be seen, if you are a Christian and I hope you are or about to convert over, welcome into the house of believes. We are the light of the world, we should stand out in this dark world. God says, His children are the light of the world a town built on a hill cannot be hidden. Besides, No one lights a lamp and then puts it under a basket. Instead a lamp is placed on a stand, where it gives light to everyone, (Everybody, Everywhere) in the house. (All over the world Christians must shine!) Matthew 5:14-15

The Care Plan, is for the lost and the found! All those who are still struggling with sin, Please get on your knees, read, repeat after me:

I am guilty of living a lie, I have not been living the way I should, I have blended in a lot, with the world, I am just trying to live and enjoy my life while I can. I like being with others and having fun but in doing so, I have compromise my faith, my walk has not been right. I've done things I ought not to have done. Lord, I'm sorry! Please forgive me! I repent! But I'm still living in sin, I'm in bondage, I don't know how to undo what I have done. There are individuals in my life that like things just the way they are, I am afraid if I make any kind of moves, I may lose some of them. I know this sounds like I am choosing them and this world over you God, but what am I to do? I'm in bondage, I need help Lord, I need a savior, I cannot undo this all by myself, Father God, I need you, I need you, I want to turn my life over to you now, today, I want to change, get born again; I want to live right, I need help, rescue me! in Jesus name **Amen**

Here's what I say to all of you who feel this way place your **"Trust In The Lord"** He will help undo your life. He will never leave or forsake you. Just take it one day at a time.

So, if you just prayed that prayer, and really meant what you just said, hold on, help is on its way! It is never too late to start over, I did and so can you. Remember this always, how we live and carry ourselves matters to God, now let it matter to you. Be a person of God, follow Christ! **"Read Your Bibles Daily"** meditate on it day and night! Start over, **"Stop The Madness"** "YOU" don't have to keeping living broke, confused, miserable and uptight!

Just Simply, Live Right!

We don't compromise our walk with God, we live for him and him only!

Quality Of A Real Christian

1. We don't have sex outside of marriage.
2. We live for Christ and it shows.
3. We stay Fit, Focus, and Faithful!
4. We love our enemies.
5. We don't retaliate, We don't sue, We put it all in God's hand.
6. We Practice forgiveness and love.
7. We hate gossip and strife.
8. We love Everybody, Everywhere.
9. We seek the Lord's counsel, before others.
10. We Practice righteous living.
11. We enjoy reading our bibles every day.
12. We have uncompromising Christian values.
13. We are beautiful inside and out.
14. We will fight the good fight of faith.
15. We love being Christians!
16. We respect marriage.
17. We believe in tithing, serving too.
18. We are cool headed, slow to anger.
19. We are givers, not takers.
20. We work toward excellence.
21. We love people, we help strangers.
22. We help win souls for Christ.
23. We live quiet and peaceful lives.
24. We have a prayer life.
25. We put God first in all they do.

There are countless of things we do to stay in right standing with God, too many to list but, the most important thing we do is obey his word, we are loyal to our God! We worship and adore him!

Jesus Makes My "Heart Sing"!

Quality Attributes of a Christian

1. **Alertness,** know God's voice when you hear him.
   "But after I have been raised, I will go before you to Galilee." (Mark 14:28)

2. **Attentiveness.**
   Showing the worth of a person by giving undivided attention to his words and emotions.

   "For this reason we must pay much closer attention to what we have heard, lest we drift away from it." (Hebrews 2:1)

3. **Availability**
   Taking time out to serve others gladly.

   "For I have no one else of kindred spirit who will genuinely be concerned for your welfare." (Philemon 2:20)

4. **Boldness**
   Confidence that what I have to say or do is true and right and just in the sight of God.

   "And now, Lord take note of their threats, and grant that Thy bondservant may speak Thy word with all confidence." (Acts 4:29)

5. **Cautiousness**
   Gets the facts before it acts!

   "Also it is not good for a person to be without knowledge, and he who makes haste with his feet errs." (Proverbs 19:2)

6. **Compassion**
   Investing whatever is necessary to heal the hurts of others.

   "But whoever has the world's goods, and beholds his brother in need and closes his heart against him, how does the love of God abide in him?" (1 John 3:17)

7. **Contentment**
   Realizing God has provided everything I need for my present happiness.

   "And if we have food and covering, with these we shall be content." (1 Timothy 6:8)

8. **Creativity**
   Allowing The Holy Spirit to transform you, and how you look at things.

   "And do not be conformed to this world, but be transformed by the renewing of your mind, that you may prove what the will of God is, that which is good and acceptable and perfect." (Romans 12:2)

9. **Decisiveness**
   The ability to finalize difficult decisions based on the will and ways of God.

   "But if any of you lacks wisdom, let him ask God, who gives to all men generously and without reproach, and it Will be given to him." (James 1:5)

10. **Deference**
    Limiting my freedom to speak and act in order not to offend the taste of others.

    "It is good not to eat meat or to drink wine, or to do anything by which your brother stumbles." (Romans 14:21)

11. **Dependability**
    doing what I said I would do, even if it's inconvenient, I said I yes, so I take action.

    "In whose eyes a reprobate is despised, but who honors those who fear the lord; He swears to his own hurt, and does not change." (Psalm 15:4)

12. Determination

purposing to accomplish God's goals in God's timing regardless of the opposition.

"I have fought the good fight, I have finished the course, I have kept the faith; in the future there is laid up for me the crown of righteousness, which the Lord, the righteous Judge, will award to me on that day; and not only to me, but also to all who have loved His appearing." (2 Timothy 4:7-8)

13. Diligence

Visualizing each task as a special assignment from the Lord and using all my energies to accomplish it, by letting nothing get in the way of it.

"Whatever you do, do your work heartily, as for the Lord rather than for men." (Colossians 3:23)

14. Discernment

The God-given ability to understand why things happen to others and to me.

"But the Lord said to Samuel, 'Do not look at his appearance or at the height of his stature, because I have rejected him; for God sees not as man sees, for man looks at the outward appearance, but the Lord looks at the heart." (1 Samuel 16:7)

15. Discretion

The ability to avoid words, actions, and attitudes which could result in undesirable consequences that keeps us from being all we can be in the Lord.

"The prudent sees the evil and hides himself, but the naive go on, and are punished for it." (Proverbs 22:3)

16. **Endurance**
The inward strength to withstand the stress to accomplish God's best.

"And let us not lose heart in doing good, for in due time we shall reap if we do not grow weary." (Galatians 6:9)

17. **Enthusiasm**
Expressing the goodness of the LORD wherever we go, for He is worthy to be praised!

"Rejoice always; pray without ceasing; in everything give thanks; for this is God's will for you in Christ Jesus. Do not quench the Spirit." (1 Thessalonians 5:15-16)

18. **Faith**
Simply trusting God for everything and in every situation know that, God is going to work it out in our favor.

"Now faith is the assurance of things hoped for, the conviction of things not seen." (Hebrews 11:1)

19. **Flexibility**
Not setting my affections on ideas or plans, which could be changed by God or others.

"Set your mind on the things above, not on the things that are on earth." (Colossians 3:2)

20. **Forgiveness**
Clearing the record of those who have wronged me, and love them anyway!

"And be kind to one another, tenderhearted, forgiving each other, just as God in Christ also has forgiven you." (Ephesians 4:32)

21. Generosity

Realizing that all I have belongs to God and using it for His purposes.

"Now this I say, he who sows sparingly shall also reap sparingly; and he who sows bountifully shall also reap bountifully." (2 Corinthians 9:6)

22. Gentleness

Showing personal care and concern in meeting the needs of others gently.

"But we proved to be gentle among you, as a nursing mother tenderly cares for her own children." (1 Thessalonians 2:7)

23. Gratefulness

Making known to God and others that you appreciate what they have done in your life.

"For who regards you as superior? And what do you have that you did not receive? But if you did receive it, why do you boast as if you had not received it?" (1 Corinthians 4:7)

24. Hospitality vs. loneliness

Cheerfully sharing food, shelter, and spiritual refreshment with those whom God brings into your life.

"Do not neglect to show hospitality to strangers, for by this some have entertained angels without knowing it." (Hebrews 13:2)

25. Humility

I Cannot make it this world without God! No way, now how, that's Humility in the most humble form.

"But he gives a greater grace. Therefore it says, "God is opposed to the proud, but gives to the humble." (James 4:6)

26. Initiative

Recognizing and doing what needs to be done before you're asked to do it.

"Do not be overcome by evil, but overcome evil with good." (Romans 12:21)

27. Joyfulness

The result of knowing that God's light is in me and it shows everywhere I go!

"A joyful heart makes a cheerful face, but when the heart is sad, the spirit is broken." (Proverbs 15:13)

28. Justice

Personal responsibility to God's unchanging laws.

"He had told you, O man, what is good; and what does the Lord require of you but to do justice, to love kindness, and to walk humbly with your God?" (Micah 6:8)

29. Love

Giving to others' without having personal rewards as my motive.

"And if I give all my possessions to feed the poor, and if I deliver my body to be burned, but do not have love, it profits me nothing." (1 Corinthians 13:3)

30. Loyalty

Using difficult times to demonstrate my commitment to God and to those whom he has called me to serve.

"Greater love has no one than this that one lay down his life for his friends." (John 15:13)

31. Meekness

We don't make a move without Him! God is in control of every aspect of our lives.

"My soul, wait in silence for God only, for my hope is from him." (Psalm 62:5)

32. Obedience

Reading and Doing God's Word.

"We are destroying speculations and every lofty thing raised up against the knowledge of God, and we are taking every thought captive to the obedience of Christ." (2 Corinthians 10:5)

33. Orderliness

Arranging my life and surrounding so that God has maximum freedom to achieve His goals through me.

"But let all things be done properly and in an orderly manner." (1 Corinthians 14:40)

34. Patience

Accepting a difficult situation from God without giving Him a deadline to remove it. Trusting that God allowed it for a reason, remember, 'patience is a virtue, not meant to deny or hurt you!'

"And not only this, but we also exult in our tribulations, knowing that tribulation brings about perseverance; and perseverance, proved character; and proven character, hope." (Romans 5:34)

35. Persuasiveness

Using words, which cause the listener's spirit to conform that he is hearing truth.

"And the Lord's bondservant must not be quarrelsome, but be kind to all, able to teach, patient when wronged." (2 Timothy 2:24)

36. Punctuality

Showing respect for other people and the limited time that God has given to them. Punctuality is on time!

"There is an appointed time for everything. And there is a time for every event under heaven" (Ecclesiastes 3:1)

37. Resourcefulness

Wise use of that which others would normally overlook or discard.

"He who is faithful in a very little thing is faithful also in much; and he who is unrighteous in a very little thing is unrighteous also in much." (Luke 16:10)

38. Responsibility

How we live our lives matters to God, who did we choose, this world or God?

"So then each one of us shall give account of himself to God." (Romans 14:12)

39. Reverence

Awareness of how God is working through the people and events in our lives to produce the character of Christ in us.

"Do not let your heart envy sinners, but live in the fear of the Lord always." (Proverbs 23:17)

40. Security

Structuring our lives around what is eternal and cannot be destroyed or taken away by people.

"Do not work for the food which perished, but for the food which endures to eternal life, which he Son of Man shall give to you, for on Him the Father, even God, has set His seal." (John 6:27)

41. Self-control

Instant obedience to the initial prompting of God's Spirit, not led or controlled by the flesh anymore. Hate sinning against God.

"Now those who belong to Christ Jesus have crucified the flesh with its passions and desires. If we live by the Spirit, let us also walk by the Spirit." (Galatians 5:24-25)

42. Sensitivity

Knowing by the prompting of God's Spirit what words and actions will benefit the lives of others. What we do and say matters! Words can heal, words can destroy! Action can build, actions can tear down.

"Rejoice with those who rejoice, and weep with those who weep." (Romans 12:15)

43. Sincerity

Eagerness to do what is right with transparent motives.

"Since you have in obedience to the truth purified your souls for a sincere love of the brethren, fervently love one another from the heart." (1 Peter 1:22)

44. Thriftiness

Not letting myself or others spend that which is not necessary. Don't do or take too much!

"If therefore ye have not been faithful in the unrighteous mammon, who will commit to your trust the true riches?" (Luke 16:11)

45. Thoroughness

Realizing that each of our tasks will be reviewed and rewarded by God. What we sow, we reap!

"The mind of the prudent acquire knowledge, and the ear of the wise seeks knowledge." (Proverbs 18:15)

46. Tolerance

Viewing every person as a valuable individual whom God created and loves. We don't always have to agree, but we always have to love. Love one another like sisters and brothers!

"Make my joy complete by being of the same mind, maintaining the same love, united in spirit, intent on one purpose." (Philemon 2:2)

47. Truthfulness

If we don't have the facts, we don't speak!

"Therefore, laying aside falsehood, speak truth, each one of you, with his neighbor, for we are members of one another." (Ephesians 4:25)

48. Virtue

Believing what God believes, sex outside of marriage is wrong.

"Seeing that His power has granted to us everything pertaining to life and Godliness, through the true knowledge of Him who called us by His glory and excellence." (2 Peter 1:3)

49. Wisdom

Seeing and responding to life situations from God's frame of reference.

"The fear of the Lord is the beginning of wisdom, and the knowledge of the Holy One is understanding." (Proverbs 9:10)

50. Zeal

God is good and so should we be, zeal is for those who love him for real! If you got it

'Flaunt it'!

Those who I love, I reprove and discipline therefore be zealous and repent. (Revelations 3:19)

Miss Asondra StarN'air

Christ Will Save The Day!

Get Out Problems, "You Can't Stay!"

Qualities of a Christian Care Plan

Make These Your Realities Day and Night

- Read your Bibles daily, grow up in Christ!
- Remove everything out of your life that is not pleasing to God. And get away from anything or anyone that's a hindrance. We do not need those kinds of problems in our lives anymore.
- Realize change takes time, so be patient. Trust the holy spirits guidance.
- Stop hanging out with non –believers that refuse to give their lives to Christ. Love and pray for them but, move on...
- Remember, if you are living for Christ, you will be hated and rejected. But God's got your back, you will be protected!
- Reframe from sex, wait on God to send you a mate. If it's too tempting, then **"Don't Date!"**
- If you are not fit, get fit. God needs us healthy and in good shape, it may take years but you can do it! Just say, I can do everything through Christ who gives me strength.
- Fall in love with being a Christian, it's wonderful and peaceful too!
- **Do The Care Plan** with others! Grow strong in the Lord together! Study and learn these qualities from A to Z . Shout out loud **"Greatness Is In Me!"**

In Jesus name **Amen!**

Get The Care Plan
Open The Care Plan
Do The Care Plan

Is with You!

My Care Plan

From now on, I commit to ______________________________

I will make necessary changes because ______________________________

I will allow God to ______________________________

I want to be more and more like Jesus in this area because __________

My prayer is ______________________________

Reflection Diary Journal

Date ___________

Father God,

____

____

____

____

____

____

____

____

____

____

____

____

____

____

____

Amen.

THE CARE PLAN for God's People!

How We Think and Live Matters!

"Knowing these teachings will mean true and good health for you."
Proverbs 4:22

Read Your Bibles Everyday!

RIGHTEOUSNESS

Whoever pursues righteousness and love finds life, prosperity and honor.

—Proverbs 21:21

THE LORD DETEST the ways of the wicked, but he loves those who pursue righteousness — yes, God loves it when we flee from doing wrong.

Another way to look at Righteousness is, God is Righteous! Therefore, if we say we are born again then we must live life God's way. We are his people and he is our God.

The bible also tells us that the righteous will live by faith, Hebrews 10:38 which means we are not to worry at all, about anything, what shall we eat? What shall we drink? Or what shall we wear? — Matthew 6:31 No worries, because we know the God we serve, will always be there. Yes, God will supply our every need. But in the meantime, **"EVERYBODY"** understand this, how we behave here on the planet matters.

Righteousness vs, Unrighteousness, it's a choice we all have to make each day we walk this earth. Christ had to make that choice and so must we. Righteous says, "each day" sisters and brothers we must choose whom we will serve. **"Be Wise, Choose Christ!"** Embrace **"Righteousness"!** Be discipline—obedient and full of faith. Remember to love, never hate! If we do all that, we can't go wrong. Know this too, **"We're Human"** we make mistakes but we correct them and move on.., God keeps us strong.

As for the "Unrighteous", a whole different song! Keep praying for them, hate the sin, love the sinner but still, wrong is wrong! We can't save someone who loves this world and don't want to be saved! For it is written, that people love unrighteousness, "SIN". Yes the verdict is in! *Light has come into the world, but people love darkness instead of light because their deeds were evil.* **John 3:19**

The unrighteous cares nothing about helping others or loving their neighbors. On the contrary, their robbing their neighbors, full of destruction and crime. Bottom line, they hate God! They're lost, wretched and miserable. And full of iniquity, they're in bondage to their sins and oppressed, poor and the bibles says blind too and naked! My heart breaks and aches for the unrighteous because they're not going to make it! What ah wasted life! And still, with all that being said, "The World" and every soul in it, will be made humbled! 'Every knee shall bow, and every tongue shall confess, that Jesus and his righteousness is **LORD!**' Romans 14:11

All I can say is, 'Stop in the name of **"Righteousness",** which is God, which is also **"LOVE"**. Before you break God's heart, think it over, hasn't our creator been good to you? Hasn't he been true to you? Think it over! Right now, as it stands here today on planted earth, (righteous) good is bad and (unrighteous) bad is good.

Question now is, which one do **"YOU"** practice? Righteousness or Unrighteousness? But before you answer, Christ speaks, listen to this

"Do you not know that the unrighteous will not inherit the kingdom of God? Do not be deceived: neither the sexually immoral, nor idolaters, nor adulterers, nor men who practice homosexuality, nor thieves, nor the greedy, nor drunkards, nor revilers, nor swindlers will inherit the kingdom of God. And such were some of you. But you were washed, you were sanctified, but you were justified in the name of the Lord Jesus Christ and by the Spirit of our God. I Corinthians 6:9-11

Yes, many of us, changed, got born again, gave this world up for the sake of "Righteousness"! All I can say now is. "I hope you have too!"

God Bless You!

"Listen"

Little children, make sure no one deceives you, the one who practice righteousness is righteous, just as He is righteous. 1 John 3:7

"You should diligently keep the commandments of the Lord (read your bibles) your God, and his testimonies (those disciples who wrote the bible) and his statues which he has commanded you." You shall do what is right and good in the sight of the Lord, that it may be well with you and that you may go in and possess the good land which the Lord swore to give your fathers. Deuteronomy 6:17-18

Now may the goodness of the Lord, be bountiful in your life, may you have the desires of your heart. Do what's right and good.

Live For God, Be Righteous!

Righteousness Care Plan

Make These Your Realities Day and Night

- Let them reject you, **"RIGHTEOUSNESS"** is an excellent way to be.
- God rewards those who are faithful to him and his word.
- Pursue the kingdom of God and his righteousness, and all else will be given unto you (Matt. 6:33).
- We are in the world but not of it and that should place a lot of 'Do's and Don'ts' in our lives. I believe the more 'Do's and Don'ts', we have for this wicked and evil world, the more we'll stay out of trouble, and the more righteous we'll become. At least that's what I discovered.
- Read your bibles, find out what God has to say about righteousness.
- Remember what Christ told us, if we are one of his, we will be hated and persecuted. This world is not righteous, it's unrighteous, it loves evil, it loves doing wrong, — the power that be, hate God, in their wicked and evil minds, like I said, and the bible reminds us of this too, good is bad, and bad is good. Isaiah 5:20. So keep your armor on everybody, the bible teaches we'll know them by their fruits, so from now on become a fruit inspector. Don't worry, God is our protector. Just be righteous like out Father in heaven is.
- To Everybody, Everywhere, all you good and righteous people out there who worship and adore our God, join hands with me, lets be strong and courageous in the Lord, for he will never let the righteous person stumble, **Never!**

Pray For The Unrighteous!

Tell them to:

Get The Care Plan
Open The Care Plan
Do The Care Plan

Is with You!

My Care Plan

From now on, I commit to ____________________________________

____

____

____

____

____

I will make necessary changes because ________________________

____

____

____

____

____

I will allow God to ____

____

____

____

____

I want to be more and more like Jesus in this area because _________

____

____

____

____

____

My prayer is ____

____

____

____

____

____

Reflection Diary Journal

Date ___________

Father God,

Amen.

THE CARE PLAN for God's People!

How We Think and Live Matters!

"Knowing these teachings will mean true and good health for you."
Proverbs 4:22

Read Your Bibles Everyday!

SIN

If we claim we have no sin,
we deceive ourselves and the truth is not in us
—1 John 1:8

EVERYBODY, EVERY WHERE HAVE SIN. But the question is, why do we keep inviting it in? Why do we think we can win, with sin? We can't!

Some of you are playing a very dangerous game with your life. Yes it's true Jesus died for our sins, but it's still up to us to say no to sin. All of us have a choice, **To Sin** or **Not to Sin**! Just like we have a choice to follow Christ or not to make him Lord over our lives. This free will has been given to Everybody, Everywhere!

God put it out there like this, "choose whom this day you will serve? Either you will love one and hate the other. Matthew 6:24.

Another way to look at it, either you give your life to Christ, or you will give your life over the this world where Satan rules. Think it over, don't be a fool! And another thing, while we're on the subject of sin, although Jesus died for our sins, the wages of continual sin, is still death! I encourage you to choose the latter, get to know Christ better! As for me and my house we will serve the Lord!

Again it's your choice, The Care Plan can't force you, but If you know what I know, choosing this world over God is a huge mistake, but some of you may have to learn the hard way, choosing this world means you will keep on sinning, you will feed your flesh whatever it desires, and it also means that you have absolutely no fear of God. And if this is "YOU" you're through! It's just a matter of time! Your life will never be stable or fine.

See, sin people is destructive, it's hellish in nature, it ruins everything! Sin destroys lives, marriages, families, economies, nations, minds, you name it, sin is truly the root to all evil.

Why destroy your lives and this world like that? Why, why, why? Put an end to your sin, let Jesus come in. Repent! Change directions, before it's too late. If you are reading this book right now, it' not too late, let this book help you.

Some of you out there are so lost in sin, it feels normal—right, even— "everyone else is doing it", no one else is trippin but **The Care Plan**, No! **The Bible** is trippin too, I guess, listen to this, *"There is a way that seems right to a person, but its end is death."* Proverbs 14:12. What do you have to say now?

As I was saying, some of you may not be aware that you are sinning at all, I wasn't always aware when I was out there in the world doing my own thing. But I changed, I got saved. Now I've come back for all of you.

So let's talk about what sin is, and what it looks like, shall we. What is sin? First let me say this, I am not a bible scholar, I don't pretend to be, all I am is a born again Christian that's become madly in love with Jesus Christ. When I am not writing for him, I'm studying his word; I know the fundamentals and I know the truth when I hear it. So you scholars out there reading this, correct me, if I am wrong, but I don't think I am wrong here: Sin from the way I understand it now, is a form of transgression against doing what is right, good vs evil! Righteousness vs Unrighteousness what we just covered, From a Christian standpoint, it's a transgression against God. It's a willingness to ignore, what's written in the bible! A deliberate act to go on sinning, regardless of the consequences. Let me put it this way, so even a child can understand,

Sin is No Fear of GOD, Whatsoever!

This is what **SIN** looks like here on earth:

Adultery, idolatry, homosexuality, covetousness, filthy immoral Lifestyles, lying a withholding from others what's do them, cheating, stealing, negativity, gossiping, putting family and friends before God, attachment to riches and material things, lust of the eyes and ears, lover of self, vanity, sport obsessions, violent TV, Internet hackers, female and male sex symbols who lure viewer with their bodies, false witnesses, Shack -uppers, one night stands, strippers, nudity, illegitimacy, children born out of wedlock, poverty, uncleanliness, violent and lust sex filled TV, reality shows and soap operas,pornography, lewd dance and offensive behavior, immorality, schemers, jealousy, hatred, deceit, slanderers, loud and lude personalities, greed, disobedience, waywardness, drunkenness and drugs, whoremongers, prostitutes, disrespectful children, thieves, robbers, pride, gamblers, rapist, cheaters, wife beaters, drug dealers, murderers, fakes that do whatever it takes, disguiser's, angels of light, political and cruel fights....I can go on and on but Christ said, I got it just about right! So, I'll stop here, you get the gist of it, **"We Can't Win When We Practice Sin!"** Sinning against God is terrible, it's ugly, but to this dark and evil world, it's beautiful. It's called freedom, it's called money and power, no matter if souls are dying and dropping dead by the hour... But unfortunately those who belong to this world still want power!

As you see, sin is very dark and ugly indeed, and one of the main reasons why we suffer and are so miserable today. Please don't misinterpret what I'm trying to say, or get mad, and throw this book away, we all are sinners, **"Me Too"** me too, me too, but if we can control a lot of it, we should and we must, especially if we say in God we trust. We don't have to do the things we do, we have a choice, we can either live in the will of the Almighty God, where sin dies out of us or we can continue to live in the world where sin (the devil) breaks us down, lures us away from God. By giving us everything our flesh wants, then destroys us, one by one, **Dead, "Gone", The End!**

I don't know how to say it any other way, so I'll sum it up like this: **Denounce Sin! Choose Christ and Win!**

Sin

In

Nothing, make up your mind, say no more, Walk through God's Open Door!

This world is not worth going to hell for, walk through a different door, The door that leads to "Everlasting Life" **Choose Christ!**

Sin Care Plan

Make These Your Realities Day and Night

- Know that sinning against God is going to cost you something, in the end and let me tell you it's not worth it!
- Stay in God's Word as if your life depends on it and it does.
- Ask God to remove anything that is not pleasing to him out of your life.
- Pray for righteousness, righteous living too.
- Pray for Christ to overtake you with his kindness and mercy.
- Tune into The Trinity Broadcasting Network (TBN), on a regular bases **"Hear The Word, Do The Word"** 24/7.
- Take inventory of your life, ask yourself this question, am I living right?
- Don't hang out with men or woman who fornicate, have nothing to do with them, less you become like them. Love them, of course, pray for them too, but, stay away, be the example they need to see. Be done with sinning, **"Be Free"!**
- **S**in **I**n **N**othing, say to yourself, no more, **"Get Born Again"** walk through God's open door!
- Watch what you watch at the movies and on TV. Ask yourself, would Jesus, be watching this? If the answer is no, turn it off, and keep it off.
- Reframe from sex outside of marriage, if it's hard to do, don't date.
- Remember, if you don't take **The Care Plan**, seriously you'll stay sick in sin. But if you want to heal, be blessed and enter the kingdom of God you're going to have to put your cloves on too, and fight against sinning, so that means you are going to have to do some work, you are going to have to study the bible on a regular bases, and practice obedience and disciple so, mightiest well get started.

"Go, Go, Go, Don't Walk, Run:

Get The Care Plan
Open The Care Plan
Do The Care Plan

Is with You!

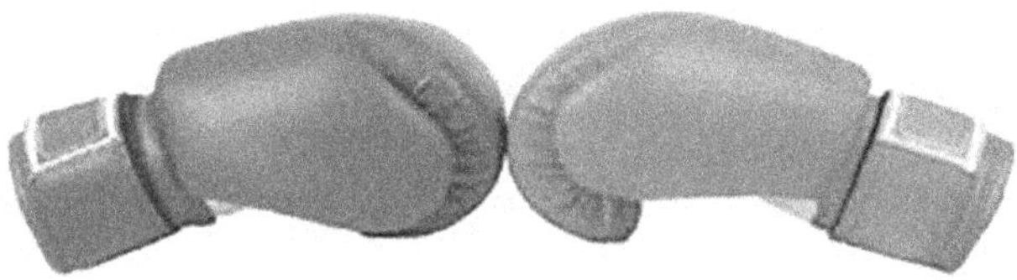

"Good" Vs. "Evil"

Woe to those who call evil good
and good evil,who put darkness for light and light for darkness,
who put bitter for sweet and sweet for bitter.
Isaiah 5:20

My Care Plan

From now on, I commit to ______________________________

I will make necessary changes because ______________________________

I will allow God to ______________________________

I want to be more and more like Jesus in this area because ______________________________

My prayer is ______________________________

Reflection Diary Journal

Date ___________

Father God,

____

____

____

____

____

____

____

____

____

____

____

____

____

____

____

Amen.

THE CARE PLAN for God's People!

How We Think and Live Matters!

"Knowing these teachings will mean true and good health for you."
Proverbs 4:22

Read Your Bibles Everyday!

TRUST

Trust in the LORD with all your heart and lean not on your own understanding.

—Proverbs 3:5

TAKE A LOAD OFF! Trust in the Lord! When things go wrong in our lives and they will sometimes, know this, "God is our refuge and strength, a very present help in time of trouble" (Ps. 46:1). Trust him!

Trusting God means, we have to surrender our entire life to him, some say just the heart, but I say the healthiest way is with, Everything You Got, Your Heart — Your Mind — Your Body — Your Spirit — and Your Soul.

When we trust God with all that, we can breathe, we can sit back and chill, take a load off! This is what I say to the world and to all my troubles:

The Lord is my shepherd, I shall not want. He makes me lie down in green pastures; he leads me beside still waters; he restores my soul. He leads me in right paths for his name's sake. Even though I walk through the darkest valley, I fear no evil; for you are with me; your rod and your staff—they comfort me. You prepare a table before me in the presence of my enemies; you anoint my head with oil; my cup overflows. Surely goodness and mercy shall follow me all the days of my life, and I shall dwell in the house of the Lord my whole life long.

Psalms 23! That's Me, Let That Be YOU!

I put all my trust in him and only him, that's where my strength come from. I pray you do the same. Trust In the Lord from now on, call on his holy name!

Miss Asondra StarN'air

Trust Care Plan

Make These Your Realities Day and Night

- Trust no one, not even yourself. Just God!
- Cast all your cares on Jesus.
- When you are afraid or in trouble, put your trust in God.
- Read your Bibles daily, trust in God's promises.
- Be trustworthy yourself, live holy and true.
- Trust in the blessing of the Lord, he rewards those who wait on him.
- Trust God to find you a soul mate, not you.
- Trust and believe you can do all things in Christ.
- Don't put your faith or trust in people, they will always disappoint you.
- **"Don't Worry, Be Happy"** *Trust God! He is Our Shepard', you are his sheep! He will guide and protect you always if you trust and rely on him.*
- Guard your heart; there are many deceivers out there. Put your 'Trust' only in the Lord!
- Today, if you are going through something, trust that God is going to work it all out in your favor.
- Keep God first he'll take you places you never dreamed of.

Trust Him With It All!

- **Heart**—that loves like he does.
- **Mind**—that stays focused on him.
- **Body**—belongs to him not us.
- **Spirit**—is holy and true.
- **Soul**—longs to be with Our Father in "Heaven".

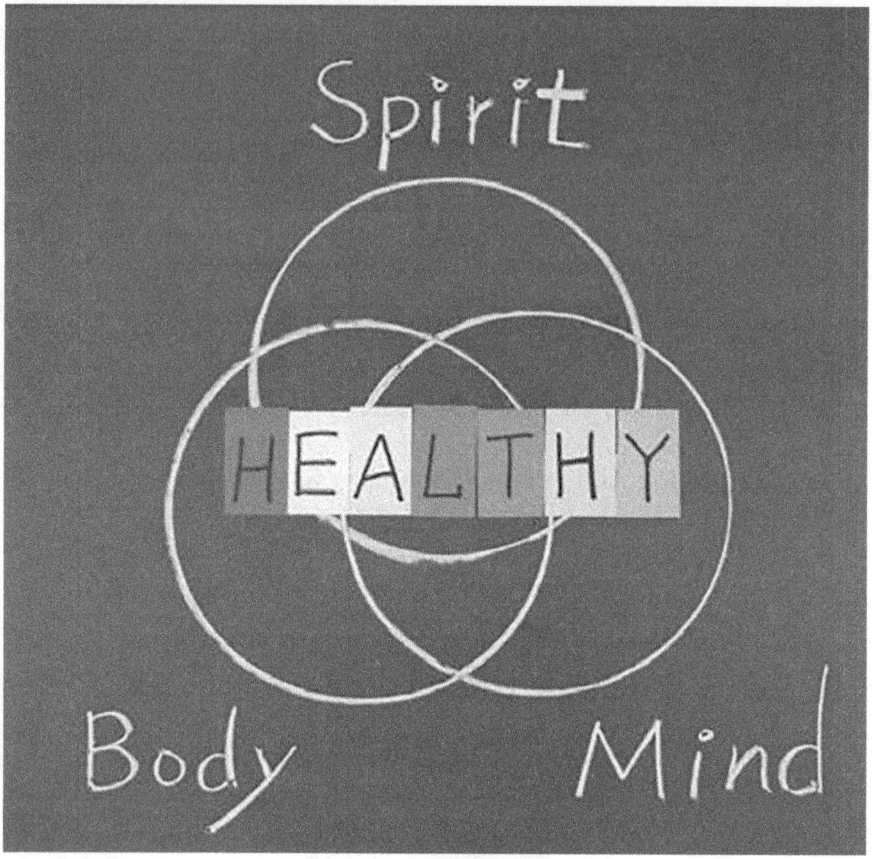

If you trust him with all that, then get busy and stay focus!

Get The Care Plan
Open The Care Plan
Do The Care Plan

Is with You!

My Care Plan

From now on, I commit to ____

____

____

____

____

____

I will make necessary changes because ______________________________

____

____

____

____

____

I will allow God to ____

____

____

____

____

I want to be more and more like Jesus in this area because __________

____

____

____

____

____

My prayer is ____

____

____

____

____

____

Reflection Diary Journal

Date __________

Father God,

Amen.

THE CARE PLAN for God's People!

How We Think and Live Matters!

"Knowing these teachings will mean true and good health for you."
Proverbs 4:22

Read Your Bibles Everyday!

UNITY

ONLY CONDUCT YOURSELF in a manner worthy of the gospel of Christ, so that whether I come and see you or remain absent, I will hear of you that you are standing firm in one spirit, with one mind striving together for the faith of the gospel. Philippians 1:17

Whether you are a believer of the gospel of Jesus Christ or not, regardless, **Unity Matters! 'Everybody, Everywhere'** need to come together as one and stop all the hatred and violence. We are supposed to be loving one another like sisters and brothers.

I have a question for all of you, 'Do we not all have one father? Has not One God creator us? Then why do we act so treacherous with each other? Why do we hate each other so much? Malachi 2:10. Give that kind of heart up! Where there is hate, there can be no love or unity. Something has got to change if we are going to move forward in peace, love and happiness don't you think so? I hope so.

Well, today, let's all agree to respect and love one another like sisters and brothers. We don't always have to like or agree with the things people say or do, God will deal with all that stuff but, **"Everybody"**, it is written, that we **"MUST LOVE"!** Yes, we still must find a way to love and come together in unity, throughout the world and in your community. When that happens, **"Life is Good!"**

> *Behold, how good and how pleasant it is for brothers and sisters to dwell together in unity!* **Psalms 133:1**

> *For just like we have many members in one body and all the members do not have the same function, so we, who are many are one body in Christ and individually members one of another.* **Romans 12:4-5**

Love Your Sisters And Brothers!

Be Smart, Keep A Child's Like Heart, Love, Unify!

Change The World, Fly!

Unity Care Plan

Make These Your Realities Day and Night

- Be kind to others, make new friends.
- Help each other, "Unify' come together, show love!
- Share your material things with others.
- Offer to do something for someone you don't know.
- Sit with others, don't always sit alone.
- Do daily acts of kindness.
- Invite a stranger to your home for dinner or go out to eat.
- Help care for the poor, or those in need.
- Don't hold on to grievances, work things out!
- Don't single anyone out because they are different; although we are one, no two people are alike.
- Agree to disagree, but stay in unity!
- Don't be cruel, Be kind to people!
- Love the Lost and Found, Love Everybody, Everywhere!
- Tithe, unify, come together for the good of humankind.
- Love one another like sisters and brothers!

Join Hands, Let Us All Become One Body In Christ!

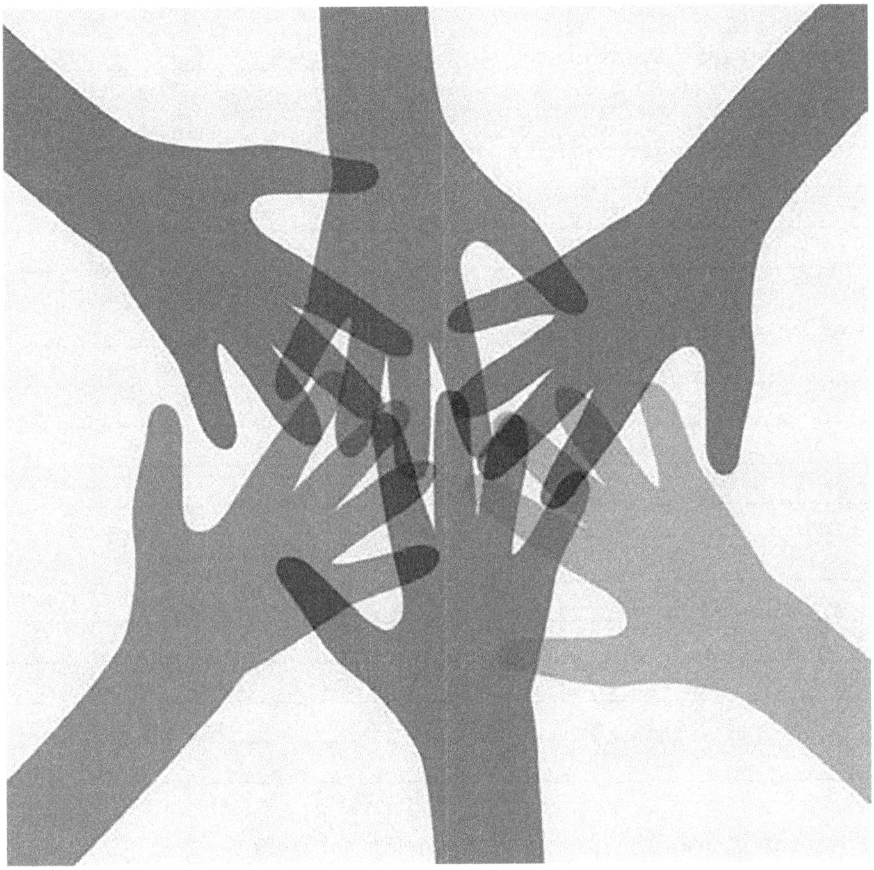

Get The Care Plan
Open The Care Plan
Do The Care Plan

Is with You!

My Care Plan

From now on, I commit to ____
____
____
____
____
____

I will make necessary changes because ____________________________
____
____
____
____

____
I will allow God to ____
____
____
____
____

I want to be more and more like Jesus in this area because _________
____
____
____
____
____

My prayer is ____
____
____
____
____
____

Reflection Diary Journal

Date ___________

Father God,

Amen.

THE CARE PLAN for God's People!

How We Think and Live Matters!

"Knowing these teachings will mean true and good health for you."
Proverbs 4:22

Read Your Bibles Everyday!

VICTORY

HOW IMPORTANT IS victory to you? Would you do anything to defeat the other person? Where I come from, victory is loving your enemies. We do nothing to retaliate, "We Wait!"

Victory, victory, victory happens when we wait on God!

Beloved, never avenge yourselves, but leave it to the wrath of God, for it is written "Vengeance is mine, I will repay, says the Lord." To the contrary, "if your enemy is hungry, feed him; if he is thirsty, give him something to drink; for by so doing you will heap burning coals on his head." Do not be overcome by evil, but overcome evil with good. ***Romans 12:21***

Never leave the love position, remember, and just keep praying for evil doers, for their days are numbered.

People of God, let's stay alert and focused on the real enemy, Sin! That's our everyday battle, not the chick down the street, or other fools we meet. Our victory cup is won when we overcome sin and corrupt men (People).

> For everyone born of God overcomes the world. This is the Victory that has overcome the world, even our faith. Who is it that overcomes the world? Only the one who believes that Jesus is the Son of God. **1 John 5:4-5**

I believe, do you believe? Then act according.

Triumph, Live For Christ!

Victory Is Mine!

Victory, victory, victory, in Christ
This is what I've found
We live in a world that slanders
Hate those who are good,
They try to knock us down
Gang up on us, throw us in pits
They're liars, they'll never admit
They hate God, Insanely Jealous,
And wicked too,
They'll smile in your face and say, I love you.
But in their hearts, they can care less about us, they really don't want us around
Victory, victory, victory in Christ
This is what I found
When rejected, lied on and falsely accused
Set-up, 'nailed to the cross'
If you are in Christ,
Wait! Don't retaliate!
'Nope', don't make a sound,
Jesus rose on the third day,
Say, **"Me Too!"** "How Profound!"

I'm Still Here!

We have the **Victory**, hatred can never hold Love Down!

"For the LORD your God is the one who goes with you to fight for you against your enemies to give you victory"
Deuteronomy 20:4

Remember this always Christians, we have the power to defeat anything, sin, the devil and this world when we wholeheartedly obey and live for Christ. If God is for us, who can be against us? Nobody!

In the name of Jesus **"WE"** have the **Victory!** So let's walk in that **"POWER"** Every day, Every Minute and Every Hour!

Victory Care Plan

MY
CHILDREN
WILL BE
MIGHTY
IN THE
LAND

PSALMS 112:2

Make These Your Realities Day and Night

- Know that the battle is not yours; it's the Lord's.
- Know that you are going to have trials and tribulations like everyone else, but those of us who put their trust and faith in God will always have the last laugh **"VICTORY!"**
- Love and forgive your enemies this is part of dying on the cross.
- Hatred toward those who hate you is *not* acceptable; we *must* love our enemies. It's hard—yes, I know—but once you get used to doing it, it will become easier and easier, and you will become more and more like Jesus.
- Don't fight back, vengeance is mine says the Lord.
- God called me at age seven and these were his exact words to me: **LOVE NO MATTER WHAT — LEARN TO TURN THE OTHER CHEEK— MAKE FOOTPRINTS ON THE HUMAN HEART!** Now I'm asking **'YOU'** to do the same.
- Remember, in the name of Jesus, we have the victory, be gone devil "flee"! For those who want what I got, Jesus says pick up your cross and follow me......

In Christ We Have The Victory!

Hold Your Head Up High!

But thanks be to God, who always leads us in triumph in us the sweet aroma of the knowledge of him in every place.
2 Corinthians 2:14

You Want Victory? Then, 'Die to Self!'

Get The Care Plan
Open The Care Plan
Do The Care Plan

Is with You!

In Christ We Rise Again!

Love Conquers All!
1 Corinthians 13

My Care Plan

From now on, I commit to ______________________________

____

____

____

____

____

I will make necessary changes because ____________________

____

____

____

____

____

I will allow God to _____________________________________

____

____

____

____

I want to be more and more like Jesus in this area because ________

____

____

____

____

____

My prayer is ____

____

____

____

____

____

Reflection Diary Journal

Date ___________

Father God,

Amen.

THE CARE PLAN for God's People!

How We Think and Live Matters!

"Knowing these teachings will mean true and good health for you."
Proverbs 4:22

Read Your Bibles Everyday!

WOMEN

LADIES, IF YOU are going to be a woman, be a woman of God!

"She is clothes with strength and dignity, and she laughs without fear of the future." — Proverbs 31:25

Yes, **"WE Laugh"!** We laugh because we are with God, we know, that no weapons formed against us will prosper and we laugh because we know, the first will be last, and the last will be first! Matthew 20:16, Ha, ha, ha, Women of God, we can't help it, **"We Laugh"!**

But, not so, for the women of the world, they are in trouble, real big trouble! every day is a struggle to survive. We want to help! There are so many women out there today, that have turned their backs on God, — they have put the sinful desires of man and themselves first, and are suffering because of what they've done. Many of these women end up pregnant and eventually abandon by that man or boy. A lot of these woman, — some are very, very young too, perhaps a teen, are left to carry the load; the person they chose over God, Is Gone!

Now they are by themselves, they've become single moms, some struggling to make 'ends meet'. Forced on welfare, food stamps, low housing, if not that, many are working two jobs just to keep shoes on their child's feet. The scripture says in Jeremiah 17:5 Curse is the man (woman) who trust in man and make flesh his/her strength, whose heart turns away from the Lord.

(THIS BOOK IS TRYING TO GET YOU SAVED, I AM NOT GOING TO TELL YOU WANT YOU WANT TO HEAR!) I'M NOT THAT KIND OF WRITER.)

If you are reading this right now, rethink your life and your choices. A life without Christ has a price and it ain't nice! "Everybody, Everywhere" 'KEEP GOD FIRST PLACE IN YOUR LIFE', Not Man. Again, let me repeat myself, **If You Are Going To Be A Woman, Be**

A Woman of God! Stop Your Foolishness, Grow Up! Females who love God, we don't put man first nor do we put ourselves first. That's right, only **"GOD"** holds that number one spot, not our mothers, fathers, sisters or brother, friends and certainly not a boyfriend, please, **"Really"!**

Grow Up! Grow up In Jesus, for he is the only one who really cares for you, it is written and I have found it to be true blue, Man will disappoint "YOU"! Before we move on let me just say this, I am not male bashing here, but this is what I've found out after I gave my life to Christ, If that man is not with Jesus, saved or born again, **"Look Out"!** "Good Morning Heartache", **"Sit Down!"** Females Get Your Priorities Straight and Keep Them Straight!

"Don't Fall For Fakes"! And learn from your mistakes; sex outside of Marriage, will always hurt women the most, plus it's wrong in God's Eyes. And shacking -up together, clearly lets God know you don't respect him or his wishes. You are going to do what you want to do, He's not running the show!

When we disrespect and brush our Lord off like this, we will reap what we sow! "Forget You" some say, but "I'll pray for you"! For those of you that don't want to listen, when you come back to this page, this banner is for you: **"SISTER I TOLD YOU SO!"** to the rest, Go and sin no more!

Ladies, stop having babies out of wedlock, don't be part of a generational curse, instead, from now on, walk in obedience to all that the Lord your God has commanded you, so that you may live and prosper and prolong your days in the land that you will possess. **Deuteronomy 5:33**. Lastly, To The Women of God, You are so beautiful to God inside and out. God loves us. His love for us endures FOREVER! That's right! I tell you the truth, his love is constant and it never ends! Psalms 136:26

Keep Laughing, Thanks God, that **"WE"** don't belong to this world! No matter what, never blend or try to fit in! Like a tree, stay rooted in Christ! Love the Lord and obey his voice. Deuteronomy 30:20

Now, may God continue to shine his light upon you!

In Jesus name, Amen, **Laugh!**

No weapons formed against us will ever prosper! **Laugh!**

Be Women of God, Stay Women of God!

Women Care Plan

Make These Your Realities Day and Night

- From now on I will keep God first in my life.
- I will not be with men who fornicate anymore.
- I will date Jesus for one year or more so that I can learn of his ways and allow him to mold me into the kind of bride I should be. Cliche: **Text Can Wait, Sex Can Wait!**
- I will tell men up front, "I don't fornicate. I don't believe in sex outside marriage." If you don't respect that, we can't date.
- Repent from all your worldly ways, start taking God and his word serious from now on.
- Get yourself a bible, a nice one too, because you will be using it a lot from now on, God is getting ready to clean house, he is going to make you into the kind of person he wants you to be.
- Ladies, move on, leave your past in the past, God can still use you if you have ten kids, so what! If you give your life to him right now, today, you can still get blessed, children are innocent in God's sight! And it is written that once you repent, give your life to Christ. **"YOUR SINS I WILL REMEMBER NO MORE"** Hebrews 8:12, 1 John1:9...
- Keep sinful opportunities out of your home, off your phone, off your TV, out of your ear, and away from your children, if you want a new life in Christ the old life has to go, him too, if he won't marry you.
- Stay away from fornicators and God haters.
- Tell Everybody, Everywhere, your friends and family too, that you just got born again, you have to be around Godly friends.
- Stay in constant prayer because the flesh is weak and can be tempted, but if you are constantly in his Word, the flesh will not prevail, follow Christ, live to tell!
- Woman of God, find someone to mentor to, help save the lost.

- Develop a prayer life, find a special place to be with God, a prayer closet of some kind, for just the two of you. You and God need to become ONE!
- Be at peace when trials and tribulations come. Some kind of way, find that strength and joy spot in your heart, Laugh! You know God's got your back he'll put you back on track!
- To all the babes in Christ, if you want all the promises of God, you are going to have to change. You cannot live and do the things you use to. And you are going to have to study his world to make thyself approved. If you're not reading the bible on a regulars bases it will show in your lifestyle and gives God a pretty good idea of this scripture, **Matthew 6:21**, For where your treasure is, there your heart will be also. So women and young ladies, if it's "the streets" or with "fleshly and lustful driven men" Our Father will know, he sees and knows everything. Also those close to you will know too, so get serious, and get right with God and stay right with him. Did I say, God sees and know everything? I said that, didn't I, well the bible says **"NOTHING"** in all creation is hidden from God's sight, **"EVERYTHING"** is naked and exposed before his eyes, and he is the one to whom we are accountable. **Hebrews 4:13,** "Question" where is your treasure?

Get The Care Plan
Open The Care Plan
Do The Care Plan

Is with You!

My Care Plan

From now on, I commit to ______________________________

____

____

____

____

____

I will make necessary changes because ______________________________

____

____

____

____

____

I will allow God to ______________________________

____

____

____

____

I want to be more and more like Jesus in this area because __________

____

____

____

____

____

My prayer is ______________________________

____

____

____

____

____

Reflection Diary Journal

Date __________

Father God,

____

____

____

____

____

____

____

____

____

____

____

____

____

____

____

Amen.

WISDOM

Do not forsake wisdom, and she will protect you; love her, and she will watch over you. The beginning of wisdom is this: Get wisdom, though it cost all you have, get understanding.

—Proverbs 4:6–7

Wisdom wants to save you, it cries out, echoes in the dark, repent, change your heart!
But the flesh wants what it wants, it won't stop! — Until it's dead! — **StarN'air 5:2017**

We do not have the right to do what we want to do, give wisdom a chance, let wisdom hang out with you. "Do you not know that your bodies are temples of the Holy Spirit, who is in you, whom you have received from God? You are not your own." **1 Corinthians 6:19-20**

Therefore, wisdom says, 'Be very careful, then how you live—not as unwise but wise, making the most of every opportunity, because the days are evil, **Ephesians 5:15-16**

The days are evil that's true, and so are the nights. Wisdom warns, the thief comes in order to steal and kill and destroy. I came that they may have and enjoy life and have it in abundance. **John 10:10**

Wisdom— is Christ, and he wants to take care of us, bless us too, but sometimes when Christ looks down on us, it's hard to tell, whose, who? — **StarN'air 5:2017**

Wisdom Care Plan

Make These Your Realities Day and Night

A Person of Wisdom:

- Can't function without Christ.
- Stand out from the rest, they don't try to blend in.
- Read their bibles daily, they stay in the word!
- Really believes that, The fear of the Lord is the beginning of wisdom.
- Sits with Jesus, often, a lot and learns as much as they can from him and his teaching.
- Practice holiness and disciplines themselves in righteousness daily.
- Respect and obey God's word.
- Loves to tithe, they are givers not takers.
- Is not jealous or envious of others.
- Is not ruled by their flesh or desires, God takes them higher!
- Will not comprise what's in the bible, they stands firm on God's words.
- Knows the word, applies the word.
- Laughs, at the devil, because no weapons forms against us ever prospers.
- Listens to others, accepts constructive criticism.
- Loves and Forgives!
- Shares
- Is very humble.

Wisdom is a gift from God to all who embrace her, like nature, she will help protect you in any kind of storm be it, rain, pain, poverty or fame. Get with her, remember her name! Wisdom is invincible and like God, **"Unseen."** When we reject her, we bleed. — **StarN'air 6:2015**

Wisdom From A to Z!

Get It, Grab a Hold of Me!
Won't cost You Anything, I'm A Gift, I'm Free!

Get The Care Plan
Open The Care Plan
Do The Care Plan

Is with You!

My Care Plan

From now on, I commit to ____

____

____

____

____

____

I will make necessary changes because _________________________________

____

____

____

____

____

I will allow God to ____

____

____

____

____

I want to be more and more like Jesus in this area because ___________

____

____

____

____

____

My prayer is ____

____

____

____

____

____

Reflection Diary Journal

Date ___________

Father God,

Amen.

WELLNESS

WELLNESS IS AN active process of becoming aware of making choices toward a healthy and fulfilling life. Wellness is more than being free from illnesses, it multidimensional too, —lifestyle, environment, finances, spirituality, faith, and social life, all these areas contributes to our overall happiness.

The Care Plan, is a wellness book too, it's a book you can use for the rest of your life. **The Care Plan** will work if you stay on it. It will help keep you mentally healthy, vibrant and strong. Your **Care Plan** has personalized care plan pages that you can use to help track you growth and development. **How we think and live matters!**

I just want to make sure sisters and brothers we are living the best life possible. In your Care Plan I have also given you some tips on how to improve your life and it does include physical exercise. Come on, you know you have to exercise, "Move" you have to do some work. Being in shape is very, very, important! Fitness is good for us, it matters how we look and feel. Our bodies are the temple of God, therefore we must take excellent care of it. Let's not waste any more time talking, we got work to do! Get your workout gear on "grab your water bottles too **"Let's Get Physical!"**

Listen, before we get started let's hear what saith the lord *"Let's not become weary in doing good, for at the proper time we will reap a harvest if we do not give up."* **Galatians 6:9. Lecture:** Living the best life possible, is possible, it means we have to put the forth effort. If you want it, work hard and stay focus. And we also have to stay commitment and disciplined too, if we want to see results. Well same goes for our walk with Christ, we must spend time with him. Besides, Jesus is the

'Wellness Plan' He can heal anyone throughout the land. Others charge a fee, they may have a different plan. I don't know about you, but I want Jesus "Wellness Plan"! For in **"HIM"** we move and have our **"Well-Being"** don't get it twisted!

Move That Body!

It's Time, **"Lets Get Physical!"**

Fitness is the Key to Longevity!

Take care of your body and your body will take care of you.

Let's Get Fit For God, Lets' Stay Fit For God!

My weight is ________
My desired weight is ________
Today I will get in shape and stay in shape!

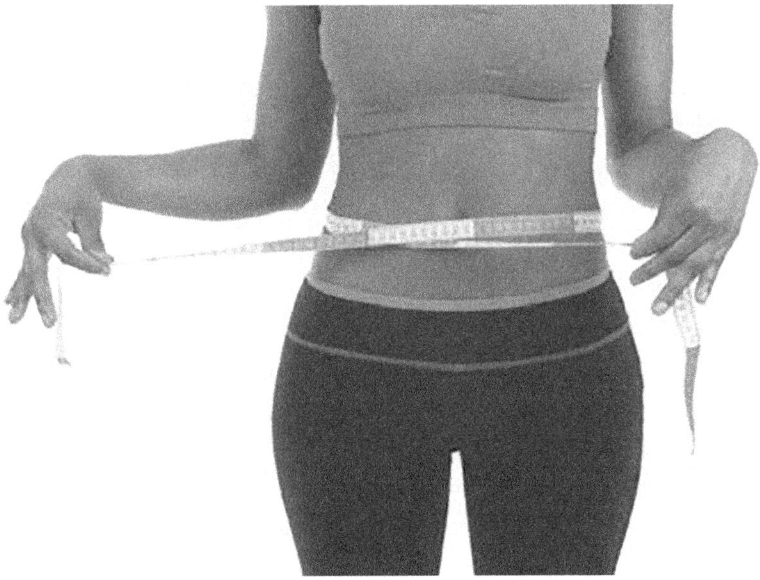

The Wellness Plan

- Drink plenty of water every day, give up sweet drinks, soda pops, and mocha coffees.
- Get seven to eight hours of sleep each night.
- Read Your Bibles Daily!
- Set up a prayer room for yourself, a place you can be alone with God and ask him to help you get in shape and he will.
- Develop Smart spending habits.
- Tithe, tithe, tithe, a tenth or more! Be a giver, stay a giver!
- Choose your friends who want to win!
- Choose positive environments to go in.
- Keep a clean house.
- Keep a clean mind.
- Work to get out of debt, and stay out.
- Invest in your happiness, save some money.
- Welcome Joy and laughter back into your life, it good chicken soup for the soul!
- Start a Prayer life, pray for your enemies always, keep wishing them well!
- Pursue all your goals and dreams, go back to school if you have to.
- Do monthly breast exams and yearly physicals too.
- Do something good for yourself. It can be something as simple as taking a hot candlelight bubble bath, or buy yourself some flowers — pamper thyself.
- Live for Christ, be righteous and proud of it!
- Help those less fortunate than you.
- Be a blessing to others, do random acts of kindness daily!
- Be a Helper of humankind, give to a charity or come up with one yourself.
- Practice celibacy, wait for God to send you a mate.
- Workout 4 to 6 days a week, vary your workouts, make it a lifetime habit.
- Watch how much you eat, overeating means overweight!

- Layoff fast food restaurants! — Cook at home, prepare nutritious meals for yourself and your family.
- Stay humble and patient too, God is going to do what he said he will do.
- Stay in love with Jesus!
- Watch what you watch, don't let your eyes cause you to sin against God. Get away from it, turn it off.
- Don't spit, cuss or chew or hang out with folks that do!
- Choose programs that are pleasing to God. And good for your mind body and soul.
- When you live for God, faithfully and righteously, Expect good results, expect a harvest too, those are his promises to you.
- Take advantage of **The Care Plan**, use this book as a personal diary, — a journal too, write in it often, keep growth alive. Tell everyone you know what this book has done for you, it certainly has changed my life, I read it over and over again, From **A** to **Z**, this book is not just for you this book is for **"Me Too"!**

Wellness Care Plan

Make These Your Realities Day and Night

W—Work out, keep a job, wait on God, and be willing to serve God when called upon.

E—Expand your horizon, go around enriched environments like museums, art galleries, science centers etc. visit other cultures, travel.

L—Lifestyle is very important to God and your health too; remember, the wages of sin is death.

L—Learn from Christ and his teachings! Spend time with him, pray, read your bibles every day.

N—New Creature In Christ! Wellness at its highest level.

E—Eat Smart! **"Read Your Bibles Too"** Remember our bodies don't belong to us, it belongs to God, so take excellent care of it!

S—Save but give too, we are to be the head and not the tail; the lender, not the borrower.

S—Shout for Joy, praise his **'HOLY'** name! Hopefully, when you finish **The Care Plan**, nothing about you will be the same!

Our Bodies are Not Ours!

Don't you realize that your body is the temple of the Holy Spirit, who lives in you and was given to you by God? You do not belong to yourself, for God bought you with a high price, so you must honor God with your body. **1 Corinthians 6:19-20**

A Healthy Body, is a Strong and Vibrant Body!

Get The Care Plan
Open The Care Plan
Do The Care Plan

Is with You!

Wellness Plan
Simple, "Keep God's Book in Your Hand!"

Live for Christ, not Man!

"You Are What You Eat!"

Eliminate Unhealthy Sweets

Junk Food Junkies!

Junk food is for those who want to get fat and stay fat!

Junk food is just that JUNK don't eat it!

Rest!

It is vain for you to rise up early, to retire late. To eat the bread of painful labors, For He gives to His beloved (us) even in his sleep.
Psalms 127:2

Does The Body Good!

God Rested on the Seventh Day!

Genesis 2:2-3

From Now On Let Sleep Have Its Way!

My Care Plan

From now on, I commit to ______________________________________
____
____
____
____
____

I will make necessary changes because __________________________
____
____
____
____

____
I will allow God to ____
____
____
____
____

I want to be more and more like Jesus in this area because _________
____
____
____
____
____

My prayer is ____
____
____
____
____
____

Reflection Diary Journal

Date ____________

Father God,

____

____

____

____

____

____

____

____

____

____

____

____

____

____

____

Amen.

THE CARE PLAN for God's People!

How We Think and Live Matters!

"Knowing these teachings will mean true and good health for you."
Proverbs 4:22

Read Your Bibles Everyday!

X FACTOR

WHAT DOES X Factor mean? By definition an X Factor it's a variable in a given situation that could have the most significant impact on the outcome. Let's take a Christian and a non- Christian, and use that, as our example, okay, now I'm being asked to be one of the judges in a singing competition between these two, but I could not see them, only hear their voices and both contestants had to sing the same song. The song was a pop song, and after listening to them both, found it hard to choose, because they both were excellent! But one had a spark, an anointing power that stayed with me long after the performance. For me, the choice would be a no brainer, that's the one I'd choose, that person has **The X Factor!**

Well, that how it should be for us, as Christians. If we say we are Christians and love the Lord, then people all over the world should be able to see **'The X Factor of God'** in us! Because "WE" are different and it shows, not only in our voice, if we are singers, but in our lifestyle choice. Oh yes, others should clearly be able see, by how we carry ourselves and how we live, that we do not belong to this world. We stand out, we have "Jesus Light" we shine "bright" in a dark world. "WE" are It! **'The X Factor of God'!** And that godly **'X Factor'** must go everywhere **"WE Go"!**

- On our jobs
- In the mall
- At school
- Out at parties
- In our homes
- In our children's lives
- In our marriages
- In our business dealings
- At church where we fellowship

- Long lines in the grocery stores
- In our appearance and wardrobe
- In our love and compassion toward others
- Stadiums
- Social setting
- Public libraries
- Amusement parks
- In our speech and conduct
- On stage and off stage
- On vacations
- During political debates
- In management
- In how we treat our employees
- In how we treat our employers
- In how we give care for our seniors and the sick
- In how we love and forgive our enemies
- In our giving and tithing
- In our praises and worship to the Lord

The X Factor of God, is a factor, it weeds out the real from the fake! That's why it is written, we shall know them by their fruits!

No matter what, **The X Factor of God**, must remain in us if we call ourselves Christians. If you got **'The X -Factor,** Use What Your Father Gave You! Jesus did, he went on to rebuke and save as many souls as he could with ***His*** **X Factor**, now so should we. Let's help win souls and set others free, I hope you're with me...

Jesus said, "It is not the healthy who need a doctor, but the sick. I have not come to call the righteous, but the sinners". **Mark 2:17**

Jesus our LORD, The X Factor of The World!

X Factor, Help Fish For Lost Souls!

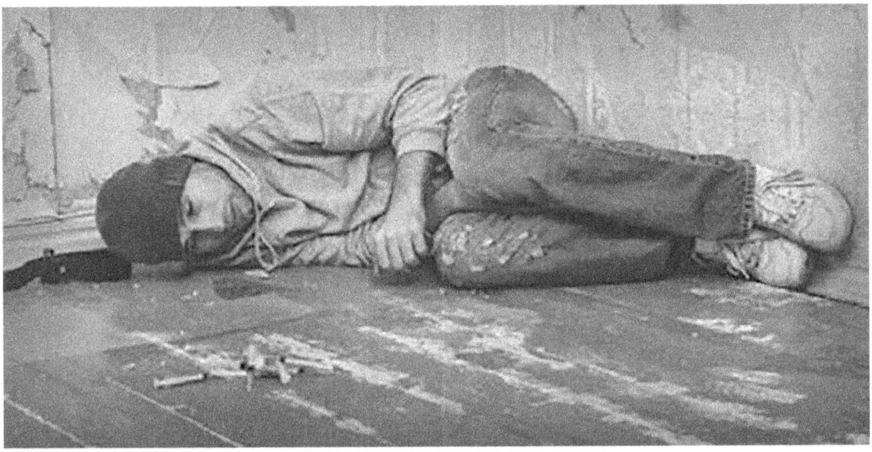

For the Son of man is come to seek and save that which is lost. Luke 19:10

Xenial

Faithful

Answers the call

Christ-like

Trusting

Obedient

Ready to serve.

The world should be able to tell, "WE" do not belong to this world. If you have the X-Factor **"SHOW US"**! Be kind, hospitable "Xenial" and "Faithful" to God, "Answer" when called. Be "Christ-like" in all your ways. "Trusting", being "Obedient" and always "Ready to serve"!

If this is you, and you have that X-Factor, go on, use what your **"Father" Gave YOU!**

The X Factor of God, is Yours for the Taking!

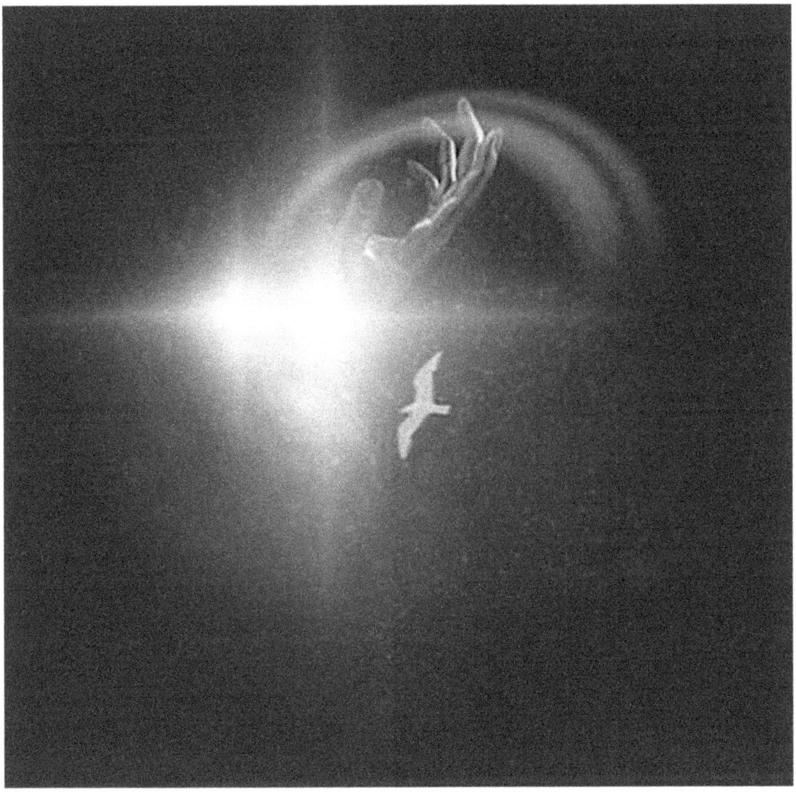

For all those who chose the latter, our hearts are breaking.. God is not willing that any should perish.

2 Peter 3:9

Rethink Your Life, X Factor With Christ!

The X Factor Care Plan

Make These Your Realities Day and Night

Be an X Factor of God!

- Reads your bibles daily
- Stay holy, practice celibacy.
- Use your gift wisely.
- Stand out from the crowd.
- Take care of your temple (body).
- Take God everywhere you go!
- Live for Christ.
- Stay humble.
- Say no to fast money, earn a living the right way.
- Make Jesus your role model.
- Set your heart on doing good for others.
- Never give up on your dreams, but don't compromise your walk with God either.
- Live An Uncompromised Life, Keep God First!
- Don't date fornicators, get far away from people like that. Protect what you have built with Christ.
- Be around like minded people, people who also practice righteous living.
- Count your blessing, share them too!
- Tithe, give a tenth or more.
- Live righteously, let your **X Factor** shine!
- Watch what you put on, dress appropriately.
- Exercise daily, watch what you eat.
- Everyday, Choose whom this day you will serve.
- Be good to your co-workers, have no favorites, love everybody!
- Support the pastor and the church, be good Stewards
- Be a Good Samaritan, help Everybody, Everywhere!

Tell Everybody, your friends and family too, to:

Get The Care Plan
Open The Care Plan
Do The Care Plan

Is with You!

X

Factor

The X Factor Of God!

'The X Factor of God', Use What Your Father Gave You! Go out and help win as many souls as you can for Christ!

- In the streets
- In the bars and clubs
- In the prisons

Everywhere, go..

> ***The fruit of the righteous is a tree of life, And he who is wise wins souls.***
>
> **Proverbs 11:30**

My Care Plan

From now on, I commit to ______________________________

____

____

____

____

____

I will make necessary changes because ______________________________

____

____

____

____

____

I will allow God to ______________________________

____

____

____

____

I want to be more and more like Jesus in this area because __________

____

____

____

____

____

My prayer is ______________________________

____

____

____

____

____

Reflection Diary Journal

Date __________

Father God,

____

____

____

____

____

____

____

____

____

____

____

____

____

____

____

Amen.

THE CARE PLAN for God's People!

How We Think and Live Matters!

"Knowing these teachings will mean true and good health for you."
Proverbs 4:22

Read Your Bibles **Everyday!**

"YES" LORD!

YES LORD SEND ME, I will go! Are you ready to start saying YES LORD? How much more time do you need out in the world before you come back home to your creator "GOD" your first love? Answer, what in the world are you thinking of? There's nothing better than **"His"** love.

Do you not know that obedience to God is the true sign of love?

And the only way you can know that kind of love is to read God's word, once you start doing that, no problem, you'll say **"YES" LORD,** I'm on board, send me I will go…

But, you can't do, what you don't know!

God speaks, listen: *Now if you obey me fully and keep my covenant, then out of all nations you will be my treasured possession. Although the whole earth is mine,* Exodus 19:5

As the Father has loved me, so have I loved you. Now remain in my Love. John 15:9 say **"YES" LORD!**

Reading God's word, obeying him and spending time with Christ is the key to it all, no worries anymore, God promises to catch us when we fall. However, you have to get fed up with this world, before God can send you out and use you for his glory, no more excuses or sad stories.

At some point, **"YOU"** have to choose between this world and God's.

If you are ready for that, today say, **"YES" Lord!** Be Ready, Answer **'The Call!'**

Yes Lord, Send Me, I will Go!

I Will Tell The Whole Wide World,
"Jesus Lives!"

"YES" Care Plan

Make These Your Realities Day and Night

- Say "YES" to God always, use me in thy service.
- If you are asked to forgive those who hurt you, do it, say **YES!**
- Say, Yes I am my brothers and sisters keepers
- Say, Yes and Amen to the Christian life!
- Yes I will start exercising and eating right!
- Yes things get challenging but I can do all things in Christ who strengthens me.
- From now on, I will let my **YES** be **YES** and my no be **NO!**
- Yes I will praise and honor God everywhere I go!
- Yes I will practice obedience
- Yes I will start a prayer life
- Yes I will live a holy life
- Yes I will reframe from sex until I get married, I believe 'male' to be husband and female to be wife! No doubt in my mind about it, never have to think twice. **YES, YES, YES,** God way is perfect and right!
- Yes I will bless the lord at all times, his praise shall continually be in my mouth.
- Yes I was give God a tenth of whatever, I make from now on.
- Yes I will undo all the things I know are not pleasing to God.
- Yes I will end toxic relationships and I will not shack up again, or hang out with those you refuse to let God in.
- Today I will make that change, **"YES LORD"** will no longer feel so strange.
- Yes I want to get born again, because with God, **"Life Never Ends".**

Repeat After Me

"Dear God"

I know I am a sinner, but I'm tired of sinning against you, right now in my heart I am asking you to please forgive me. I believe that your one and only begotten son Jesus, he came into the world and gave his own life up for me, so that I would be free and live eternally.

Yes I know Jesus died and that, you father God, you are the one who raised him back up again. Now today, right now, I want to put my trust in your son Jesus, rely on him and make him my Lord and Savior.

Father God, forgive me of all my wrongdoings. Forgive me for all the lies I told and all the people I hurt too. From this day forward, Lord come into my life and save me, save me, oh save me from me and this corrupt and evil world. I'm ready, take over, and guide my life moving forward. Jesus, please I'm asking, where I am weak, help me, keep me focus, help me to be brave and strong, finally help me to tell this cruel and evil world, so long!

In Jesus name I turn my life all over to you now. Take me I'm yours!

Amen

If you just prayed that prayer from your heart and meant every word you just said, then Hallelujah, God is about to use ya!

Don't Wait, Celebrate!!!!!

You're Saved "Now"!

Bid the world farewell, **"Goodbye",** say, I just got
"BORN AGAIN!!"

Everybody, Everywhere, Hurry, Hurry, **"Hallelujah":**

Get The Care Plan
Open The Care Plan
Do The Care Plan

Is with You!

"No One Can Serve Two Masters. Either You Will Hate One and Love the Other".

Matthew 6:24

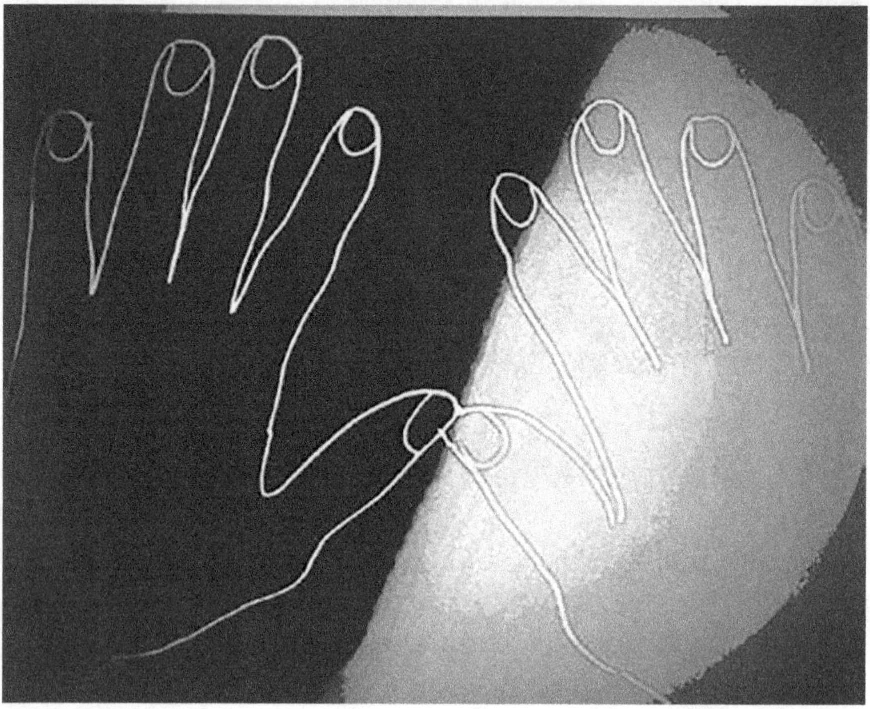

"PICK ONE!"

I pick the one on the right, God, and his Holiness,

Righteousness, the one full of **Light!**

My Care Plan

From now on, I commit to ______________________________

I will make necessary changes because ______________________________

I will allow God to ______________________________

I want to be more and more like Jesus in this area because ______________________________

My prayer is ______________________________

Reflection Diary Journal

Date ___________

Father God,

____

____

____

____

____

____

____

____

____

____

____

____

____

____

____

Amen.

THE CARE PLAN for God's People!

How We Think and Live Matters!

"Knowing these teachings will mean true and good health for you."
Proverbs 4:22

Read Your Bibles Everyday!

ZEALOUSNESS

CHRISTIAN'S GET READY it's time for Zealousness. It time to get your Zeal on! Time to go out with a bang! Get fired up for the Lord! It's time to show the world, what we are made of. We are soldiers in the army for the Lord, 'The Joshua's' of our time, on the battlefield to win souls for Christ! We need Everybody, Everywhere out there fighting too. Yes, we need all of YOU!

Help us, get up, get dress, be a Warrior! Show your **Zeal**, Put on **'The Full Armor of God',** for crying out loud, have no fear "FIGHT"! God is with us, and if God is with us, "tell me" who can be against us? "NOBODY!" Get Up, Get Dress, and "Suit Up"! Wear this:

- **The Belt of Truth,** in the beginning was the word and the word was with God.
- **The Breast Plate of Righteousness,** be perfect like our father in heaven is.
- **The Shoes of the Gospel of Peace,** be still and know that I Am GOD!
- **The Shield of Faith**, my God shall supply all my needs according to his riches.
- **The Helmet of Salvation** there is no condemnation to them which are in Christ.
- **The Sword of the Spirit!** No weapons formed against us shall will prosper.

Why the **'Full Armor?'** Because sisters and brothers, if God has saved **"YOU"** from your sin, He has called **"YOU"** to serve too.

Every Christian Is Saved To Serve!

So, Come on...... Get Zealous, Show your Zeal for real!

'Fight The Good Fight Of Faith!'

The Armor of God!

Ephesians 6:10-18

Finally, be strong in the Lord and in his mighty power. **Put on the full armor of God,** so that you can take your stand against the devil's schemes. For our struggle is not against flesh and blood, but against the rulers, against the authorities, against the powers of this dark world and against the spiritual forces of evil in the heavenly realms. Therefore put on the **full armor of God,** so that when the day of evil comes, you may be able to stand your ground, and after you have done everything, to stand. Stand firm then, with the **belt of truth** buckled around your waist, with the **breastplate of righteousness** in place, and with your feet **fitted with the readiness** that comes from the **gospel of peace**. In addition to all this, take up the **shield of faith**, with which you can extinguish all the f laming arrows of the evil one. Take the **helmet of salvation** and the **sword of the Spirit**, which is the word of God.

And pray in the Spirit on all occasions with all kinds of prayers and requests. **With this in mind, be alert and always keep on praying for all the Lord's people.**

Zealousness Care Plan

Make These Your Realities Day and Night

- Get some godly zeal in your walk and talk.
- Listen to praise and worship music often.
- Read the book of Joshua. He was full of zeal!
- Celebrate the promises of God daily! Praise him!
- Testify, tell Everybody, Everywhere about the goodness of Lord!
- Be ready to act when God calls you.
- Keep your full armor on at all times.
- Repeat after Joshua and me, "As for me and my house, we will serve the Lord." Hey, why don't cha' do Deuteronomy 6:9, Write them on your door frames of your houses and on thy gates. get busy, start posting, let **'Everybody, Everywhere'** know who you belong to, I do!
- Stay on the mission fight and win souls. **Be Zealous, "Be Bold"!**
- Be deliberate in your moves toward Christ, honor and obey him, keep praising him, give him all the zeal you got! I hope like me, you got a lot!
- Sing too, make a joyful noise, lift him up for he is worthy to be exalted and praised, if you don't sing, praise him in other ways.
- Say, "Hallelujah, world, I'm not trying to do ya!"
- Be Bold and Courageous for the Lord!
- Be Zealous! Be Brave! Help someone that's lost, "Get Saved"! Once found, tell'em to:

Get The Care Plan
Open The Care Plan
Do The Care Plan

Is with You!

My Care Plan

From now on, I commit to ______________________________

____

____

____

____

____

I will make necessary changes because ________________

____

____

____

____

____

I will allow God to ___________________________________

____

____

____

____

I want to be more and more like Jesus in this area because ________

____

____

____

____

____

My prayer is ____

____

____

____

____

____

Reflection Diary Journal

Date ___________

Father God,

Amen.

The Good Morning Care Plan

Praise Him, in the Morning!

- Wake up and thank God for waking you up this morning.
- Wash up, brush your teeth, and grab your coffee or tea.
- Go sit with God!
- Make sure you have your Bible with you.
- Find a room in your house, apartment or dorm room to be with God. This should become your sanctuary—a place where you and God will not be disturbed, close the door behind you.
- Now invite the Holy Spirit in. You can say, "Lord, I am here. I've come to you for direction and guidance. I praise your holy name." (That should do it.) Soon, this will become so easy and natural; like friends, you and Jesus will bond wonderfully. I love my time with Christ. Soon, you will too.
- If you are troubled, cast it all on the Lord at this time. This is what he wants us to do, he never wants us to go it alone. Jesus is there to help us and keep us from worrying about life stuff, for instance, what am I going to eat, wear, or how am I going to get there? I don't driver or have a car etc. **"Don't Worry Be Happy"** trust God he'll find a way. Our God knows how to make a way out of no way. Stay with him and pray!
- Pick a scripture for the day. Meditate on it throughout the day. Be prepared to tell God how you applied it to your day before your evening ends, okay!
- Pray and ask God to bless your day, your comings and goings.
- Pray also for Everybody, Everywhere, including your enemies.

Now, **Okay, Now You're Off To A "Godly Start"** but don't forget to take care of the Lord's body too. **"Workout"** get physical, then get ready for work or school. Don't forget to apply the scripture you chose for this day, Okay you're all set! "Get Going"!

Rising Early!

Now Abraham arose early in the morning and went to the place where he had stood before the **LORD**.
Genesis 19:27

The Good Afternoon Care Plan

Praise Him in the Afternoon!

- Lunchtime—enjoy it! But make smart food choices. Remember our bodies belong to Christ, we don't feed him junk food or overeat, — He would not like that!
- Meditate on your daily scripture. Find a way to use it, at work, or at school, with a co-worker, or you choose, but choose! Scriptures don't work if you don't apply them to your everyday life. When situations or problems arise, apply scriptures, they work each and every time. That's why God gave "His People" ("my sheep listen to my voice. I know them, and they follow me". Jhn.10:27) this manual to help us when we get stuck, and to know what's expected of us. Oh, I almost forgot, it's noon, lunch time, instead of taking in all those high fat calories, **"STOP", "WAIT"** do this instead; start off with something light like a salad and a great glass of water. And for the main course, I want to introduce you to a different kind of food, "Scriptures", they're "Scrumptious" extremely appetizing and delicious too and check this out, "No Dishes!" I tell you the truth, "Scriptures works" so well on the mind, body and soul. And check this out, there's are no additives or artificial flavoring. You'll stay nourished and full the whole day! So what are you waiting for? Grab some napkins and a clothes protector, tie it around your neck, and get comfortable, unbutton your buckle, get ready to wet your appetite. Try some "Scriptures" for lunch, go ahead, taste for yourself and see that the Lord is good! He's so good plus, he'll get you fit and looking the way you should. I love his food, it'll keep you healthier too, you'll look and feel Mmmmmm Gooood!
- Tell others about **The Care Plan** and what it is doing for you.
- Now that you're saved, time to go out and help save others. Remember we are all sisters and brothers! The goal is always to win souls for Christ. — We must not forget that! Jesus came

for the lost not the found, (Mark 2:17). Remember, we are his disciples now, our job is 24/7. **"The Mission never Stops"!**

- Check in with God. Let him know how your day is going.
- Praise him too throughout your day, keep acknowledging his goodness.
- Thank him for lunch, now get back to excellence/work. After that, come home and do the **'Good Evening and Good Night' Care Plan!**

Stay Focused, Be Blessed!

Oh My, I Just Tasted, and The LORD is Good!

Wow!

The Good Evening Care Plan

Praise Him in the Evening!

- Thank God for the entire day.
- Thank him for bringing you and your family together again safely.
- Take off your work clothes and put on comfortable wear—you are home now. Put on some Godly music while you unwind and prepare for dinner.
- Ask God to help you start preparing healthier meals for you and your family.
- Greet the members of your household, see how their day went before you get busy in the kitchen or..
- Enjoy your evening, praise God, for your life with him, smile!
- This evening find a quite area to have Bible study. Study time should last for one to two hours, each night. Grab you some tea and crackers, make study time, wonderful time. Look forward to it each evening.
- Those who work nontraditional hours, you still need to do **The Care Plan** just put together a nontraditional schedule for yourself, that's important if you want real change to occur, this book will help change your life, if you let it!
- If you are going to be a **"Champion" Choose Righteousness!"** And stay on fire for the Lord, you are going to have to be **"ALL-IN"** No time to straddle or bend. So, make up your mind, are **"YOU" "ALL-IN"?** If you are, and I do hope that you are, then, you are going to have to find the time to study his word period! End of story if you want to witness the blessing and join him in his glory, then we have to spend time reading his word, Yes, we have to **"Study To Make Thyself Approved" (2 Tim. 2:15)**
- Also, this evening, watch what you watch on TV tonight! Christian programs are best, and most pleasing to God, I'm just 'sayin'! We are not to pollute out eyes and ears with filth, violence

and sex filled soap operas and TV shows, and call ourselves a child of God. **"Flea From Ungodly Entertainment"!** Don't let this go on in your home. *"But if serving the LORD seems undesirable to you, then choose for yourself this day you will serve. But as me and my household,"* **WE SHALL SERVE THE LORD!**

Josh. 24:15

"Watch what you Watch"
I'm just sayin' God's not playin!

Enjoy your evening, choose wisely, do something that is pleasing to God. **Say "NO"** to your Flesh! Why? Because **"The Scriptures" Knows Best!**

The Call To Guard Your Ears, Eyes And Heart!
Tonight, Would Be A Good Time To Start!
Proverbs 4:20-27

The Good Night Care Plan

Praise Him in the 'Midnight Hour'!

Thank him for your day, tell him how much you love and need him. Bow down, worship him, get on your knees if you can, if not that's okay, just lay there for a while and praise him, for he is worthy to be praised all day, afternoon, evening and night. Hallelujah, praise Him, because he's more than alright! Pretty soon, you'll notice new light entering your life, that's God. And oh how exciting that will be, see when you get close to God, God gets even closer to you, and wonderful things starts to happen, you'll see, don't take it from me, you'll see.

God has been waiting so long for you to come to him this way. You'll be amazed by all the love God has in his heart for you. Once you're **"All-In"** with 'God', you two will become eternal friends, Hallelujah, the world lose, **"YOU WIN"**!

Time to pray! This is where I exit, only you know what's in your heart to say. **Goodnight!** stay in the light, live right! **Night, night, sleep tight!**

Congratulations,

You Did It! You finished **'The Care Plan'** all the way, from **A to Z**. Now all you do is start over, do it again, and keep doing it. Repetition is the key to change! Make **'The Care Plan'** a lifelong practice. **"Do The Work, Reap The Results!"**

Get The Care Plan
Open The Care Plan
Do The Care Plan

Is with You!

Get on **The Care Plan**, Stay on The Care Plan!
It's got you covered from **A to Z!**

Until We Meet Again!

Our journey together has finally come to and end, but In my heart, it feels like we've only just begun, let's go out and win some! Yes, **"TOGETHER"** we'll win souls for Christ. Because when **"WE"** get saved, We help save others, Everybody's our sisters and brothers, black and white alike, "Praise The Lord!"

Last thing, before I depart, and it's from my heart, I have something for all of you. I Put together a ★ N'air Grab bag, and it's loaded too! Inside it, you'll find lots of foundational scriptures and tools you can quickly use when you need them. I also added some journaling pages so that you can keep track of your walk with Christ! Plus, "more stuff" like I said, like a baked potato, this bag is loaded. Grow with it, fill up on it! Overall, everybody should be all set, from A to Z, I'm satisfied; I feel that I have given you more than enough stuff to help set you free. Each one of you have been given a wealth of information and now a **"Grab Bag"** too, to help jumpstart your life with Christ, the rest is on **"YOU"!** I do hope you love it and use it, it's a gift, **Enjoy It!**

★ Go in peace, "Now" may God shine his **'Light'** upon you, and keep you faithful, healthy and strong always and forevermore ★
In Jesus Name, Amen

Peace! *Miss Asondra StarN'air*

Miss Asondra StarN'air

★ N'air's Grab Bag!Take One...

Grab One

Enjoy it!

Get Ready N.O.W!

No One Works, but **Jesus!**

1. **Almighty One** – *"...who is and who was and who is to come, the Almighty."* Rev. 1:8
2. **Alpha and Omega** – *"I am the Alpha and the Omega, the First and the Last, the Beginning and the End."* Rev. 22:13
3. **Advocate** – *"My dear children, I write this to you so that you will not sin. But if anybody does sin, we have an advocate with the Father—Jesus Christ, the Righteous One."* 1 John 2:1
4. **Author and Perfecter of Our Faith** – *"Fixing our eyes on Jesus, the author and perfecter of faith, who for the joy set before Him endured the cross, despising the shame, and has sat down at the right hand of the throne of God."* Heb. 12:2
5. **Authority** – *"Jesus said, 'All authority in heaven and on earth has been given to me."* Matt. 28:18

6. **Bread of Life** – *"Then Jesus declared, 'I am the bread of life. Whoever comes to me will never go hungry, and whoever believes in me will never be thirsty.'"* John 6:35
7. **Beloved Son of God** – *"And behold, a voice from heaven said, "This is my beloved Son, with whom I am well pleased."* Matt. 3:17
8. **Bridegroom** – *"And Jesus said to them, "Can the wedding guests mourn as long as the bridegroom is with them? The days will come when the bridegroom is taken away from them, and then they will fast."* Matt. 9:15
9. **Chief Cornerstone** – *"The stone which the builders rejected has become the chief corner stone."* Ps. 118:22
10. **Deliverer** – *"And to wait for his Son from heaven, whom he raised from the dead, Jesus who delivers us from the wrath to come."* 1 Thess.1:10
11. **Faithful and True** – *"I saw heaven standing open and there before me was a white horse, whose rider is called Faithful and True. With justice he judges and wages war."* Rev.19:11
12. **Good Shepherd** - *"I am the good shepherd. The good shepherd lays down his life for the sheep."* John 10:11
13. **Great High Priest** – *"Therefore, since we have a great high priest who has passed through the heavens, Jesus the Son of God, let us hold fast our confession."* Heb. 4:14
14. **Head of the Church** – *"And he put all things under his feet and gave him as head over all things to the church."* Eph. 1:22
15. **Holy Servant** – *"…and grant that Your bond-servants may speak Your word with all confidence, while You extend Your hand to heal, and signs and wonders take place through the name of Your holy servant Jesus."* Acts 4:29-30
16. **I Am** – *"Jesus said to them, "Truly, truly, I say to you, before Abraham was, I am."* John 8:58
17. **Immanuel** – *"…She will give birth to a son and will call him Immanuel, which means 'God with us.'"* Is. 7:14
18. **Indescribable Gift** – *"Thanks be to God for His indescribable gift."* 2 Cor. 9:15
19. **Judge** – *"…he is the one whom God appointed as judge of the living and the dead."* Acts 10:42

20. **King of Kings** – *"These will wage war against the Lamb, and the Lamb will overcome them, because He is Lord of lords and King of kings, and those who are with Him are the called and chosen and faithful."* Rev. 17:14
21. **Lamb of God** – *"The next day John saw Jesus coming toward him and said, "Look, the Lamb of God, who* takes away the sin of the world!" John 1:29
22. **Light of the World** – *"I am the light of the world. Whoever follows me will never walk in darkness, but will have the light of life."* John 8:12
23. **Lion of the Tribe of Judah** – *"Weep no more; behold, the Lion of the tribe of Judah, the Root of David, has conquered, so that he can open the scroll and its seven seals."* Rev. 5:5
24. **Lord of All** – *"For this reason also, God highly exalted Him, and bestowed on Him the name which is above every name, so that at the name of Jesus every knee will bow, of those who are in heaven and on earth and under the earth, and that every tongue will confess that Jesus Christ is Lord, to the glory of God the Father."* Phil. 2:9-11
25. **Mediator** – *"For there is one God, and one mediator between God and men, the man Christ Jesus."* 1 Tim. 2:5
26. **Messiah** – *"We have found the Messiah" (that is, the Christ)."* John 1:41
27. **Mighty One** – *"Then you will know that I, the Lord, am your Savior, your Redeemer, the Mighty One of Jacob."* Is. 60:16
28. **One Who Sets Free** – *"So if the Son sets you free, you will be free indeed."* John 8:36
29. **Our Hope** – *"…Christ Jesus our hope."* 1 Tim. 1:1
30. **Peace** – *"For he himself is our peace, who has made the two groups one and has destroyed the barrier, the dividing wall of hostility,"* Eph. 2:14
31. **Prophet** – *"And Jesus said to them, "A prophet is not without honor, except in his hometown and among his relatives and in his own household."* Mark 6:4
32. **Redeemer** – *"And as for me, I know that my Redeemer lives, and at the last He will take His stand on the earth."* Job 19:25
33. **Risen Lord** – *"…that Christ died for our sins according to the Scriptures, that he was buried, that he was raised on the third day according to the Scriptures."* 1 Cor. 15:3-4

34. **Rock** – *"For they drank from the spiritual Rock that followed them, and the Rock was Christ."* 1 Cor. 10:4

35. **Sacrifice for Our Sins** – *"This is love: not that we loved God, but that he loved us and sent his Son as an atoning sacrifice for our sins."* *1* John *4:10*

36. **Savior** – *"For unto you is born this day in the city of David a Savior, who is Christ the Lord."* Luke 2:11

37. **Son of Man** – *"For the Son of Man came to seek and to save the lost."* Luke 19:10

38. **Son of the Most High** – *"He will be great and will be called the Son of the Most High. The Lord God will give him the throne of his father David."* Luke 1:32

39. **Supreme Creator Over All** – *"By Him all things were created, both in the heavens and on earth, visible and invisible, whether thrones or dominions or rulers or authorities—all things have been created through Him and for Him. He is before all things, and in Him all things hold together…"* 1 Cor. 1:16-17

40. **Resurrection and the Life** – *"Jesus said to her, "I am the resurrection and the life. The one who believes in me will live, even though they die."* John 11:25

41. **The Door** – *"I am the door. If anyone enters by me, he will be saved and will go in and out and find pasture."* John 10:9

42. **The Way** – *"Jesus answered, "I am the way and the truth and the life. No one comes to the Father except through me."* John 14:6

43. **The Word** – *"In the beginning was the Word, and the Word was with God, and the Word was God."* John 1:1

44. **True Vine** - *"I am the true vine, and My Father is the vinedresser."* John 15:1

45. **Truth** – *"And you will know the truth, and the truth will set you free."* John 8:32

46. **Victorious One** – *"To the one who is victorious, I will give the right to sit with me on my throne, just as I was victorious and sat down with my Father on his throne."* Rev. 3:21

47. – 50. Wonderful Counselor, Mighty God, Everlasting Father, Prince of Peace– *"For to us a child is born, to us a son is given, and the* *government will be on his shoulders. And he will be called Wonderful Counselor, Mighty God, Everlasting Father, Prince of Peace."* Is. 9:6

Seven Redemption Names of God

1. *Jehovah-Raah.* The Lord is my shepherd
2. *Jehovah-Jireh.* The Lord that sees and provides
3. *Jehovah-Rapha.* The Lord that heals and restores our souls
4. *Jehovah-Tsidkenu.* The Lord our righteousness
5. *Jehovah-Shalom.* The Lord my peace
6. *Jehovah-Shammah.* The Lord is present
7. *Jehovah-Nissi.* The Lord my canopy (a covering)

Jehovah refers to God's relationship to man; he is our Lord, God the Almighty, and our Creator. There are about ten different variations of Jehovah in the Old Testament. I gave you seven of them: the seven redemption names of God. Redemption is the release of a hostage or prisoner upon the receipt of a ransom—simply put, we were redeemed when Christ died on the cross. He gave up his entire life for us. These seven names show the commitment and love God has for us.

More than that, he has an individual care plan too, designed to fit each one of us uniquely. See? He knows the plans he has for each one of us that will follow him. He does not care about your past or your current situation either. In fact, he already knows. Remember, he sees everything, but that will not stop him from giving you a brand new life if you really want it. It's yours for the taking. Your care plan is already put in place; all you need to do is start spending time with Jesus to find out what God has in store for you and how to go about fulfilling your destiny.

I would encourage you to meditate on these seven redemptive names of God and begin to call on him using each name that fits your situation or matters of the heart; each name, as one can see, means something. With that being said,

Get Yourself A Bible
Open it, "Read It"
Do What the "Word" Says

Is with You!

The Lord's Prayer

1. **"The Lord is my shepherd"**
   Jehovah-Raah (The Lord is my shepherd and my guide) —"I shall not worry about nothing anymore, my way has never worked. Today I surrender all my affairs to him including my personal life. Now I allow his will to be done in my life. I make him my Lord he is truly my shepherd 'now.' He will GUIDE you into all truth" (John 16:13).

2. **"I shall not want"**
   Jehovah-Jireh (The Lord is my provider, so I do not want) —"He supplies all my needs according to His riches in glory by Christ Jesus" (Phil. 4:19).

3. **"He makes me lie down in green pastures; He leads me beside the still waters"**
   Jehovah-Shalom (The Lord is my peace, my calm in the midst of a storm) —"Now may the God of PEACE Himself sanctify you completely" (1 Thess. 5:23).

4. **"He restores my soul"**
   Jehovah-Rapha (He is my healer) —"And by His stripes we are healed" (1 Pet. 2:24 and Isa. 53:5).

5. **"He leads me in the paths of righteousness for His name's sake"**
   Jehovah Tsidkenu (The Lord is my righteousness; in Him I have right standing with God) —"For He made Him who knew no sin to be sin for us, that we might become the RIGHTEOUSNESS of God in Him" (1 Cor. 5:21). My plans now are to live righteously. Today I make that change!

6. **"Yea, though I walk through the valley of the shadow of death, I will fear no evil; for You are with me"**
   Jehovah-Shammah (The Lord is there; he is our ever-present God) —"For He himself has said 'I will never leave you nor forsake you'" (Heb. 13:5).

7. **"Your rod and Your staff, they comfort me. You prepare a table before me in the presence of my enemies"**
   Jehovah-Nissi (The Lord is my banner, my standard, he covers me)— "When the enemy comes in like a flood, the Spirit of the LORD will lift up a STANDARD against him" (Isa. 59:19). Therefore I will not fear, not even in everyday situations or problems because I know that the enemy, B.K.A. the devil comes in so many packages and forms. Therefore, I will not be afraid anymore. God's rod and staff will make me laugh at it all because with him on my side, I shall not fall!

My God! "You anoint my head with oil; my cup runs over. Surely goodness and mercy shall follow me all the days of my life; and I will dwell in the house of the LORD forever." **Amen**

The Ten Commandments (Exod. 20:2–17 NKJV)

1. "I am the Lord your God, who brought you out of the land of Egypt, out of the house of bondage. You shall have no other gods before Me.
2. "You shall not make for yourself a carved image, or any likeness of anything that is in heaven above, or that is in the earth beneath, or that is in the water under the earth; you shall not bow down to them nor serve them. For I, the Lord your God, am a jealous God, visiting the iniquity of the fathers on the children to the third and fourth generations of those who hate Me, but showing mercy to thousands, to those who love Me and keep My Commandments.
3. "You shall not take the name of the Lord your God in vain, for the Lord will not hold him guiltless who takes His name in vain.
4. "Remember the Sabbath day, to keep it holy. Six days you shall labor and do all your work, but the seventh day is the Sabbath of the Lord your God. In it you shall do no work: you, nor your son, nor your daughter, nor your male servant, nor your female servant, nor your cattle, nor your stranger who is

within your gates. For in six days the Lord made the heavens and the earth, the sea, and all that is in them, and rested the seventh day. Therefore the Lord blessed the Sabbath day and hallowed it.

5. "Honor your father and your mother, that your days may be long upon the land which the Lord your God is giving you.
6. "You shall not murder.
7. "You shall not commit adultery.
8. "You shall not steal.
9. "You shall not bear false witness against your neighbor.
10. "You shall not covet your neighbor's house; you shall not covet your neighbor's wife, nor his male servant, nor his female servant, nor his ox, nor his donkey, nor anything that is your neighbor's."

In Jesus name, I shall obey, Amen

The Sermon On The Mount
Matthew 5

Now when Jesus saw the crowds, he went up on a mountainside
and sat down. His disciples came to him, 2 and he began to teach them.

The Beatitudes

He said:
3 "Blessed are the poor in spirit,
for theirs is the kingdom of heaven.
4 Blessed are those who mourn,
for they will be comforted.
5 Blessed are the meek,
for they will inherit the earth.
6 Blessed are those who hunger and thirst for righteousness,
for they will be filled.
7 Blessed are the merciful,
for they will be shown mercy.
8 Blessed are the pure in heart,
for they will see God.
9 Blessed are the peacemakers,
for they will be called children of God.
10 Blessed are those who are persecuted because of righteousness,
for theirs is the kingdom of heaven.
11 "Blessed are you when people insult you, persecute you and falsely
say all kinds of evil against you because of me. 12 Rejoice and be glad,
because great is your reward in heaven, for in the same way they
persecuted the prophets who were before you."

Believes are Salt and Light

13 "You are the salt of the earth. But if the salt loses its saltiness, how
can it be made salty again? It is no longer good for anything, except to
be thrown out and trampled underfoot.
14 "You are the light of the world. A town built on a hill cannot be
hidden. 15 Neither do people light a lamp and put it under a bowl.

Instead they put it on its stand, and it gives light to everyone in the
house. [16] In the same way, let your light shine before others, that they
may see your good deeds and glorify your Father in heaven."

Christ Fulfills the Law

[17] "Do not think that I have come to abolish the Law or the Prophets;
I have not come to abolish them but to fulfill them. [18] For truly I tell
you, until heaven and earth disappear, not the smallest letter, not the
least stroke of a pen, will by any means disappear from the Law until
everything is accomplished. [19] Therefore anyone who sets aside one of
the least of these commands and teaches others accordingly will be
called least in the kingdom of heaven, but whoever practices and teaches
these commands will be called great in the kingdom of heaven. [20] For
I tell you that unless your righteousness surpasses that of the Pharisees
and the teachers of the law, you will certainly not enter the kingdom
of heaven."

Murder begins in the Heart

[21] "You have heard that it was said to the people long ago, 'You shall not
murder, and anyone who murders will be subject to judgment.' [22] But I
tell you that anyone who is angry with a brother or sister will be subject
to judgment. Again, anyone who says to a brother or sister, 'Raca, is
answerable to the court. And anyone who says, 'You fool!' will be in
danger of the fire of hell.

[23] "Therefore, if you are offering your gift at the altar and there remember
that your brother or sister has something against you, [24] leave your gift
there in front of the altar. First go and be reconciled to them; then come
and offer your gift.

[25] "Settle matters quickly with your adversary who is taking you to
court. Do it while you are still together on the way, or your adversary
may hand you over to the judge, and the judge may hand you over to
the officer, and you may be thrown into prison. [26] Truly I tell you, you
will not get out until you have paid the last penny."

Adulteryin the Heart
27 "You have heard that it was said, 'You shall not commit adultery.'[e]
28 But I tell you that anyone who looks at a woman lustfully has already
committed adultery with her in his heart. 29 If your right eye causes you
to stumble, gouge it out and throw it away. It is better for you to lose
one part of your body than for your whole body to be thrown into hell.
30 And if your right hand causes you to stumble, cut it off and throw
it away. It is better for you to lose one part of your body than for your
whole body to go into hell."

Marriage is sacred and Binding
31 "It has been said, 'Anyone who divorces his wife must give her a
certificate of divorce.'32 But I tell you that anyone who divorces his wife,
except for sexual immorality, makes her the victim of adultery, and
anyone who marries a divorced woman commits adultery."

Jesus Forbids oaths
33 "Again, you have heard that it was said to the people long ago, 'Do
not break your oath, but fulfill to the Lord the vows you have made.'
34 But I tell you, do not swear an oath at all: either by heaven, for it is
God's throne; 35 or by the earth, for it is his footstool; or by Jerusalem,
for it is the city of the Great King. 36 And do not swear by your head,
for you cannot make even one hair white or black. 37 All you need to say
is simply 'Yes' or 'No'; anything beyond this comes from the evil one."

Go the Second Mile
38 "You have heard that it was said, 'Eye for eye, and tooth for tooth.'[39
But I tell you, do not resist an evil person. If anyone slaps you on the
right cheek, turn to them the other cheek also. 40 And if anyone wants
to sue you and take your shirt, hand over your coat as well. 41 If anyone
forces you to go one mile, go with them two miles. 42 Give to the one
who asks you, and do not turn away from the one who wants to borrow
from you."

Love Your Enemies

43 "You have heard that it was said, 'Love your neighbor[i] and hate your
enemy.' 44 But I tell you, love your enemies and pray for those who
persecute you, 45 that you may be children of your Father in heaven. He
causes his sun to rise on the evil and the good, and sends rain on the
righteous and the unrighteous. 46 If you love those who love you, what
reward will you get? Are not even the tax collectors doing that? 47 And if
you greet only your own people, what are you doing more than others?
Do not even pagans do that? 48 Be perfect, therefore, as your heavenly
Father is perfect."

"The teaching of God's word gives light,
so even the simple can understand"
Psalms 119:130

★ Just a little bit of scriptures will do! ★

★ It works for me, it'll work for you too! ★

Anxiety

"Don't worry about anything; instead, pray about everything. Tell God what you need and thank him for all he has done. If you do this, you will experience God's peace, which is far more wonderful than the human mind can understand. His peace will guard your hearts and minds as you live in Jesus Christ" (Phil. 4:6–7).

Anger

"And don't sin by letting anger gain control over you. Don't let the sun go down while you are still angry, for anger gives a mighty foothold to the devil" (Eph. 4:26–27).

"Dear brothers and sisters, be quick to listen, slow to speak, and to anger. Your anger can never make things right in God's sight" (James 1:19–20).

Bravery

"Be strong and courageous, do not be afraid or tremble at them, for the Lord your God is the one who goes with you He will not fail you or forsake you" (Deut. 31:6–7).

Broken Heart

"The LORD is close to the brokenhearted" (Ps. 43:18).

"Trust in the LORD with all your heart and do not lean on your own understanding. In all your ways acknowledge him, and he will make straight your paths" (Prov. 3:5–6).

Depression

"The Lord hears his people when they call to him for help. He rescues them from all their troubles . . . The righteous faces many troubles, but the Lord rescues them from each and every one" (Ps. 34:17, 19).

Death

"And now sisters and brothers, I want you to know what happens to the Christians who have died so you will not be full of sorrow like people who have no hope. For since we believe that Jesus died and was raised to life again, we also believe that when Jesus comes, God will bring back with Jesus all the Christians who died" (1 Thess. 4:13–14).

Eternality

Jesus told her, "I am the resurrection and the life. Those who believe in me, even though they die like everyone else, will live again. They are given eternal life for believing in me and will never perish" (John 11:25–26).

Fear

"Don't be afraid, for I am with you. Do not be dismayed, for I am your God. I will strengthen you, I will help you. I will uphold you with my victorious right hand" (Isa. 41:10).

"THEY do not fear bad news; they confidently trust the LORD to care for them. They are confident and fearless and can face their foes triumphantly" (Ps. 112:7–8).

"For YOU are my hiding place; you protect me from trouble. You surround me with songs of victory" (Ps. 32:7).

Frustration

“PATIENT endurance is what you need now, so you will continue to do God’s will. Then you will receive all that he promised” (Heb. 10:36).

Guilt

“‘Come now and let us argue this out,’ says the LORD. ‘No matter how deep the stain of your sin, I can remove it, I can make you as clean as freshly fallen snow. Even if you are stained as red as crimson, I can make you as white as wool.’” (Isa. 1:18).

“And I will forgive their wrong doings and I will never again remember their sins” (Heb. 8:12).

Healing

“In one of the villages, Jesus met a man with an advanced case of leprosy. When the man saw Jesus, he fell to the ground, face down in the dust, begging to be healed. ‘Lord,’ he said ‘if you want to, you can make me well again.’

“Jesus reached out and touched the man. ‘I want to,’ he said. ‘Be healed!’ And instantly, the leprosy disappeared” (Luke 5:12–13).

“Confess your sin to each other and pray for each other so that you may be healed. The earnest prayer of a righteous person has great power and wonderful results” (James 5:13–16).

Impatience

“BE STILL in the presence of the LORD, and wait patiently for him to act. Don’t worry about evil people who prosper or fret about their wicked schemes” (Ps. 37:7).

Insecurity

"I am holding you by your right hand—I the LORD your God. And I say to you, do not be afraid, I am here to help you" (Isa. 41:13).

"What can we say about such wonderful things as these? If God is for us who can be against us? Since God did not spare even his Son but gave him up for all, won't God, who gave up Christ, also give us everything else?" (Rom. 8:31–32).

Insult

God blesses those who are persecuted because they live for God, for the Kingdom of Heaven is theirs.

God blesses you when you are mocked and persecuted and lied about because you are his followers. Be happy about it! Be very glad! For a great reward awaits you in heaven. And remember, the ancient prophets were persecuted too.

But I say, love your enemies! Pray for those who persecute you! In that way, you will be acting as true children of your Father in heaven. For he gives his sunlight to both evil and the good, and he sends rain on the just and on the unjust, too (Matt. 5:10–12, 44–55).

Jealousy

"But if you are bitterly jealous and there is selfish ambition in your heart, don't brag about being wise, that is the worst kind if lie. For jealousy and selfishness are not God's kind of wisdom. Such things are earthly, unspiritual and motivated by the Devil. For wherever there is jealousy and selfish ambition there you will find disorder and every kind of evil" (James 3:14–16).

"So don't be dismayed when the wicked grow rich, and their homes become splendid. For when they die, they carry nothing with them. Their wealth will not follow them into the grave" (Ps. 49:16–17).

Loneliness

"'For the mountains may depart and the hills disappear, but even then I will remain loyal to you. My covenant of blessing will never be broken,' says the LORD, who has mercy on you" (Isa. 54:10).

"No I will not abandon you as orphans—I will come to you" (John 14:18).

Low Self–Esteem

As God's messenger, I give each of you this warning. Be honest in your estimate of yourself, measuring your value by how much faith God has given you. Just as our bodies have many parts and each part has a special function, so it is with Christ's body. We are all parts of his own body, and each of us has different work to do. And since we are all one body of Christ, we belong to each other, and each of us needs all the others (Rom. 12:3–5).

Pain

"For our present troubles are quite small and won't last long. Yet they produce for us an immeasurably great glory that will last forever! . . . I have received wonderful revelations from God. But to keep me from getting puffed up, I was given a thorn in my flesh, a messenger from Satan to torment me and keep me from getting proud. Three different times I begged the Lord to take it away. Each time, he said, 'My gracious favor is all you need. My power works best in your weakness,' So no I am glad to boast about my weaknesses, so that the power of Christ may work through me. Since I know it is all for Christ's good. I am quite content with my weaknesses and with insults, hardships, persecutions, and calamities. For when I am weak, then I am strong" (2 Cor. 4:17, 12:7–10).

Sickness

"The Lord nurses them when they are sick and eases their pain and discomfort" (Ps. 41:3).

"You must serve only the Lord your God. If you do, I will bless you with food and water, and I will keep you healthy. There will be no miscarriages or infidelity [sex outside of marriage] among your people, and I will give you long and full lives" (Exod. 23:25–26).

Temptation

"God BLESSES the people who patiently endure testing. Afterward they will receive the crown of life that God has promised to those who love him. And remember, no one who wants to do wrong should ever say, 'God is tempting me.' God is never tempted to do wrong, and he never temps anyone either . . . so humble yourself before God. Resist the devil and he will f lee from you" (James 1:12–13, 4:7).

"But REMEMBER that the temptations that come into your life are no different from what others experience. And God is faithful. He will keep the temptation from becoming so strong that you can stand up against it. When you are tempted, he will show you a way out so that you will not give in to it" (1 Cor. 10:13).

Weariness

"Then Jesus said, 'Come to me all of you who are weary and carry heavy burdens, and I will give you rest. Take my yoke upon you. Let me teach you because I am humble and gentle, and you will find rest for your souls. For my yoke fits perfectly, and my burden I give you is light.'" (Matt. 11:28–30).

"But those who wait on the Lord will find new strengths. They will fly high on wings like eagles. They will run and not grow weary. They will walk and not faint" (Isa. 40:31).

Worry

"You will keep in perfect peace all who trust in you, whose thoughts are fixed on you! Trust in the LORD always, for the LORD GOD is the Eternal Rock" (Isa. 26:3–4).

"Give all your worries and cares to God for he cares about what happens to you" (1 Pet. 5:7).

"Then turning to his disciples, Jesus said, 'So I tell you, don't worry about everyday life—whether you have enough food to eat or clothes to wear. For life consists of far more than food or clothing. Look at the ravens. They don't need to plant or harvest or put food in barns because God feeds them. And you are far more valuable to him than any birds! Can all your worry add a single moment to your life? Of course not! And if worry can't do little things like that, what the use in worrying over bigger things? Look at the lilies and how they grow. They don't work or make their clothing, yet Solomon in all his glory was not dressed as beautiful as they are. And if God cares so wonderfully for f lowers that are here today and gone tomorrow, won't he more surely care for you? You have so little faith!" (Luke 12:22–28).

"Light" is More Powerful than Darkness!

Friendship

Whoever walks with the wise will become wise; whoever walks with the fools will suffer harm.

"DON'T be selfish; don't live to make a good impression on others. Be humble, thinking of others as better than yourself. Don't think only about your affairs, but be interested in others, too, and what they are doing" (Phil. 2:3–4).

Injustice

"In his Kingdom God called you to his eternal glory by means of Jesus Christ. After you have suffered as little while, he will restore, support, and strengthen you. And he will place you on a firm foundation. All power is his forever and ever. Amen" (1 Pet 5:10–11).

Love

"I have loved you even as the Father has loved me. Remain in my love. When you obey me, you remain in my love, just as I obey my Father and remain in his love. I have told you this so you will be filled with my joy. Yes, your joy will overflow! I command you to love each other in the same way that I love you. And here is how to measure it—the greatest love is shown when people lay down their lives for their friends. You are my friends if you obey me. I no longer call you servants, because a master doesn't confide in servants. Now you are my friend since I told you everything the master has told me. You did not choose me. I chose you. I appointed you to go produce fruit that will last, so that the Father will give you whatever you ask, using my name" (John 15:9–16).

Marriage

"And FURTHER, you will submit to one another out of reverence for Christ. You wives will submit to your husband as you do to the Lord . . . and you husbands must love your wives with the same love Christ shows the church" (Eph. 5:21, 25).

Parents

"And now a word to the fathers, don't make your children angry by the way you treat them. Rather, bring them up with the discipline and instructions approved by the Lord" (Eph. 6:4).

Children

"CHILDREN, obey your parents because you belong to the Lord, for this is the right thing to do. 'Honor your father and mother.' This is the first of the Ten Commandments that ends with a promise. And this is the promise: If you honor your mother and father, you will live a long life, full of blessing" (Eph. 6:1–3).

Money Management

"Those who love money will never have enough. How absurd to think that wealth brings true happiness" (Eccles. 5:10)!

"And the same God who takes care of me will supply all your needs from his glorious riches, which have been given us in Christ Jesus" (Phil. 4:19).

"Owe nothing to anyone except love one another, for he who loves his neighbor has fulfilled the law" (Rom 13:8).

"Just as the rich rule the poor, so the borrower is servant to the lender" (Prov. 22:7).

"For where your treasure is, there your heart will be also" (Matt. 6:21).

"'Bring the whole tithe into the storehouse, that there may be food in my house. Test me in this,' says the LORD Almighty, 'and see if I will not throw open the f loodgates of heaven and pour out so much blessing that there will not be room enough to store it'" (Matt. 3:10).

Debt

"Keep out of debt and owe no man anything, except to love one another; for he who loves his neighbor [who practices loving others] has fulfilled the Law [relating to one's fellowmen, meeting all its requirements]" (Rom. 13:8).

"When the Lord your God blesses you as He promised you, then you shall lend to many nations, but you shall not borrow; and you shall rule over many nations, but they shall not rule over you" (Deut. 1:6).

"But don't begin until you count the cost. For who would begin construction of a building without first getting estimates and then checking to see if there is enough money to pay the bills" (Luke 14:28)?

Trust

"Trust in the lord with all your heart; do not depend on your own understanding. Seek his will in all that you do, and he will direct your path" (Prov. 3:5–6).

Faith

"So then Faith come by hearing and hearing by the word of God" (Rom. 10:17).

Simply put, read your Bibles daily. Get in a good Bible-living and -teaching church.

"Truly I tell you if you had faith as small as a mustard seed, you can say to this mountain, move from here to there and it will move" (Matt. 17:19).

Born Again

"Jesus replied, 'I assure you, unless you are born again, you can never see the Kingdom of God . . .

"Those who have been born into God's family do not sin, because God's life is in them. So they can't keep on sinning, because they have been born of God" (1 John 3:9).

Finding God

"HIS PURPOSE in all of them was that the nations should seek him after God and perhaps feel their way toward him and find him—through he is not far from anyone of us. For in him we live and move and exist. As one of your own poets says, 'We are his offspring's'" (Acts 17:27–28).

"'For I know the plans I have for you,' says the LORD. 'They are plans for good and not for disaster, to give you a future and a hope. In those days when you pray, I will listen, if you look for me in earnest, you will find me when you seek me'" (Jer. 29:11–13).

Knowing God

"However at that time, when you did not know God, you were slaves to those which by nature are no gods. But now that you have come to know God, or rather to be known by God, how is it that you turn back again to the weak and worthless elemental things, to which you desire to be enslaved all over again" (Gal. 4:8–9)?

"And this I pray, that your love may abound still more and more in real knowledge and all discernment, so that you may approve the things that are excellent, in order to be sincere and blameless until the day of Christ; having been filled with the fruit of righteousness which comes through Jesus Christ, to the glory and praise of God" (Phil. 1:9–11).

"By this, the children of God and the children of the devil are obvious: anyone who does not practice righteousness is not of God, nor the one who does not love his brother" (1 John 3:10).

Knowing Jesus Christ

"But seek first His kingdom and His righteousness, and all these things will be added to you" (Matt. 6:33).

"Many will say to Me on that day, 'Lord, Lord, did we not prophesy in Your name, and in Your name cast out demons, and in Your name perform many miracles?' And then I will declare to them, I never knew you; **DEPART FROM ME, YOU WHO PRACTICE LAWLESSNESS** (Matt. 7:22–23).

"For the LORD is a great God and a great King above all gods" (Ps. 95:3).

Prayer

"But you, when you pray, go into your inner room, close your door and pray to your Father who is in secret, and your Father who sees what is done in secret will reward you. And when you are praying, do not use meaningless repetition as the Gentiles do, for they suppose that they will be heard for their many words. So do not be like them; for your Father knows what you need before you ask Him" (Matt. 6:6–9).

"If my people, who are called by my name, will humble themselves and pray and seek my face and turn from their wicked ways, then I will hear from heaven, and I will forgive their sin and will heal their land" (2 Chron. 7:14).

"Therefore I tell you, whatever you ask for in prayer, believe that you have received it, and it will be yours" (Mark 11:24).

Love Your Enemies!
Luke 6:27-36

Love your enemies, do good to those who hate you, bless those who curse you, pray for those who mistreat you. If someone slaps you on one cheek, turn to them the other also. If someone takes your coat, do not withhold your shirt from them. Give to everyone who asks you, and if anyone takes what belongs to you, do not demand it back. Do to others as you would have them do to you.

"If you love those who love you, what credit is that to you? Even sinners love those who love them. And if you do good to those who are good to you, what credit is that to you? Even sinners do that. And if you lend to those from whom you expect repayment, what credit is that to you? Even sinners lend to sinners, expecting to be repaid in full. But love your enemies, do good to them, and lend to them without expecting to get anything back. Then your reward will be great, and you will be children of the Most High, because he is kind to the ungrateful and wicked. Be merciful, just as your Father is merciful.

There's No Place Like Home!

When you are lost, there is no place like home, the bible is home! Not the streets, and not in the bed of strangers we meet!

For we know that if the earthly tent we live in is destroyed, we have a building from God, an eternal house in heaven, not built by human hands. Meanwhile we groan, longing to be clothed instead with our heavenly dwelling, because when we are clothed, we will not be found naked. For while we are in this tent, we groan and are burdened, because we do not wish to be unclothed but to be clothed instead with our heavenly dwelling, so that what is mortal may be swallowed up by life. Now the one who has fashioned us for this very purpose is God, who has given us the Spirit as a deposit, guaranteeing what is to come.

Therefore we are always confident and know that as long as we are at home in the body we are away from the Lord. For we live by faith, not by sight. We are confident, I say, and would prefer to be away from the body and at home with the Lord. So we make it our goal to please him, whether we are at home in the body or away from it. For we must all appear before the judgment seat of Christ, so that each of us may receive what is due us for the things done while in the body, whether good or bad. **2 Corinthians 5:1-10**

Question?

What Has The World Done For **"YOU"** Lately? **Nothin!**
Enough Is Enough!
Give It UP!
Come Home, God Left the **'Light On"!!!!**

"Thy word is a lamp unto my feet and a light unto my path"
Psalms 199:105

"Knowing these teachings will mean true and good health for you."
Proverbs 4:22

Read Your Bibles Everyday!

How do you like your Grab Bag so far? I hope you love it, I do, The Care Plan, like I told you, is for **"Me Too"!**

Just remember always to include God in
"Your Everyday Life!"
There is 'Nothing' in Your Life God Can't Fix

Always Remember This, "Nothing"!

And if you need Him, do what I do, "Call Him"!

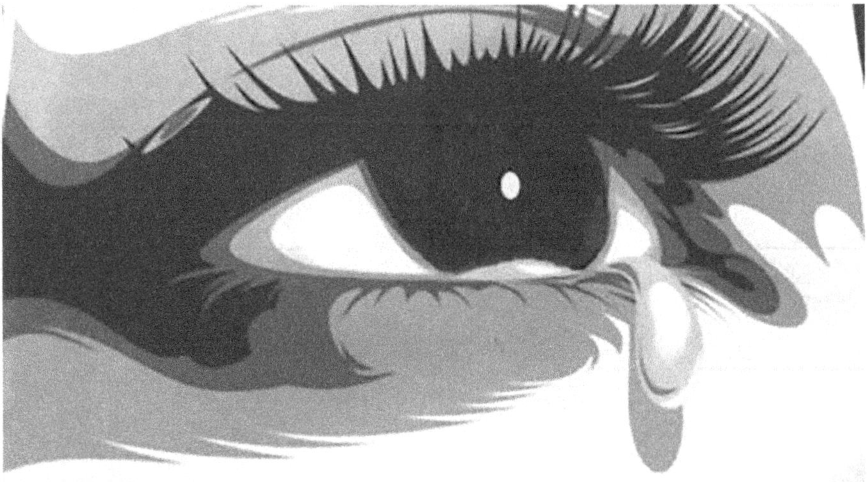

Then they cried to the LORD in their trouble, and he saved them from their distress. He sent out his word and healed them, he rescued them from the grave. **Psalms 107:19-20**

He's just an ear away, Him today!

His 'Word' **'WORKS'** "My sheep listen to my voice,
I know them, and they follow me."
John 10:27

The Care Plan Phone Directory

• When your heart is troubled	Call	John 14
• When you feel abandoned and alone	Call	Psalm 23
• When God seems far away	Call	Psalm 91
• When you are being set up or attacked	Call	Psalm 27
• When you are bitter and want to get even	Call	Ephesians 4:31
• When you are overwhelmed	Call	Isaiah 40:28
• When you are being tempted	Call	James 1:13–18
• When you need help	Call	Psalm 46:1–2
• When you are worried	Call	Philippians 4:6–7
• When you are weak and need strength	Call	Isaiah 41:10
• When you need love	Call	Jeremiah 31:3
• When you need prosperity	Call	Malachi 3:10
• When you need wisdom	Call	Proverbs 1–31
• When you need rest	Call	Psalm 127:2
• When you need answers to life questions	Call	Ecclesiastes 3:2
• When you need a friend	Call	Proverbs 18:24
• When you need a new life	Call	Colossians 3:10 and 4:16
• When you lack patients	Call	Galatians 6:19
• When you need peace	Call	Philippians 4:6
• When you are worried	Call	Matthew 6:25–34
• When you are lied on, slandered, and persecuted	Call	1 Peter 4:12-14 and John 15:18
• When you are afraid	Call	Isaiah 41:10
• When you are betrayed	Call	Proverbs 19:5 and Ephesians 6:10–18
• When you are sick	Call	James 5:14 and 1 Peter 4:19
• When you are down and out	Call	Matthew 11:28–30
• When you need joy	Call	Romans 12:12 and James 1:2–4

Don't Worry, Trust "GOD"!

He already knows what you need before
you even ask, be patient and wait!
He is working everything out in your favor, so go get some rest!

Maybe he's doing a 'Faith Test'
Will You Pass?

WEEPING MAY ENDURE FOR A NIGHT BUT JOY COME IN THE MORNING!

Psalms 30:50

The Holy Bible Care Plan

Sets Us All FREE!

READ
YOUR
Bible
FIRST
IN THE MORNING
LISTEN TO GOD FIRST

The New Me!

Reflections Of The Way My Life Use To Be

Your image goes here

Who I Use To Be!

Who I Have Become!

What Matters To Me "NOW"

My Goals, Dreams, Hopes and Desires!

My Contribution to the World

God's Care Plan for My Life **"N.O.W."**

No **O**ne **W**orks but **Jesus!**

"For I know the plans I have for you,"
declares the LORD, "plans to prosper you and not to harm you,
plans to give you a future."
—Jeremiah 29:11

My Favorite Scripture's!

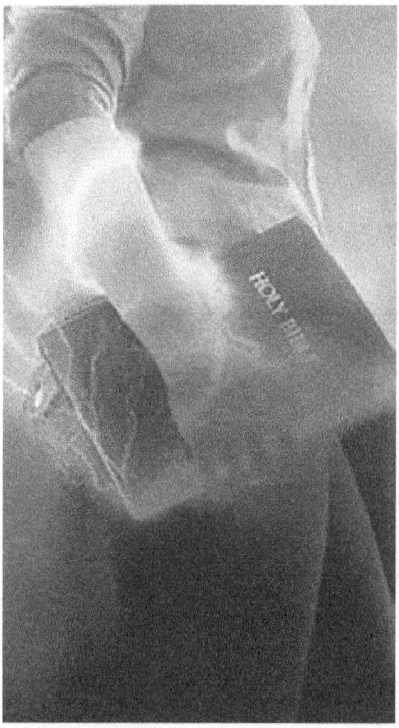

Goes Where I Go...

The Books of the Bible			
Order	**Book Title(s)**	**Chapters**	**Verses**
I. Law			
1.	The First Book of Moses Called Genesis	50	1,533
2.	The Second Book of Moses Called Exodus	40	1,213
3.	The Third Book of Moses Called Leviticus	27	859
4.	The Fourth Book of Moses Called Numbers	36	1,288
5.	The Fifth Book of Moses Called Deuteronomy	34	959
II. Old Testament Narrative			
6.	The Book of Joshua	24	658
7.	The Book of Judges	21	618
8.	The Book of Ruth	4	85
9.	The First Book of Samuel	31	810
10.	The Second Book of Samuel	24	695
11.	The First Book of Kings	22	816
12.	The Second Book of Kings	25	719
13.	The First Book of Chronicles	29	942
14.	The Second Book of Chronicles	36	822
15.	The Book of Ezra	10	280
16.	The Book of Nehemiah	13	406
17.	The Book of Esther	10	167
III. Wisdom Literature			
18.	The Book of Job	42	1,070
19.	The Book of Psalms	150	2,461
20.	The Book of Proverbs	31	915
21.	The Book of Ecclesiastes	12	222
22.	The Song of Songs (or Song of Solomon *or* Canticles)	8	117
IV. Major Prophets			
23.	The Book of Isaiah	66	1,292
24.	The Book of Jeremiah	52	1,364
25.	The Book of Lamentations	5	154
26.	The Book of Ezekiel	48	1,273
27.	The Book of Daniel	12	357
V. Minor Prophets			
28.	The Book of Hosea	14	197
29.	The Book of Joel	3	73
30.	The Book of Amos	9	146
31.	The Book of Obadiah	1	21
32.	The Book of Jonah	4	48
33.	The Book of Micah	7	105
34.	The Book of Nahum	3	47
35.	The Book of Habakkuk	3	56
36.	The Book of Zephaniah	3	53

37.	The Book of Haggai	2	38
38.	The Book of Zechariah	14	211
39.	The Book of Malachi	4	55
VI. New Testament Narrative			
40.	The Gospel According to Matthew	28	1,071
41.	The Gospel According to Mark	16	678
42.	The Gospel According to Luke	24	1,151
43.	The Gospel According to John	21	879
44.	The Acts of the Apostles	28	1,007
40.	The Gospel According to Matthew	28	1,071
41.	The Gospel According to Mark	16	678
42.	The Gospel According to Luke	24	1,151
43.	The Gospel According to John	21	879
44.	The Acts of the Apostles	28	1,007
VII. Pauline Epistles			
45.	The Epistle of Paul to the Romans	16	433
46.	The First Epistle of Paul to the Corinthians	16	437
47.	The Second Epistle of Paul to the Corinthians	13	257
48.	The Epistle of Paul to the Galatians	6	149
49.	The Epistle of Paul to the Ephesians	6	155
50.	The Epistle of Paul to the Philippians	4	104
51.	The Epistle of Paul to the Colossians	4	95
52.	The First Epistle of Paul to the Thessalonians	5	89
53.	The Second Epistle of Paul to the Thessalonians	3	47
54.	The First Epistle of Paul to Timothy	6	113
55.	The Second Epistle of Paul to Timothy	4	83
56.	The Epistle of Paul to Titus	3	46
57.	The Epistle of Paul to Philemon	1	25
VIII. General Epistles			
58.	The Epistle to the Hebrews	13	303
59.	The General Epistle of James	5	108
60.	The First Epistle of Peter	5	105
61.	The Second Epistle of Peter	3	61
62.	The First Epistle of John	5	105
63.	The Second Epistle of John	1	13
64.	The Third Epistle of John	1	14
65.	The Epistle of Jude	1	25
IX. Apocalyptic Epistle			
66.	The Book of Revelation (*or* The Apocalypse of John)	22	404
	Total number of Chapters and Verses	**1,189**	**31,102**

THE CARE PLAN for **God's People!**

How We Think and Live Matters!

"Knowing these teachings will mean true and good health for you."
Proverbs 4:22

Read Your Bibles Everyday!

My favorite Scriptures

Found in the book of ____________________ The scripture ____________________
Notes: ____
Found in the book of ____________________ The scripture ____________________
Notes: ____
Found in the book of ____________________ The scripture ____________________
Notes: ____
Found in the book of ____________________ The scripture ____________________
Notes: ____
Found in the book of ____________________ The scripture ____________________
Notes: ____
Found in the book of ____________________ The scripture ____________________
Notes: ____
Found in the book of ____________________ The scripture ____________________
Notes: ____
Found in the book of ____________________ The scripture ____________________
Notes: ____
Found in the book of ____________________ The scripture ____________________
Notes: ____
Found in the book of ____________________ The scripture ____________________
Notes: ____
Found in the book of ____________________ The scripture ____________________
Notes: ____
Found in the book of ____________________ The scripture ____________________
Notes: ____
Found in the book of ____________________ The scripture ____________________
Notes: ____
Found in the book of ____________________ The scripture ____________________
Notes: ____
Found in the book of ____________________ The scripture ____________________
Notes: ____
Found in the book of ____________________ The scripture ____________________
Notes: ____
Found in the book of ____________________ The scripture ____________________
Notes: ____
Found in the book of ____________________ The scripture ____________________
Notes: ____
Found in the book of ____________________ The scripture ____________________
Notes: ____

Found in the book of ____________________ The scripture ____________________
Notes: ____
Found in the book of ____________________ The scripture ____________________
Notes: ____
Found in the book of ____________________ The scripture ____________________
Notes: ____
Found in the book of ____________________ The scripture ____________________
Notes: ____
Found in the book of ____________________ The scripture ____________________
Notes: ____
Found in the book of ____________________ The scripture ____________________
Notes: ____
Found in the book of ____________________ The scripture ____________________
Notes: ____
Found in the book of ____________________ The scripture ____________________
Notes: ____
Found in the book of ____________________ The scripture ____________________
Notes: ____
Found in the book of ____________________ The scripture ____________________
Notes: ____
Found in the book of ____________________ The scripture ____________________
Notes: ____
Found in the book of ____________________ The scripture ____________________
Notes: ____
Found in the book of ____________________ The scripture ____________________
Notes: ____
Found in the book of ____________________ The scripture ____________________
Notes: ____
Found in the book of ____________________ The scripture ____________________
Notes: ____
Found in the book of ____________________ The scripture ____________________
Notes: ____
Found in the book of ____________________ The scripture ____________________
Notes: ____
Found in the book of ____________________ The scripture ____________________
Notes: ____
Found in the book of ____________________ The scripture ____________________
Notes: ____
Found in the book of ____________________ The scripture ____________________
Notes: ____
Found in the book of ____________________ The scripture ____________________
Notes: ____

Ending Remarks From Miss StarN'air

Wisdom for the Soul!

No matter what we do in life or what we become—super rich, famous, or second to none—a life without Christ is a wasted life! You've accomplished nothing, you may have won over men, but your soul will not go on, it will end. My advise, is simply this,

Don't Blend!
Don't Follow The Trend
Fight The Good Fight
Until Christ Comes Back Again

So Long, My Friend!

Miss. Asondra StarN'air

PRAYER OF JABEZ

JABEZ cried out to God of Israel

OH, THAT YOU would bless me and enlarge my territory! Let your hands be with me and keep me from harm, so that I will be free from pain "And God granted his request.

1st Chronicles 4:10

Flesh and Spirit!

Let's Hear It!

The Prayer of StarN'air

My God 'oh how do I love Thee
Take over my life and never give it back to me.
Tame the ego mind
Make it stay behind,
Free me from fear,
Remind me a **Messiah** lives here.
Give me all that I need to succeed.
Never let my wealth turn into greed.
Keep Godly spirits in my life to help me grow and learn,
Let your light shine in me, forever burn.
When my time is over, help me to step aside, give someone else a turn.
"Oh my Lord **STAY** in the mist, keep your hands in all I do
Keep reminding me, the day I was born, a diamond grew.
Lord take me, my gifts, and the music in me, use it for humankind,
Send me out in the world to do your work no matter what I find.
Keep me thriving and living on **FAITH**
My Lord, Let me love all my enemies and never hate.
Help me to walk the narrow path,
Be there with me, together, let's skip, sing and laugh.
Keep me meek and humble all the time
Don't let me forget where I came from
Stay in me, keep me saying **"YES"** to those who say
Sister, can you spare a dime?
Yes, Jesus make me over
I want to be just like you
Going back for the lost
Leaving no one behind!

And God also granted her request.
The Book of StarN'air
Written, 21st Century AD, Two Thousand -Seven

People, "There Is A Heaven!"

My Eyes Have Seen "The Light of God!"

Final Remarks

Before I go, I must share this with all of you never in a million years did I ever think I would be called by God to write a care plan for the world, I use to be such a shy and timid girl. Besides who am I anyway? Well I'll tell you who I am, I am someone that got born again, I came out of the world and changed. I am not the same! Today, I've committed my entire life to serving Christ, I'm not looking back. My life is saved, for all eternality, like Jesus, the world can't touch me, I'm free. I belong to Jesus now. I have been under **God's Care Plan** for so many, many years. Right now, it brings 'tears', just thinking about all he's done for me, how he's helped me in my darkest hour., **'My O' My', what Glory and Power!** "Hold on StarN'air" Be still and know I am God, he whispered, weeping may endure for a night, but joy cometh in the morning! His words gave me something to hold on to and he'll also be there for you. **God's *Care Plan***, is the greatest one known to man, it saved me, it brought me back to life again. Just when I was about to give up, his, "Son" Jesus showed up! And he will show up for you, and for **Everybody, Everywhere** that call on him. So don't do it, don't give up, **"Our God Can Fix It!"!** Whatever it is; loneliness, debt, depression, suicidal thoughts (we get those too sometimes) illnesses, cancer, joblessness, broken heartedness, divorce (God hates divorce) whatever, whatever, "Our GOD" He can fix it, all of it! I'm a witness, I tell you the truth, 'He' can put you back together again. There is nothing God can't fix, remember this, Nothing! If 'He' helped me, 'He' can help you. People all you have to do is call on him, live for him, and make him Lord over your life. **"Choose Christ"!**

With all my love, Be Healthy, Be Bright, Be Light!

Miss Asondra StarN'air

Calling Out: Hey, Everybody, Everywhere "Globally", All Around The World, Get on 'The Care Plan' It's Got us Covered From A to Z Get, "Free" With Me!

Get The Care Plan
Open The Care Plan
Do The Care Plan

Is with You!

This book was inspired by God for me to write I just know it. But beloved, let me make it "Crystal Clear" **The Care Plan** is not a replacement for **"The Holy Bible",** No book on earth will ever be. This book is a topical scriptural reference to help win souls over to Christ and help you deal with your everyday life. But the **"Holy Bible"** is **The Universal "Care Plan"** for the entire existence of man and the universe. Therefore, The Bible must always be number one, **"FIRST'!**

God Bless You!
Let God's Word Do What It Do "**SAVE YOU**"!

Holy Spirit Speaks, "Well Done!"

StarN'air 'Well done, good and faithful servant! You have been faithful with a few things; I will put you in charge of many things. "Come and share your master's happiness"!!!!!!!

Matthew 25:21

I was lost but, **N.O.W.** I'm found! God turns my life around and he can do the same thing for you.

God is Good, God is Great!

"Whatever you do, work at it with all your heart, as working for the Lord, not for human masters, since you know that you will receive an inheritance from the Lord as a reward. It is the Lord Christ you are serving" (Col. 3:23-24).

"God will repay each person according to what they have done" (Rom. 2:6).

"Therefore, my dear brothers and sisters, stand firm. Let nothing move you. Always give yourselves fully to the work of the Lord, because you know that your labor in the Lord is not in vain" (1 Cor. 15:58).

"Let us not become weary in doing good, for at the proper time we will reap a harvest if we do not give up" (Gal. 6:9).

"Let love and faithfulness never leave you;
bind them around your neck,
write them on the tablet of your heart.
Then you will win favor and a good name
in the sight of God and man"
(Prov. 3:3–4).

I will bless those who bless you, and him who dishonors you I will curse, and in you all the families of the earth shall be blessed."(Genesis 12:3)

"A gift opens the way and ushers the giver into the presence of the great" (Prov. 18:16).

“Blessed is the one who perseveres under trial because, having stood the test, that person will receive the crown of life that the Lord has promised to those who love him” (James 1:12).

“Walk in obedience to all that the Lord your God has commanded you, so that you may live and prosper and prolong your days in the land that you will possess” **Deuteronomy 5:33**

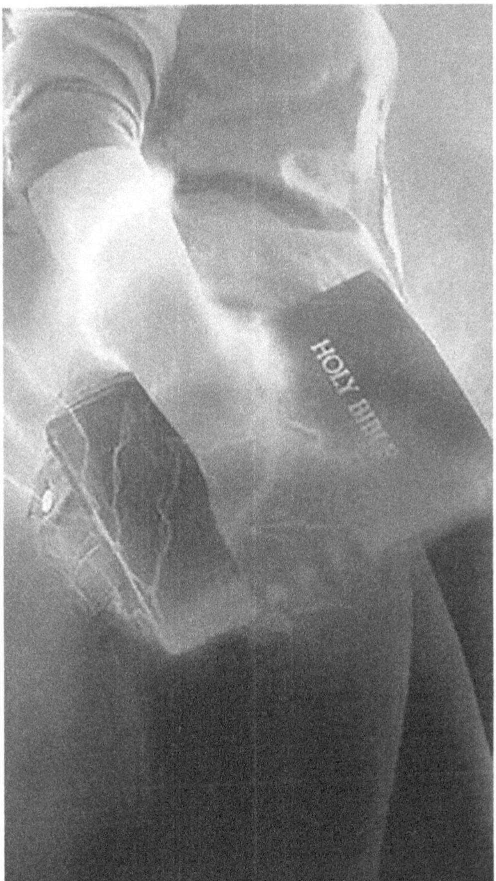

The Care Plan, From A to Z

We've Only Just Begun!
To all of God's People
"Well Done!"

Barren Land!

*Jesus said to them, "I am the bread of life.
Whoever comes to me will never go hungry and
whoever believes in me will never be thirsty."*
—John 6:35

Remember this: If you stay out of the Word, the Word stays out of you.

THE CARE PLAN for **God's People!**

How We Think and Live Matters!

"Knowing these teachings will mean true and good health for you."
Proverbs 4:22

Read Your Bibles Everyday!

Holy Spirit

Holy Spirit come and fill this place
Bring us healing with your warm embrace
Show your power, make your presence known
Holy Spirit come, fill this place
(CeCe Winans)

I can hear CeCe's incredible voice right now, as this book comes to an end, what a beautiful voice she has. I love you CeCe! If you haven't heard her you should. That song, 'Holy Spirit'is so fitting right now.

Right before Jesus's departure, he spoke to his disciples, he told them, he was leaving them soon, that he had to go away. "Nevertheless, I tell you the truth: it is to your advantage that I go away, the ***Helper*** will not come to you, but if I go, I'll send him to you." John 16:7

In that same way, Jesus sent the Holy Spirit to and gave me this assignment, **'The Care Plan'** write it, he said, then I'll put it in my people's hand. Well I have done that, it is finished! And now I must go. Otherwise, **"YOU"** won't Grow or come to know Jesus for yourself, but I'll leave the world with **'The Care Plan'** you're on your own now, but remember if you Get **The Care Plan,** Open **The Care Plan,** and Do **The Care Plan**, what's going to happen 'yawl'? **Everybody, it's your turn to say it, "God is with You"!** So you see, I can't stay, I feel that I have done what I've been called to do, **The Care Plan** is done, "Through". Now the rest is up to you, what yawl do with it, is entirely up to you. People, loved ones, I hope you've taken a lot in, learned something and also had fun! Someone, pass me the tissue,  It's time for us to part! I know this sounds corny, but it's really true, you'll always be in my heart!

Good –Bye, O' How I Sigh.. How I Sigh
More Work To Do, **Got to Go, Got to FLY...........**

I Love You!

Miss Asondra StarN'air

Get Yourself On The Ball? Let's Stay On One Accord!

Christ Is LORD!

Come To The Cross!

Die Out of This World...

Everybody, Everywhere, Christ is Not For Sale

Come Out This World!

Don't Go Back There!

Moving On

Now, may the God of Abraham, Isaac and Jacob be with you all, and until we meet again, tell **Everybody, Everywhere**, your friends and family too, to:

Get The Care Plan
Open The Care Plan
Do The Care Plan

Is with You!

Blessings, Blessings, and More Blessings to 'YA'!

Love always, ***Miss Asondra StarN'air***

Jesus Is Calling Out To "YOU"!

I stretch down my hand to you, won't you come?

**Come to me, all who are weary and burdened,
and I will give you rest.
Matthew11:28**

Get Saved Now!

"I am the way and the truth and the life.
No one comes to the Father except by me."

John 14:6

There will be a time when it's too late, so don't wait,

"COME NOW!"

The Invitation To Come!

If you are someone out there whose lost, in need of a savior, **Good News Today**, God sent you one, his name is **Jesus**, yes **God sent** his only begotten son, to die for you, so you could live, but first you must accept him, and know that although you can't see or touch him, He's **"REAL"** and He's coming back again. He will rule over this earth along with his 'people' us, the ones who have been faithful and true.

Next, you must **NOW**, right now! **Accept him fully in your heart**, allow him to take over your life, make you over into the kind of person **HE** wants you to be. Along with all that, today you also **Agree to study his word and be obedient to it for the rest of your life.** Do you agree? Well, If you are ready, **Repeat after me:** Lord I am ready right now to give my entire life over to you, I can no longer go on without you, I am in need of help, a savior, **I cannot make it on my own anymore,** please come and be my Lord and Savior. **Allow your holy spirit** to take over everything now. **I want to be made over; I want to get "Born Again". I want to be free from this world, for once and for all. "God Please Rescue Me"!,** I want to be **"FREE"!**

If you prayed that prayer, I do believe you just got "Born Again"!

Start cleaning house now! Get away from all that has kept you in bondage, depressed and defeated. **G**et a bible, **O**pen it up, and start reading it for one full years non -stop, **D**o what God's word is telling you to do and not to do. And know through your obedience **God is with You!** Yes He is, God is getting ready to do something amazing in your life now! And On behalf of every disciple in the bible, including me, we all say, **"Welcome Home"**, we remember your sins no more, you have been given a fresh start, a brand new beginning, God loves you and so do we. **Together in Christ we are FREE!**

The Care Plan

The Care Plan will change your life forever, if you let, let it! Because you have nothing to lose. This book is for all those who are sick and tired of how things have been going in their lives and want change. But this time around, You have come to realize, you can't do it by yourself, you need a savior "JESUS", The Son of the "Almighty GOD" and his holy spirit to come in your life and help guide and save you. Well I do believe that **The Care Plan** is "Just **What The Doctor Ordered"** to help get you up and well again. So that you can come to know Christ and make Him **LORD** over your life. You've lived life your way, it didn't work, **"Now Try God" for 'Crying Out Loud'!!!** Do something, take action, don't be stubborn or **"Proud."** Take charge:

Get The Care Plan
Open The Care Plan
Do The Care Plan

Is with You!

Congratulations!

Don't be afraid anymore, you are born again now, for I am with you; do not be dismayed or worried, for I am your God, I will give you all the strength you need now, my child, and I will help you! You can depend on that and never worry, I'm going to be there for you, like I promised in my word. I will bless you, protect you too, yes, I will hold you up with my right hand. **Isaiah 41:31**

Wow, Praise God, You Just Got Saved!

The Day I Gave My Life To Christ!

For He Is Worthy To Be Praised!

New Wine and Old Wineskins!

Luke 5:36-39

STUDY THIS PARABLE, APPLY IT TO YOUR NEW LIFE: "No one tears a piece out of a new garment to patch an old one. Otherwise, they will have torn the new garment, and the patch from the new will not match the old. And no one pours new wine into old wineskins. Otherwise, the new wine will burst the skins; the wine will run out and the wineskins will be ruined. No, new wine must be poured into new wineskins. And no one after drinking old wine wants the new, for they say, 'The old is better.' Mark2:22

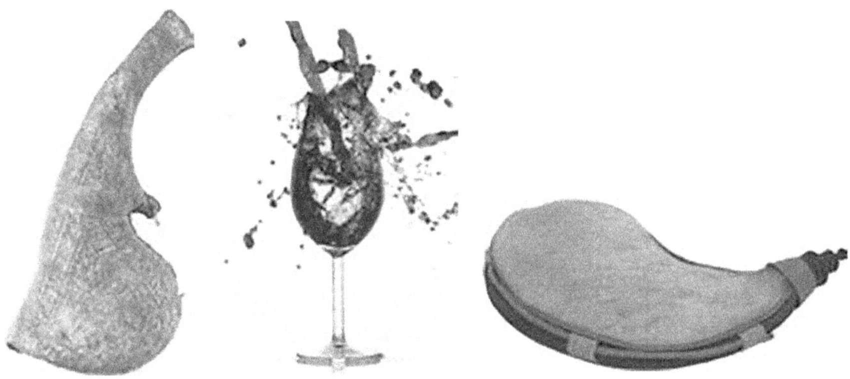

Now that you are saved, you cannot live the way you use to.
You cannot mix your **"Old Life"** with **"The New!"**

'New Life, Means You Live For Christ!'

Recommendation for the Lost and the found!

Turn your channel to:

- Trinity Broadcasting Network (TBN)
- Tri-State Christian Television (TCT)
- Joyce Meyer's Ministries
- Cref lo Dollar's Ministries
- In Touch Ministries with Charles Stanley
- Billy Graham Evangelical Association /you-tube the classics.
- T. D. Jakes, Potter's House
- The 700 Club with Pat Robertson
- If you live in Ohio, W VIZ ideastream, PBS.
- Kenneth Copeland Ministries
- Joel Osteen

DVDs

War Room: by Stephen Kendrick
Fireproof by Samuel, Goldwyn
CeCe Winans: Live in the Throne Room
Courageous: by Kendrick

If you don't want to watch anything, that's okay too!

Literature

The Battlefield of the Mind by Joyce Myers
A Caregiver's Bible to Excellence by Miss Asondra StarN'air
Removing Sin and Guilt by Cref lo Dollar
The Prophet by Kahlil Gibran
And of course the only book you'll ever need,

The Holy Bible!

Taste and **"SEE"** that the Lord is Good!

Watch Your Weight, Exercise Like You Should!
Ooh-Wee, "The Lord Is Good!" **He's Mmmmm Gooood!**

okay, not in the mood for reading, then how about some Music!

La Donna's *Peace and Healing*
Yolanda Adams's *More than a Melody* and *Believe*
Joey and Rory's *Inspired: Songs of Faith & Family*
CeCe Winans, Never Have To Be Alone
wait, I got it, how about some Kenny G, Heart and Soul

Whatever your musical taste, choose wisely!
Don't pollute your soul with garbage anymore, I just sayin"
Remember you are a new creature in Christ!

Live Well, Enjoy Jesus and Your New Life!

The Care Plan
for
God's People!
How We Think and Live Matters!
HOLY BIBLE
HOLY BIBLE
Miss Asondra StarN'air

Beauty For Ashes!

Get on, **'The Care Plan'** it can turn back the hands of time....

That face you are seeing is **"MINE"!**

Special Thanks

Thank you goes out to my publishers for all the hard work in getting this book realized. **'The Care Plan'** is now, in their hands! Thank you!

Thanks to my two toy poodles, Amanican Latt'e and Mariah Autumn. I know this book was cutting in on our time and bike rides together. Hopefully I made up for it during mealtime. You had lots of extra goodies as much as possible, plus I gave you both vanilla ice cream during the hot, hot days. I love you two little girls. You are the most wonderful precious toy poodles on the planet. Thank you for being patient while I wrote. May God keep you healthy and full of joy.

Finally, I'd like to thank those who turned their backs on me over the years, because I was different, thank you, I am different, I don't belong to you or this world, I belong to Christ, and he had already warned me in his word that I would be persecuted and hated because of who I belong to. 'He Was Right! But He also said forgive them for they know not what they do. And the good news is "I Have", yes I have already forgiver all who wronged me, lied on me and turned their backs on me too. I still love you and want the best for you. **The Care Plan,** is not just for you, but it's for me too. Together we can change into the kind of person God is calling us to be. Get on The Care Plan , Stay on The Care Plan. Keep saying "Yes I Can", "Yes I Can" be strong , happy and free!

So long, I'm with God and right where I'm supposed to be! SeeeeeeeeeeeYa!

Love you always, Miss Asondra StarN'air

Get The Care Plan
Open The Care Plan
Do The Care Plan

Is with You!

Special Thanks

Can't forget Ms. Darlene Jones, My **"Karaoke Buddy"** and **"Emotional Support."** Thank you for being a friend. Your heart is true, you're a pal and a confidant!

God Bless You!

Special Page, Special Message!

To my darling daughter Jazz, you've come a long way baby! You and all that Jazz never cease to amaze me of just how resilient you are, But don't forget about Christ, especially if you want to live a long a prosperous life. The **"Special Message"** I send, two words, **DON'T BLEND!** Stay far away from sin, Let "God In" and be ALL-IN, Stay ALL-IN too. Because daughter God really wants to love and take good care of you. My work is done, **"NOW" YOU MUST CHOOSE**, him or this world, I'm on a mission, Good-bye Baby Girl! **The Care Plan** is for Everybody, Everywhere including you dear daughter, but this goes for "Me Too" see **The Care Plan** is not going to work if we don't work it! Each individual must put in the work to reap the rewards, we must read the bible always, no options on that, The Bible is God's voice and our **B**asic **I**nstructions **B**efore **L**eaving **E**arth book, **So Get Hooked!**

This book is dedicated to the one I love my darling daughter Jazz. No matter what ,"YOU" are all that Jazz to me and more! Always remember this with God by your side there's nothing you can't Do, Nothing!

People were bringing little children to Jesus for him to place his hands on them. But the disciples rebuked them. When Jesus saw this, he was indignant (pissed off). He said to them, Let the little children come to me and do not hinder them, for the kingdom of God belongs to such as these. Mark 10:13-14

Love Always God, Love Always
"YOUR MOM!"

Special Photo

Miss Aaleeyah Sade Amor'Rose Lovett! OOOh "I LOVE IT!
Jazz daughter, My grandchild ☺!
Hello, little Lee, Lee, **Welcome to 'Planet Earth!'**

Amanican Latt'e and Mariah Autumn

My Two Toy Poodles!

About The Author
Miss Asondra StarN'air

Miss StarN'air remains single and lives in the state of Ohio with her two toy poodles. She has one adult daughter who she loves very much and now she's a grandmother for the first time! congrats! Socially, Miss Asondra StarN'air is an advocate for caregivers all over the world. She wants to see increases in wages and more respect for caregivers. Her debut book, *A Caregiver's Bible to Excellence*, is expected to sell millions. Because it is truly a caregivers bible, hence the title. More than scriptures, it has everything in it a caregiver or family providers can think of. I kid you not, it even has medical terminology, and a caregiver's fitness boot camp, unlike any other book on the planet. You'll have to get it and see for yourself, you will be blown away by all the hard work put into this incredible book. StarN'air is a very hard working writer and very creative too as you can see from this book, and she is also wise and courageous, she is not afraid to speak the truth, and can back it up with scriptures. Along with all of that, StarN'air, the name with the 'flair' is also an unknown recording artist too, soon to be discovered I'm sure! Miss StarN'air has a very 'Bright' future indeed. Can't not wait to hear her first single, it's going to be huge, **"WATCH"!** Miss Asondra StarNair's, time has finally come. Just look at **'The Care Plan'**, don't underestimate what God has done. I'll say it again, **"Her Time Has Finally come"!**

Seek the kingdom of God above all else and live righteously, and he will give you everything you need.

Matthew 6:33

Then I heard a voice of the Lord saying, "Whom shall I send as massager to his people?

Who will go for us?" At age seven, this little girl, now a woman, said, send me, I will go!

Isaiah 6:8

Miss Asondra StarN'air

No other book, can ever replace the Bible,
Everything we need, it's in there!

I'm Free Now, Time To Possess The Promise Land!

How long will you wait before **'YOU'** take back what God has already given you? Tell me, how long? **Joshua 18:3**

Sisters and brothers if you want freedom, you have to fight for it! God's word is our sword. Climb and fight the good fight of faith. Don't you dare stop! God said, I have given you this land. Go in and take possession of it. So, no more excuses, no time for fear, be bold and courageous. Like Moses and Joshua, Your God will be with you. Triumph, don't stop, "Think" **"Mountain Top!"**

Daily

Put on The Full Armor of God!

Don't Get Dressed Without It!

Will Protect You!

Ephesians 6:10-18

Glory To God!

Look to the **LORD** and his strength; seek his face always.

1 Chronicles 16:11

The Care Plan

Get The Care Plan
Open The Care Plan
Do The Care Plan

Is with You!

Lord, Where To Next? Send Me, I'm Free, I Will Go!

Miss Asondra StarN'air!

Lost and Found

Please Return This Book to the owner.

My name is ____.
My address is ______________________________________.
My contact number is _________________________________.
My E-mail address is _________________________________.

May God bless you for returning this book it's a treasure, this book is very, very special to me and my family. Thank you so much for returning it. **God Bless You!**

If this book is not lost, I leave this book behind to the ones I love—my family.

I want ____________________________________to have this book.

This book is a blessing from God. May you always cherish it, "I have."

Signed Sealed Delivered, It's Yours!

I will never forget how much I love you. Until we meet again

Be Blessed, Stay Faithful and Obedient to His Word Always.

In Jesus name, **AMEN!**

INDEX

P

R

S

T

W

CPSIA information can be obtained
at www.ICGtesting.com
Printed in the USA
LVHW100002181022
730905LV00003B/17

9 781959 143079